MY ONLY SUNSHINE

SHANNON JUMP

Editing by Librum Artis Editorial Services
Cover created with Canva by Shannon Jump

First edition

ISBN: 978-0-578-85766-4 (Paperback)
ASIN: B08QQFW9TG (Kindle Edition)

For my husband,
for understanding why I needed to write this

For Denim and Landon,
my only sunshine through many cloudy days

For my family and dear friends
who helped me find the voice to tell this story

AUTHOR'S NOTE

Hello, Reader! First off, a heartfelt **THANK YOU** for choosing *my* book! As a debut author, I'm especially appreciative of you and truly hope you enjoy *My Only Sunshine.*

Like Brynn, I am a domestic abuse survivor. Her story is loosely based on my own but is by no means a true recollection of events or a true account of my personal experience; this is a work of fiction, although the elements of truth lie within. Those closest to me will recognize similarities in our stories, and their voices are heard throughout this book, having inspired several of the secondary characters that you will meet in the pages that follow.

For years I struggled with the realization that putting this story out there would raise questions; from my family, my friends and anyone I encountered during these pivotal years of my life. But that fear outweighed the compelling notion to write and share this story.

Roughly thirteen years ago I sat down at my computer and drafted the first words to Brynn's story. It had a different title and even a different purpose at that time. I was on the "I got out" end of my ordeal, and while I'd given therapy a shot for a few short months—not a huge effort on my part, I know—when it didn't "fix" me the way I'd hoped, I returned to my love of writing instead. Those first words are now sprinkled throughout what is now, Chapter One of *My Only Sunshine*. They've changed, of course, since the first draft, as does the version of any story we tell, as we ourselves change and grow. I'm now older and hopefully wiser than I was then. I'm not the same person.

For years, I had this super-rough version of a manuscript tucked away in the confines of my computer, and while I had so much inspiration for the story, I had little knowledge of how I actually wanted to tell it and whether or not I even could. I didn't know if I had the skills to write it, let alone the content necessary to make it a complete novel. I was a single mom, working full time and going to school online, so instead of hunkering down and drafting out an entire book, I wrote only when I needed to —when life was tough, or I was feeling especially emotional and vulnerable but didn't want to talk about it with anyone.

Even then, I still wasn't sure that I could tell this story the way it was meant to be told, that I could finish it, or whether or not I would do it justice and be able to shed light on what has always been a touchy topic for me. But that was never the goal back then. The goal was for me to come to terms with what I'd been through and the choices I made during those years. The goal was to heal, to be a better person and a good mother for my kids. And, in the meantime, I went on living my life and raising my kids, letting the ending of the story write itself.

Then 2020 happened—the year of the pandemic— which for many people proved to be a difficult year. My heart goes out to anyone who lost a loved one or experienced hardship during this time. Not that it was all sunshine and rainbows for me either, but it did give me the gift of time and the concentration I needed to really sit down and figure out the true direction of this story. Somehow, the ideas started flowing and slowly but surely, I was able to piece together random notes, phrases, scenes, character names, scraps of song lyrics and poetry that I'd written so many years ago—and somehow it just clicked.

Then I read just about anything I could get my hands on. I needed to get into an author's mindset—into their world. So, I started following authors on Instagram and joining their Facebook groups, signing up for their newsletters, and not just reading their books but actually writing reviews for them, too—who knew that was a thing? I mean, I *did*, but I'd never really participated in that side of things as a reader. I used to read a book and then move on to the next without considering why I'd picked up that book in the first place. Shame on me! (Seriously, if you're an avid reader, do your favorite authors a favor and review their books; it's the best 'thank you' you can give them!)

In that time, I learned as much as I possibly could about writing and about what it means to be a good reader —to be a good fan—and when I felt like I had learned enough to roll my chair up to the computer and give this writing thing a shot, I placed my hands on my keyboard and miraculously turned what was originally only about 6,000 words into over 70,000 words in a little over eight months, all while working full time and doing my best not to alienate myself from my husband and kids. (I failed only slightly in the art of alienation.)

And now here we are. I've published my first book— my debut novel—and a very personal and raw version of it, at that. The longest and most difficult chapter of my life (to date) has officially been closed.

Deep breath, Shannon.

Now I wait patiently for your thoughts...this is the scary part. I hope this story speaks to you the way it's intended. I hope you find inspiration in Brynn's struggles and triumphs and through her most personal thoughts and fears; many of them are my own, even though Brynn is not me. Her voice speaks for many of us—and we are not alone. I hope you have sunshine in your life and someone who loves you just as hard as you love them.

Thank you for reading this book, for rooting for Brynn and the many real-life victims and survivors of domestic violence. Thank you for giving me the opportunity to share this story.

#SurvivorsNotVictims

~ Shannon

Wherever you go, no matter what the weather,
always bring your own sunshine.

~ Anthony J. D'Angelo

PROLOGUE

I AM a victim of domestic abuse and marital rape.

There, I said it.

I fucking hate that there's a name for it. I hate this hell that I've lived. *Victim.* But that's the reality, and apparently, there are others like me. This haunting *thing* that tainted me beyond recognition has a definition, a distinct classification and meaning.

I am a victim of domestic abuse and marital rape.

Ugh.

I will always be a victim. Kind of like how an addict is always an addict, their addiction the result of something bigger than them, something out of their control. And while I often convinced myself that what happened to me was *my* fault, I now know that it wasn't. I didn't ask to be raped by my husband; I didn't ask to be abused. But I did choose to marry him. And then I chose to stay, even after the abuse started. Just as an addict makes a choice each time they slip the heroin-laced needle into their veins, snort the white shit up their nose, or replace the water in their tumbler with a liter of vodka, I chose to stick by my despicable husband, which did nothing more than enable him to further neglect the tenets of societal norms and overall basic human decency.

Hindsight sure is a bitch.

I am a victim of domestic abuse and marital rape.

While I hate to say I didn't know better, I didn't know any better. My parents, who have been married more than thirty years, had never once been violent toward one another. Sure, they argued sometimes, just like any other married couple, but they loved each other. And they loved me—I grew up happy, I grew up content. We went on vacations, they watched me play sports and participate in extracurricular activities. They supported my hobbies and piled more than enough Christmas gifts under the tree every year. They weren't bad parents by any means—although at times I'm sure I made them feel as if they were, thanks to my love of all things F-word related and an over-whelming desire to do as I pleased. The good example had been set for me, but for some reason, I was ignorant to that knowledge when I met Nathan. I looked the other way and pretended there wasn't a problem. I dismissed the warning signs of abuse and instead fell into bed with a handsome face who liked to use sex, drugs and manipulation as a form of discipline.

That's how—seventeen years ago at the ripe young age of nineteen—I stood in front of a judge and two cler-gymen and vowed to love, honor and cherish, in sickness and in health, until death do us part, a manipulative and evil man. I signed a few pieces of paper, changed my last name and became the wife of an abusive addict.

I just didn't know it at the time.

A handful of my close friends and family suspected what I'd gotten myself into. That's why Nathan and I were married at the Wright County Courthouse in the first place. My best friend, Jerilyn, hated Nathan. My mother despised him and likely would have murdered him if such a thing were legal. My father would have helped her bury the body. It turns out it only costs about three hundred dollars to get married by a judge in their chambers, and apart from having to sit through Judge Vesser's final case of the day, it was over in less than thirty minutes.

Nathan didn't buy a ring, make a grandiose proposal or ask for my parent's permission—I assure you they wouldn't have given it to him. I didn't buy a wedding dress, book a honeymoon or send out a single wedding invitation. We merely applied for a marriage license, and when it came in the mail a few weeks later, headed to the courthouse and had the least romantic ceremony in the history of wedding ceremonies. It was a Wednesday afternoon.

I'd like to say that my new husband eventually got his shit together and grew into the man that I desperately wanted him to be, but that would be a lie. Not that it mattered—I was bound by the laws of marriage. I did, after all, vow to love him in sickness and in health, until death do us part.

I am a domestic abuse and marital rape survivor.

PART ONE

I see you looking at me,
your face a blur.
Everything you say to me
hurting me,
killing me.

CHAPTER ONE
SEPTEMBER 2006

I ARRIVED home after a long day of work as the administrative assistant at Regions Marketing Agency, where I'd been working for the past thirteen months. It was only Tuesday and already I'd had the week from hell, dealing with clients who had nothing better to do with their time than bitch and moan.

I picked our two-and-a-half-year-old daughter, Ava, up from daycare and as I pulled into the driveway of our Albertville, Minnesota townhome, an uneasy feeling slithered in my core. I hadn't heard from my husband, Nathan, for several hours. This wasn't by itself alarming but was unusual for us, considering that my husband often expected me to be at his constant beck and call.

I turned off the ignition to the piece-of-shit car I'd purchased for next to nothing when Nathan decided it'd be a great idea not only to "borrow" my Pontiac Sunfire indefinitely but also to chain smoke his Camel Lights in it. The lingering cloud of smoke that resulted had made it uninhabitable for our toddler.

I dropped my keys into the pocket of my worn purse

and glanced into the rearview mirror; Ava was asleep in her car seat, her little head lolling haphazardly to one side and her auburn curls splattered across her freckled cheeks.

Must have played hard today.

I let out a heavy sigh, and even though it went against every parenting rule I'd ever heard, made a swift decision to leave Ava in the car while I made sure it was safe to bring her inside. I rolled down the driver's side window and stepped out, jogging up the sidewalk. Pausing at the door with my hand on the knob, a *thump, thump, thump* pounded in my chest.

I pushed the door open and stepped into the foyer, my eyes struggling to adjust to the sudden darkness. All the shades had been drawn over the windows, even though I'd opened them before I left for work. A labored breath escaped my lips as I flicked the light switch to the on position, my gaze dropping to the figure sprawled on the floor in the living room. His back was against the tattered sofa, his head limp and tilted backward at an awkward angle. His hazel eyes were closed and his mouth agape, his boxer shorts and wrinkled Tupac T-shirt soaked with sweat. I ran to him and fell to my knees.

"Nathan? Nathan, wake up!" I shouted, shaking his broad shoulders. There was a foam-like substance in the corner of his mouth and a needle hanging from the crook of his arm, the rubber tourniquet still tied around his biceps. Five days shy of entering rehab at the Hazelden facility, and here I was, certain I'd just found my husband dead on the living room floor.

Check his pulse.

I pressed my fingers into the side of his neck and found a beat; it was weak, but he was alive. I stood, taking in the scene. An empty bottle of vodka lay at his side, along with an upturned plate and a half-eaten pizza, crumbs and marinara sauce littering the carpet where it slid off the plate and onto the floor.

A sense of dread overwhelmed me, and I ran to the adjoining kitchen in search of drug paraphernalia. There was nothing in sight: no fine particles of white powder left behind on the counter, no rusty spoon, not even a lighter. Just the tourniquet and the needle that protruded from a vein in his track-laced forearm. I dug my Samsung flip phone from my pocket and glanced between my husband and the door, trying to decide if I should call 9-1-1.

But all I could think about was Ava asleep in the back-seat of my car.

The last thing I wanted was for my baby girl to see her daddy wheeled out of the house on a stretcher.

Or worse, a body bag.

"Goddamn it, Nathan," I muttered, crouching down to check his pulse one more time.

Thump...thu...th...

I cupped his face in my hands and planted a quick kiss on his forehead. "I'll be right back," I promised before darting through the front door and slamming it closed behind me.

My phone still in my hand, I sprinted to the car and hit the speed dial button for Nathan's sister. Landing hard on the seat, I fished my keys from my purse and scrambled to start the engine.

Voicemail.

Please be home.

"Natalie, it's Brynn. I need a huge favor. I can't really explain right now, but I need you to watch Ava for a bit. I'll be there in a couple minutes." I buckled my seatbelt, threw the car in reverse and backed out of the driveway. My mind raced as I imagined the many ways the evening could turn out. Being the wife of an addict wasn't what I had signed up for when I married Nathan two years earlier, but fight or flight mode had engaged and I knew what needed to be done.

In sickness and in health.

The dash clock read 5:04 p.m. as I turned onto First Street and spotted Natalie's split-level on the corner. She and Isabelle, her three-year-old daughter, were chasing each other around the front yard. Natalie stopped running and looked up, waving as I parallel parked my car on the street. My breaths erratic, I threw the door open and stepped out with the engine still running—time was a luxury I wasn't sure I had. I pulled the handle on the back door and unbuckled Ava from her car seat, lifting her up and securing her on my hip while Natalie made her way over to greet us on the curb. Ava stirred and fussed in my arms, never one to appreciate being woken from a nap.

"Brynn! What a nice surprise!" Natalie said, offering me a hug and pinching Ava's cheek. "Isabelle was just saying she wanted a play date with Ava." Ava nestled her head into my shoulder, groggy as she came to. "Was she asleep?"

"Auntie Brynn!" Isabelle squealed, skipping across the well-manicured lawn.

"Hi, sweetie." I patted her head of curly brown hair.

"Nat, I'm so sorry to barge over. I tried calling and left you a voicemail; can you watch Ava for a bit?" Without waiting for an answer, I handed Ava over to Natalie and turned back to my car to retrieve her diaper bag. "I just...have an emergency and need to get home."

"Brynn, what's going on? Are you okay?" Natalie's brows furrowed as she was hit with the realization that something was wrong. She took the diaper bag from me, and I pecked a kiss onto Ava's forehead, smoothing her hair from her face.

"Mommy will be back in a little bit, sweet pea," I said to Ava and then turned back to Natalie. "No...everything is not okay. I have to go. I'll call you in a bit when I know more, okay?"

She nodded, having understood that my emergency stemmed from her reliably unreliable brother; it wasn't an uncommon occurrence for me to drop by unannounced, my daughter in tow.

Weak pulse.

Hopping back into my car, I dialed 9-1-1 and willed the operator to pick up while making a mental checklist.

~~Ava~~

Drive.

Get help.

Get home.

"9-1-1, what is your emergency?"

"Yes, this is Brynn Reeves. I think my husband OD'd, and I need an ambulance right away."

"Okay, Mrs. Reeves, remain calm. We're sending an ambulance now. What's your address?"

"1066 Third Street North."

"Is your husband breathing, Mrs. Reeves?"

"Umm...his pulse is weak."

Almost there.

"Can you tell me how many beats per minute? Do you know how to read a pulse?"

"I do, but I can't answer that." I made a left turn at the stoplight, grateful it was green for once.

"Mrs. Reeves, are you with your husband now? It sounds like you may be driving. Are you in danger?"

"I'm fine. I had to bring my daughter to my sister-in-law's. I'm pulling into our driveway now. Please hurry." I clicked the phone off, threw the car in park, grabbed my purse from the passenger seat, and darted toward the house.

What if he stopped breathing?

When I reached the living room, Nathan was still slouched over against the couch, his usually burly frame seemingly reduced to half its size. I knelt next to him and checked his pulse again; it was barely recognizable, but I could feel the beat. I debated pulling the needle out of his arm and untying the tourniquet but decided against it. I didn't want my prints on anything and had no idea what to do with them once they were removed anyway.

Sirens wailed in the distance. My heart thudded in my chest, and a wave of nausea came over me. I focused on my breathing: deep breaths in, deep breaths out.

An ambulance pulled up to the curb, and two EMTs emerged, one male and one female, their medical bags and a stretcher in tow. They jogged up to the house, the front door left open for them, and I pointed to where Nathan sat slumped on the floor. An officer unfolded from a squad car that pulled up right behind them, his hand resting on the holster at his hip.

"I'm Officer Ryan Randall," he stated, extending his hand to me and stepping through the door behind the EMTs, who were already working on Nathan. He led me into the kitchen and asked me to sit down at the table, his tall frame looming over me. I slumped into the rickety wooden chair, and a cluster of nerves fluttered in my stomach, dread hanging over me once again.

"Can you tell me what happened when you arrived home?" He pulled out a tiny notepad and flipped to a clean sheet, his pen hovering over the page.

"I just...saw him on the floor. He had a slow pulse." I glanced over at Nathan as the female EMT slid an oxygen mask over his nose and mouth.

"Mr. Reeves, can you hear me?"

Despite being six feet tall, he looked almost childlike next to her, still and unrecognizable from the first time I had laid eyes on him at the Reebok Outlet nearly three years earlier, luring me in with a cheesy pick-up line that echoed in the back of my mind. *"Are your feet tired? You've been running through my mind all day!"*

"Mrs. Reeves, do you know what drugs your husband was taking?" Officer Randall asked, snapping me from the memory.

"Today?"

"Yes, today," he replied, a look of disappointment across his face as he made a note on his pad.

"Um, he's on Clonazepam for anxiety. Wellbutrin for depression, Seroquel, I can't remember what that's for, though. Um...Percocet. I don't know why he's taking Percocet, but apparently, he has a prescription for it. His name is on the bottle. Other than that, whatever the hell he shot into his arm...heroin, I assume. And vodka. The bottle is next to him." I pointed at the offender still lying on the floor, suddenly aware that I was rambling. My mouth snapped shut.

"Does your husband typically use illegal drugs for recreation?" He scanned the room and made another note on his pad. I opened my mouth to speak but could muster no more than an exasperated sigh as I sank further into my chair.

"Officer, my husband is an addict. He's due to check-in at the Hazelden rehabilitation facility next week." *You know, the place where Chris Farley went.* "I don't know what else he was on, and I can't begin to guess where he hides his stash." I folded my arms across my chest and stared at a coffee ring on the table, wishing more than anything that I was somewhere else—anywhere else. "I didn't know he was using again."

The officer made some more notes and then stuffed the items into his shirt pocket before pulling out a chair and taking a seat next to me. I made the mistake of meeting his eyes. I knew that look. It was the same one I received on a daily basis from everyone around me. My parents, my coworkers. Even my best friend, Jerilyn, was guilty of the look. *Pity*. I diverted my eyes back to the coffee stain, debating whether to get up and grab the dishcloth to wipe it up.

"I need you to gather all of his medications and bring them with you to the hospital. The doctors will need to know what he's been prescribed so they can properly treat him."

I nodded with apprehension and stood, using the back of the chair to push myself to my feet, and then made my way to the kitchen cupboard where the sandwich baggies were kept. I grabbed a freezer-sized Ziploc bag and with heavy feet, made my way up the stairs and down the hall to our master bathroom to gather Nathan's medications. I heard the male EMT tell Officer Randall that they were about ready to transport Nathan to the hospital.

I opened the medicine cabinet and grabbed all the prescription pill bottles I could find, only mildly surprised to find a bottle of Vicodin stuffed behind the nasal spray. I picked it up and inspected the label that had been blackened out with a permanent marker. My hands shook as I stuffed the bottles one by one into the Ziploc before I sealed it shut and made my way back down the stairs. I reached the landing as the paramedics wheeled Nathan out the front door on a stretcher, his eyes closed, his body still. I watched for the rise and fall of his chest—surprised to see the motion of the rhythm more prevalent than when I'd found him.

"Miss, did you want to ride along in the ambulance?" the female EMT asked. I shook my head and handed her the plastic bag of pill bottles. She took it and nodded before she and the other EMT pushed the stretcher toward the door. She stopped halfway through and turned to me. "Monticello-Big Lake Hospital. That's where he'll be." I recognized the pity in her eyes, too, but she seemed to understand that there was a good chance I wouldn't be heading there to visit my husband as he recovered from his apparent overdose.

The ambulance pulled away, and Officer Randall came up behind me. He paused at the door and laid a calloused hand on my shoulder. "Mrs. Reeves, do you remember me?"

I looked hard at the officer: tall—about six-foot-four—muscular, well kempt brown hair and brown eyes, a splattering of freckles across his nose. A welcoming smile. It took a moment, but realization dawned that I'd seen him before, though I was unable to place him. "I...I'm not sure."

"Well, I recognize you. Recently, you were in a rough place at The Ugly Bar out in Montrose..."

Oh.

Right.

We had been out celebrating Nathan's birthday, and he'd gotten upset after seeing me talk to another man when I fetched us drinks from the bar. Never mind the fact that "the other man" was nothing more than a friend from high school who wanted to say hello.

Or that Nathan himself was checking out every girl in the place.

After a screaming match in the parking lot, where Nathan called me every derogatory name in the book, he threw his drink in my face, shoved me to the pavement and left me there on the ground. He'd taken the keys to my car and drove himself—drunk and still raging—home without me.

A bar patron had called 9-1-1 after witnessing the incident while she stood outside puffing on a menthol cigarette. She ran over and helped me to my feet, dabbing blood from my lip with a napkin she had pulled from her pocket. Officer Randall was the responding officer that night and had given me a ride home.

"I remember," I whispered, breaking eye contact and staring at the door.

"Mrs. Reeves," he said, pulling out a business card and handing it to me, "this is my personal cell phone number. Keep it in a secure place and call me anytime you feel your safety is at risk. Life is short and nobody deserves to live in fear."

Just as I had the last time he said those words, I took the card and shoved it into the back pocket of my jeans. Officer Randall headed out the front door toward his squad car. I closed the door behind him and secured the padlock, sinking to the floor with my head in my hands.

I never went to visit Nathan in the hospital.

I no longer gave a flying fuck.

CHAPTER TWO

JUNE 2020

"Mom! Have you seen my green T-shirt dress?" Ava shouted as she stomped up the stairs. I set the book I was reading down on the table and stood from the couch. Ava strolled into the adjoining kitchen wearing her gray bathrobe, a towel wrapped around her wet hair and her iPhone 7 in her hand. She was fifteen going on thirty, with bright green eyes that sparkled even without makeup, and while her raging teenage hormones were in full swing, her porcelain skin had somehow remained blemish-free.

"I'm pretty sure it's hanging in your closet, honey," I replied, grabbing my empty *Friends*-themed mug from the coaster, and walking into the kitchen to make some more coffee. I placed my mug on the faux marble countertop and reached into the cupboard for a filter and the tin of coffee grounds.

"I checked. It's not." Ava perched herself on a stool at the center island and grabbed a banana from the fruit bowl. "Can you help me look for it?"

"Yep, let me finish making this coffee first." I scooped

the coarse grounds into the filter, adding an extra scoop for good measure. "What do you need your dress for?" I leaned over the counter in front of her, my elbows resting on the counter.

"Well, I was actually wondering if I could go to Lake Rebecca with Kit and Fiona today," she admitted, raising one of her well-shaped brows. I smiled and straightened.

"Ah, I knew there was a reason you were up and moving before noon on a Saturday," I teased, opening the refrigerator and pulling out the creamer. "Who else is going to be at the lake?"

"I just told you, Kit and Fiona." Her fingers danced at full speed over her smartphone, her eyes glued to the screen. I watched her for a moment before she hit the lock button on the side of the phone and then set it down on the counter.

"That's it? A beach that big, and you'll be the only three people there?"

"Mom, seriously…" she trailed off, annoyance settling into her tone. She picked up the banana, peeled it open and took a bite before going back to her phone. "Where's Dad?"

"He went over to Grandma and Grandpa's to help with some yard work. Speaking of which, I want to talk to you about something." I reached out and placed my hand over hers in attempt to steal her attention back from the demon device.

"Mom! Stop, I'm trying to send this." She waved a dismissive hand and pivoted on the stool.

"Watch your tone, please." I turned back to my coffee maker, its short brew cycle complete. "You just let me know when I can have a minute of your time," I said with a hint of sarcasm, well aware that she wouldn't be leaving the room until I gave her an answer about going to the lake.

She sighed and shoved her phone into the pocket of her robe and then reached for the banana again. She freed the rest of the fruit from its peel, took a bite and then deposited the empty peel onto the counter.

"Okay, okay…I'm listening," she mumbled through a mouthful of banana. I poured some of the Italian sweet cream into my mug and then filled it with steaming hot coffee, bringing the mug to my nose and inhaling the aroma of the dark roast. "Grandma called earlier and said she saw one of your friends smoking out by the tennis courts."

"So?"

"So, I just want to make sure it's not you that she finds smoking out there one day," I said, taking a sip of my coffee.

"Mom, seriously? You know I don't smoke. It's gross."

"It wasn't cigarettes she smelled…"

"What, weed? Mom, *seriously!*"

"I'm just looking out for you. You know how I feel about that stuff."

"Yes, I do. And you know how *I* feel about it." Ava swiped the empty peel from the counter and tossed it in the garbage bin.

"Fair enough. Just know that it won't stop me from talking to you about this stuff."

"I know. But don't worry, Mom, I won't smoke ciga-rettes or weed. I won't vape, and I *definitely* won't get pregnant and make you the youngest grandmother in the history of grandmothers." She winked, knowing full well that her playful dig would trigger a sigh from her mother.

"Ava, come on. This is important."

"I know. But it's annoying that you think I'm dumb enough to do any of it."

"I didn't say *you're* dumb, I just want to make sure you don't *do* dumb things."

"Yeah, yeah, I got it, Mom." She rolled her eyes in my direction, but I saw a smile play on her lips. As much as Ava and I bickered, the love we had for one another was as genuine as it comes. I trusted her, but with apprehension. To date, she had yet to give me a reason not to.

"What time will Dad be home?" she asked, pushing the stool underneath the counter.

"Probably not until after you get back from the lake." My lips snaked into a smile as Ava realized I'd answered her question.

"Really? I can go?" she squealed.

"Yes, but don't forget the sunscreen," I chided. She pulled me into a hug, almost spilling my coffee as her arms wrapped around my middle.

"I won't, Mom." She released me and grabbed her phone back out from her pocket, responding to the group message with her friends.

I realized I was about to lose Ava to the demon device again and rattled off a few more instructions. "Make sure you bring water. Oh, and turn on the GPS on your phone before you leave."

"I will, Mom," she said again, in a more pleasant tone. "Can you ask Dad to take me out driving later, though? I need to get my hours in before Behind The Wheel next month."

"I'll ask him," I promised. She smiled and skipped out of the kitchen, heading toward the laundry room. "I still need help finding my dress!"

———

IT FELT like just yesterday that I was Ava's age, so carefree and filled with a sense of wonder, never realizing how much I was taking that luxury for granted. I guess that's what happens when you put your heart in the hands of the damned.

CHAPTER THREE
AUGUST 2003

AFTER HIGH SCHOOL GRADUATION, my best friend Jerilyn
and I were still trying to figure out what we wanted to be
when we grew up. We'd been the best of friends since the
age of two and had spent the majority of our childhoods
back and forth at each other's houses for endless sleepovers. We'd dedicated our early years to sitting huddled in
front of our dollhouses playing Barbies. Our teen years,
however, were more geared toward boys. If we weren't
busy crushing on the adolescent boys we'd met in grade
school, we were locked in one of our bedrooms
rummaging through *TeenBop* magazines in search of the
latest and greatest Hanson posters and then arguing over
who got to plaster which posters to their bedroom walls.

Jerilyn had spent her days that summer working full
time at Super America, where she sold cigarettes, lotto
tickets, gasoline and conveniently priced grocery items to
the good people of the city of Buffalo. Her position at the
register gave her ample opportunity to check out the so-
called "fresh meat" in our town as she rang up their items
and loaded them into flimsy plastic bags. Truth be told,

there wasn't much fresh meat to gawk at and more often than not, after my shifts at Subway I often ended up with my feet planted next to her check-out counter, where we chatted the night away in between customers. There wasn't much else to do if you were the kind of kid who liked to stay out of trouble.

Nonetheless, we still attended the occasional party and I introduced Jerilyn to Nathan the night of Harper and Jesse Harrison's End of Summer Shed Party. By that time, Nathan and I had been dating for a few weeks, and by his request, had decided to put a label on our budding relationship. We were official: girlfriend and boyfriend—even though I'd never been fond of the childish term.

Nathan had just moved into a one-bedroom apartment on the other end of town, having opted for the apartment over a car—which, in a small town nearly an hour west of the Twin Cities, meant he relied on everyone else for rides. I picked Nathan up from his apartment, and we met Jerilyn at Perkins for a bite to eat before the festivities.

I parked my car in the lot and spotted Jerilyn waiting by the front door of the restaurant, her dark, shoulder-length hair somewhat disheveled as it blew in the wind.

"That her?" Nathan asked, pointing in Jerilyn's direction.

"Yep!" I stuffed my keys in my purse and popped out of the car, slamming my squeaky door closed and running over to greet my best friend. We enveloped each other in a hug while Nathan trudged along behind me, his hands in his pockets.

"Jerilyn, this is Nathan!" He stuck out his hand and started saying, "Nice to meet—" but Jerilyn had pulled him into an awkward hug.

"I'm a hugger," she announced, bashful as she released

her grip on him. "Sorry," she added, having sensed his discomfort.

"Nah, it's okay." The corner of his lips curved into a crooked smile. "It's nice to meet you."

"Whoa, Brynn, you didn't tell me Nathan wasn't from around here!" she said, having picked up on his East Coast accent.

"I didn't?"

"Anyway, let's grab some food!" Jerilyn offered as she motioned for the door. Nathan made no effort to open it for us. I waited for an uncomfortable beat and then pulled the door open. Nathan went in first, Jerilyn and I having exchanged a look before following him inside. He took a seat on the bench in the lobby and I sat down next to him, offering him my hand. He laced his fingers through mine, Jerilyn looking on in bemusement as she took a seat on the other side of me.

"Did you put us on the list?" I smiled and kissed his cheek.

"What list?"

"The waiting list." I pointed toward the hostess stand on the other end of the lobby.

"No, sorry." He let go of my hand and walked over to the hostess, gesturing "three" with his fingers.

"You okay?" I asked, turning to Jerilyn.

"Yeah, I'm fine."

Nathan returned a moment later, none of us uttering a word while we waited for our table. Finally, the hostess called Nathan's name and we followed her through the dining room. She motioned for us to sit and laid the menus down on the table.

"I asked for a booth," Nathan said.

"Oh, this is fine, right, Jerilyn?" She nodded in agreement, but Nathan spoke again.

"I want a booth."

The hostess looked to me for help and I shrugged, asking her politely if she happened to have a booth available. She excused herself for a moment, and we waited while the awkward eyes of the families that sat around us burned holes in the backs of our heads. I tugged on Nathan's hand and he leaned his head down to me.

"Why are you being difficult?"

"I'm not, I just want to sit next to my woman in a booth," he responded, having made no effort to keep our conversation private. Jerilyn raised her eyebrows and looked away, focusing instead on a discarded French fry that sat on the floor against the baseboard.

"Okay! I have a booth ready for you right over here if you'll follow me," the hostess announced, back to her chipper self. We followed her to the smoking section—even though Nathan was the only smoker—and Nathan slid into the booth. He put his arm up over the backrest and looked at me expectantly, patting the seat next to him. I thanked the hostess and slid in beside him, his protective arm landing on my shoulder and pulling me close. Jerilyn slid in across from us and flipped her menu open, holding it in front of her face to keep her facial expressions to herself.

"What are you thinking of getting, Jer?" I asked, hoping to lighten the mood.

"Um, I'm leaning toward quesadillas. Want to share?"

"Yeah, that sounds great." I closed my menu and set it on the edge of the table. Nathan still had yet to pick one up. "Are you not eating?"

"I'm getting chicken fingers," he stated, an edge to his tone.

Jerilyn looked up and offered me a nonchalant shrug. "So, Nathan, where are you from? What brought you to Minnesota?" He cleared his throat and fiddled with the paper wrapper that held his silverware and napkin together.

"West Virginia. I needed a new start, I guess." He pulled his arm down from around my shoulder and rested it on top of my thigh, giving it a gentle squeeze, his fingers inching further up than necessary. I placed my hand on top of his and redirected his hand closer to my knee.

"Gotcha…" She trailed off. I sensed the annoyance in her voice; this wasn't going well at all.

————

Somehow, the three of us made it through the rest of dinner in awkward silence, the tone having been set by Nathan's standoffish mood. When the bill came, I reached for it and pulled my wallet out of my purse. There was no way I was going to let Jerilyn pay her portion after watching her suffer through the meal. Nathan made no effort to reach for his wallet—he hadn't yet secured a job anyway—so I pulled out an extra twenty and slid the bills under the receipt.

Nathan surprised us both a minute later when he offered to be our sober cab for the evening. Naturally, Jerilyn and I squealed like the teenage girls that we were, thanked him profusely and then ran off toward my LeBaron.

The hosts of The Shed party, twins Harper and Jesse, were in our graduating class and while both Jerilyn and I had considered Harper a good friend since our elementary days, her twin brother Jesse was an absolute douchebag. It was well known by anybody who was anybody that parties at The Shed were all the rage and until you'd been to one, you were essentially a nobody.

The Shed, as it manifested, was a decked-out pole barn on the property, complete with a full bathroom, mini kitchen and tables, several hand-me-down couches, a big-screen TV and a stereo that put out more bass than the subwoofers at a Ja-Rule concert. Of course, the usual drinking game tables made their appearance as well: beer pong, ping pong and pool. Outside, a fire pit and volleyball court filled with sand —and probably several dozen cat turds—provided added entertainment. The Shed also happened to be in the middle of nowhere, off an already secluded dirt road, and as a result, the cops were never called, and the beat-up old cars that we parked in the field couldn't be seen from the county road.

Even better was the fact that parties at The Shed happened just about every weekend, and there was never a need to worry about getting caught. See, Jesse and Harper's parents—referred to as "Ma and Pa"—figured that if their kids were going to party, they may as well have a safe place to do it. A place where everyone dropped their keys in the bowl at the door and didn't touch them again until morning. If you showed up at The Shed, you woke up at The Shed. Unless of course, it was one of the nights that Ma and Pa were supervising the shenanigans and could vouch for your sobriety. In that case, you could grab your keys and head home at any time. But of course, "you were never here."

We arrived at The Shed in typical fashion, dressed in the obligatory Silver jeans and hooded sweatshirts, our faces plastered with more makeup than necessary for such an event, and I dropped my keys into the bowl. Jerilyn and I headed over to greet Harper by the ping pong table, where she and Jesse were engaged in a one-on-one match. Ma and Pa handed each of us a wine cooler and welcomed us with hugs.

"Hey, hey!" our friend, Meg, chimed sidling up next to us. "You made it!"

"Hey, girl!" I beamed and pulled her in for a hug, her dark hair tickling my nose.

"Did you bring the new boy toy?" she asked, her eyes scanning the room.

"I did! I'm not sure where he ran off to, though."

"Well, I can't wait to meet him. Oh! There's Tatum! I need to say hi. I'll catch up with you later." She held her beer in the air and blew me a kiss before trotting off in the other direction.

Jerilyn set her drink down and joined in on a game of beer pong while I went in search of Nathan. I scanned the room and didn't see him. Assuming he must have gone out to the fire, I headed outside and spotted Nathan just as he tossed an empty beer can into the fire pit. He stood across from my tenth-grade lab partner, Carter Graham, engrossed in a conversation that I'm certain was about the size of my chest, his hands cupped under his pecks, mouthing the word "huge" and making a show of it. Carter laughed and reached into the cooler at his feet to pull out another beer, handing it to Nathan, who popped the tab and took a long sip.

So much for staying sober tonight.

He spotted me over the hill and waved me over. "There you are!" He beamed, as if he'd been looking for me. "Where did you run off to?"

"Just making the rounds." I took a sip of my wine cooler and then carefully spit the tart liquid back into the bottle, hoping Nathan wouldn't notice. I'd have to stay sober to drive us home later; I was never a fan of staying overnight at The Shed.

Nathan threw an arm around my waist and pulled me close, kissing me on the lips. "Thanks for inviting me here tonight," he said, a smile on his face. "Your friends are great!" He took another sip of his beer and then turned back to his conversation with Carter, leaving me standing awkwardly, staring at the crackling fire.

After a couple minutes I excused myself and sauntered off toward the private bathroom inside the house. I dumped the hard lemonade down the drain and rinsed out the bottle before refilling it with water from the tap and setting it down on the counter so I could relieve myself. Jerilyn barged in before I'd gotten my pants back up, my underwear still halfway down my legs.

"Oh, my God, you scared me!" I hissed. She closed the door behind her while I buttoned my jeans.

"I've been looking for you everywhere," Jerilyn slurred, leaning against the door frame. I pumped some hand soap into my palm and then rinsed my hands in the sink. "Your boyfriend's drinking."

"Oh, I told him he could," I lied, reaching for the hand towel. "I'm not really feeling it tonight so I'm just going to have water." I picked up the glass bottle and held it to her nose; she sniffed the rim and made a face.

"But it's our night out, Brynnie the Pooh," she whined, pulling out her favorite pet name for me, her lips curling into a pout.

"And I'm out! I'm here! Don't worry, everyone else will think I'm drinking. It'll still be fun." I grabbed her hand and pulled her out of the bathroom. We jogged back toward The Shed, the music growing louder with each step. "Oh! Our song is on!" I smiled and dragged Jerilyn by the arm, doing my best attempt at dancing while walking backward in the bumpy grass. Nelly's "Hot in Herre" blared across the lawn. We reached the crowd that had gathered around the fire, and I glanced through the window inside The Shed, having spotted Nathan by the pool table, one arm around a skanky blonde chick's waist while the other shoved something into his pocket.

Is he seriously macking on Tess Fucking Danielson right now?

He caught my eye and released her and then waved us over.

"There you are! Where have you two been hiding?"

"Bathroom. Who's she?" I pointed in Tess's direction, but I knew damn well who she was: the slut of our graduating class. A self-proclaimed homewrecker with a pretty face and tight body. The guys loved her because not only was she blonde, but she also had legs for days—they were even tanned to a perfect golden brown thanks to her unlimited monthly minutes at Tan on 1st—and she had no problem spreading them for any guy who showed even the slightest bit of interest. Tess *Fucking* Danielson was literally the last girl on the planet I wanted Nathan ogling, let alone talking to.

"Who? Blondie? No idea. She was looking for a deck of cards to get a game of *Presidents and Assholes* started."

"Boring!" Jerilyn chimed, clearly oblivious to Nathan's wandering hands. "Let's dance!" She smiled her flawless teeth at me and grabbed my arm, dragging me back into The Shed where a group of our friends gathered around the stereo. The air inside was thick and combined with the humidity outside—late August in Minnesota, thank you very much—I struggled to find relief; the naturally curly hair I'd spent over an hour straightening was starting to frizz. Jerilyn danced around me while I did little more than sway back and forth, my eyes locked in on Nathan as he headed out the door with Douchebag Jesse.

"I'm not really in the mood to dance," I shouted to Jerilyn over the music.

"What? You were the one pulling me over here a few minutes ago," she whined.

"I know, I'm sorry! It's so sticky in here and I need to get outside for some air." I turned and headed for the door. Nathan, Jesse, Carter and a few other guys I didn't know stood around smoking cigarettes by the fire. As I got closer, I smelled the remnants of a skunk and fanned my nose, curious where the hell such a putrid smell had come from.

"There's my girl!" Nathan shouted. He stumbled over a rock, uncoordinated on his feet. "Want a hit?"

"A hit?"

"It's a joint, Brynn. Marijuana." *Oh.*

"I didn't realize..."

"You've never smoked weed before?"

"No."

"Try it, you'll love it." He shoved the rolled joint in my direction again, but I pushed his arm away, uninterested in the rotten thing.

"No, thanks. I didn't know you smoked," I admitted.

"I didn't know you didn't," he chuckled and took another drag before passing the joint to Jesse.

Or was it a hit? Whatever.

"Oh, come on, don't be such a Goody Two-Shoes," Jesse teased, throwing his arm around Nathan's shoulders. He turned to him and said, "Don't worry, man, she's always been like this. You just need to loosen her up a bit, if ya know what I mean." He winked and threw his head back, a sadistic laugh snaking from between his lips.

"Trust me, she's far from a Goody Two-Shoes," Nathan argued, "...in the bedroom, anyway." He nudged Jesse in the ribs. I didn't care for Nathan discussing our sex life with Jesse, but I wasn't naive to the fact that guys tended to do that. Of course, women did too, but our conversations are usually a bit more respectful when the other party was standing right there.

"So, tell me, Brynn, why is it that you think you're too good for the rest of us?"

"I've never thought I was too good for anybody, Jesse," I snapped.

"No? Then how come you won't indulge in a bit of this reefer with us?" He shoved the joint in my face, challenging me with his dark eyes. Asshole or not, Jesse was a looker, which I suppose is why he got away with such dank behavior in the first place. He was a more badass version of Nathan's tall, dark and handsome but unlike Nathan, he had the tattoos and piercings—ears, nose and tongue—to back up the look. Nathan had a few tattoos, too, but nothing like the sleeve that went up the length of Jesse's arm. I recall having had a crush on him for a hot minute the summer before, but every time he opened his mouth, I was reminded of the fact that while he was hot, he was also an asshole, and that always outweighed his looks on any scale.

"Can you stop shoving that shit in my face, please?" I pivoted in the other direction.

"Where are you going?" Nathan asked.

"To find Jerilyn."

"Oh, come on! Stay a while longer. Please?" Reluctantly, I stopped in my tracks, a wave of guilt washing over me. I'd drug Nathan to this party under the assumption that my friends were wonderful and that he'd fit right in, and now that he had, all I wanted to do was leave. I sighed and took a seat in the folding chair next to Nathan. Jesse took another hit and then passed the joint over to Carter, who held it between his thumb and index finger and brought it to his mouth. He inhaled and then blew out slowly.

Nathan snaked his hand up my thigh, a coy smile on his lips. Jesse leaned over to him and nudged his arm. "She suck your cock yet?" he asked, loud enough for everyone in the circle to hear. I glared at him and willed Nathan not to answer.

"Fuck yeah! She's incredible at it, too," he said with a high-five. Nathan looked over to me and winked—as if I should thank him for the compliment. I stood and walked away without another word, ignoring the cat calls and promises that they were only kidding.

I sulked in my car for the remainder of the party, sans keys, until I could retrieve them from Ma and Pa. I was annoyed and couldn't explain why. I'd never been put in the position to say no to drugs, but something stirred inside me at that moment.

I didn't like it, and I didn't want any part in it.

CHAPTER FOUR

I HAD SHOWN up at The Shed the night before expecting to be laid up in bed with a hangover the next morning, but that was far from the case. Instead, I had the privilege of babysitting my drunk boyfriend, who I hadn't managed to pull away from the party until after 2:00 a.m. Jerilyn had passed out on one of the couches next to Harper, so I had scribbled her a quick note to let her know I'd be back to pick her up in the morning.

I'd driven Nathan back to his apartment, a tiny one-bedroom apartment located in downtown Buffalo that while offering a decent view of Buffalo Lake, was nothing to write home about.

It had taken everything in me not to drop his ass off on the curb and go home to my warm bed in my childhood home across town, where I still lived with my parents. I helped Nathan through the front door with the intention of slumping him onto the couch to sleep it off, but he had insisted I stay the night. I'd just helped him pull his shirt off and climb into bed.

"Oh, come on, baby. Stay." He attempted to unbutton

his jeans, but his level of inebriation prevented him from doing so and he looked up at me with a pout. "Help?"

I leaned over and reached for the button of his jeans, but should have known it was a ploy. Nathan's muscular arms grabbed hold and pulled me down onto the bed. "See, now you have to stay," he teased. I tried to wiggle away, but it was no use; I was no match for him and before I knew it, we were giggling and his hands were roaming my body.

"I'll make you breakfast in the morning," he offered, his eyes big like he'd just had the greatest idea in the world.

"Nathan, you're drunk." I pulled away from him and swatted at his hands. "You really need to sleep it off." Ignoring my instructions, his hand snaked up my shirt and rubbed my breast, a devious look playing on his face.

"But I'm horny…"

Had I managed to attain the same level of intoxication myself, I likely would have given in; hell, I might have even been the one initiating the foreplay. But I wasn't in the mood for sloppy sex and just wanted to sleep.

"You're too drunk, Nathan. Just go to sleep."

To my surprise, he didn't argue further and within minutes, his hand lay lifeless on my chest, the deep breaths of sleep letting me know he'd passed out. I lifted his arm and set it gently on the bed, slithering out from under him and grabbing a spare pillow and throw blanket. I slept on the tiny loveseat in the living room to avoid the inhalation of Nathan's beer breath as he snored in my face.

Morning came slowly, and I hadn't managed to get much sleep. After brushing my teeth and throwing on the fresh pair of jeans I'd remembered to pack, I fished my phone out of my purse and sent Jerilyn a text letting her know I was on my way. I knew there wasn't a chance in hell Nathan would be making breakfast and figured Jerilyn and I could stop somewhere instead.

I scribbled a sloppy note to Nathan on the back of a receipt that I'd found crumpled on the kitchen counter and then slung my purse and overnight bag over my shoulder, sliding my feet into my Doc Martens. I made my way out the door and down the five flights of stairs to my car, the unrelenting humidity smacking me in the face as soon as I stepped onto the curb.

When I pulled up to The Shed ten minutes later, Jerilyn sauntered out. She stumbled across the lawn toward my LeBaron, still sporting last night's clothes—now wrinkled—her purse lopped lazily over the crook of her arm and her dark hair in a lopsided ponytail, loose strands flying around in the warm breeze. I shoved my purse onto the floor, and Jerilyn opened the passenger door and plopped down on the seat next to me.

"You got any gum?" she asked, her voice hoarse. I pointed to my purse by her feet; she scooped it up from the floor and started to rummage through it in search of gum but pulled out a pack of assorted fruit Mentos instead. She held the packaged tower of candies up and looked at me with a raised eyebrow.

"The *fresh* maker!" we said in unison.

"Seriously, how do you not have gum?"

"I guess I must've run out. At least I have something for you to cover that breath up with," I teased before she slugged me in the arm. "Where to?"

"Hmmm...Perkins?"

"We just ate there last night."

"I know, but I need to grab my car, and I have a serious hankering for some Eggs Benedict. Pleeeeease..." she whined, pouting and batting her eyelashes. I watched as tiny flakes of last night's mascara fell onto her cheeks.

"Okay, for one, you sound like you're fresh out of the honky-tonk. Who says "hankering" anymore? And two, put that damn fresh maker in your mouth or we're not going anywhere!"

Jerilyn smiled and raised a hand to her forehead in salute. "Yes, Drill Sergeant!" she exclaimed, sporting her best Pauly Shore, *In the Army Now* impression. I threw the car into reverse and backed out of the gravel driveway.

"Now, do something about that hair. You look like shit." She feigned surprise and flipped down the visor, gasping as she caught a glimpse of herself in the tiny mirror.

———

"So, what do you think of Nathan?" I asked Jerilyn as I took a sip of my Diet Coke and opened a menu. I wasn't sure I wanted her answer, her being a truth teller and all, but I wasn't one to avoid a necessary conversation for long.

"Honestly?" She looked up from her Blackberry, her face telling of her answer. "He's kind of a dick, Brynn. I mean, I get it, he's one hell of a sexy specimen—those hazel eyes, are you kidding me? But come on. He thinks he's God's gift to women."

"Tell me how you really feel," I muttered. "That's a little harsh, don't you think?" I folded my menu and set it on the edge of the table.

"Is it?"

"You hate everyone I date," I whined. Which, in truth, was only a few other guys—most notably my first love, Brody, who happened to be the brother of my good friend, Andi. Brody and I had dated off and on throughout high school and despite his urgency to take my virginity sophomore year, he was much less enthusiastic about things like fidelity and long-term relationships. We finally parted ways halfway through my senior year. Jerilyn had wanted to kill him but settled instead of replenishing my supply of tissues and offering a shoulder to cry on.

"So date better people." She chuckled to herself and set her phone on the table. "Anyway, I just think you can do so much better," Jerilyn flagged down the waitress with a wave of her hand. "Do you know what you're getting? I'm ready to order."

"You don't even know him." I ignored her question, focusing instead on the disappointment of her apparent dislike for my boyfriend. She swiped a kid's menu and a crayon off the neighboring table and started coloring.

"Can't say I want to, hun. He's a bit of a tool."

"Jerilyn! Are you being serious right now?" I asked, shocked by her unrelenting honesty.

"Of course I am! I just want what's best for you, Brynn, and I'm sorry to say, I don't think that's Nathan." The waitress arrived and stood expectantly with her little black notebook and pen.

"What can I get you ladies this morning?" she asked. Jerilyn ordered her Eggs Benedict while I opted for a sausage and cheese omelet with hash browns. When the waitress left, Jerilyn went back to her phone, rattling off a text message before reaching for her Diet Coke and taking a sip through the straw.

"Do you really think he's that bad?" I asked quietly after a few minutes of awkward silence. "I really wanted you to like him."

"I'm not the one that needs to like him, that's all you. And you know I would never lie to you." She paused for a moment. "I'm sorry, I just don't think he's very genuine. He was pretty standoffish at dinner last night, and I hate to say it, but he seemed really possessive of you." She met my eyes, and I couldn't help but look away. "Brynn, he was supposed to be our D.D. last night and he was drinking within a half hour of that party starting. Doesn't that concern you?"

"I guess I just didn't think it was that big of a deal," I lied. "You spent the night there anyway..." I left the sentence hanging, knowing full well that Jerilyn had made the one point I'd hoped that she wouldn't. I had been more upset about Nathan's drinking after saying he wouldn't than I cared to admit, and I was still coming to terms with the fact that he smoked pot. Truth be told, most of my friends did, and that was fine, but it wasn't something I cared for in a boyfriend. But offering to be our sober cab and then drinking anyway? I was grateful I hadn't taken more than a few sips before realizing I'd have to be the one to drive us home.

"Me spending the night there isn't really the point," Jerilyn continued. "And either way, like I said, I just want you to be happy, and you definitely didn't seem happy last night after you saw him drinking. Come to think of it, I barely saw you after that. Where were you all night?"

The food arrived, and Jerilyn dug into her breakfast, giving me an out to avoid yet another unpleasant question. I picked at the omelet on my plate, suddenly having lost my appetite. My phone dinged with a text message from Nathan, one with a picture attached. I clicked on the message, double-tapped the 'OK' button and watched the grainy image of a flower bouquet appear. It looked as though the flowers were sitting on the kitchen table in Nathan's apartment—which is a fancy way to describe a fold-up Poker table shoved against the wall. The text from Nathan exclaimed, "these r 4 u!"

"Aww, see, he's not all bad," I said to Jerilyn as I shoved my flip phone in her face to show her the picture. She stopped chewing and leaned closer, squinting her eyes to get a better look.

"From where? Wal-Mart's five-dollar bin?" she asked, unimpressed. I flipped my phone closed and shoved it back into my purse.

"What's with you today?" I asked.

"I just don't want to see you get hurt again, Brynn. You've been dating Nathan for what, two weeks? Maybe three? And already you're acting like he's Prince Fucking Charming. He's not, by the way."

"Kiss your mother with that mouth?"

"I should have been a sailor, I know." She winked as she took another bite of her breakfast. Despite our disagreement over Nathan's likeability, this was one of the things I'd always loved about Jerilyn. We could disagree on just about anything, but the strength of our friendship always outweighed the argument. She'd just insulted my boyfriend—pretty aggressively—and still managed to find a way to make me laugh it off.

"Just give him a chance, okay? For me. I really like him."

She put her fork down and held my gaze for a moment as if giving me time to retract my statement. Reluctantly, she looked away and reached for her soda. "Fine. I'll do a better job of filtering my true feelings about your new boy toy. But know this: if we don't change the subject right now, the rest of breakfast will be awfully quiet because I literally have nothing nice to say about him."

I chuckled and tossed my crumpled napkin at her. "You're a snot!"

"Oh wait, I lied. I do have one nice thing to say about him. He has a nice ass. I'll give him that. Most jackasses do, though." She stuck her tongue out at me and laughed before reaching into her purse and pulling out an envelope.

"Just wait until you meet someone...I can't wait to tear him a new one," I mock-threatened.

"Meh. Okay, so, I have to tell you something..." She trailed off, holding the envelope in her hands. "Don't be mad." She held the envelope up, displaying the return address in the corner.

"Mankato State University," I read out loud.

Jerilyn applied for college?

We had mutually decided to take a year off after high school, maybe get an apartment together while we decided what to do with our lives. She apparently changed her mind at some point, neglecting to tell me.

"You're leaving?" I asked, not bothering to remove the letter from the envelope.

"I didn't know how to tell you," she admitted, her face riddled with guilt. It took me only a moment to realize I wasn't upset, that I wanted nothing more than for my best friend to be happy and chase her dreams. I chewed on my bottom lip before smiling and scooting into the booth next to Jerilyn. My arms wrapped around her and I felt her relax against me.

"I'm really proud of you," I said.

"You're not mad?"

"Only a little." I winked. "Looks like we have some dorm room shopping to do!" She hugged me again, a tear in her eye.

This moment was everything for her. But it took everything in me to swallow the jealousy that stirred at the thought of her experiencing the world without me.

CHAPTER FIVE

SEPTEMBER 2003

THE LAST COUPLE weeks of summer flew by in quick succession. Jerilyn and I shopped for her dorm room decor —Target run and done!—and together we packed up her childhood bedroom, saying our goodbyes to the slew of boyband posters that once plastered the walls, chucking them delicately into the wastebasket. She left for college on a Saturday morning, so we said our tearful goodbyes the Friday before—avoiding all conversation Nathan related— and gushing about her upcoming college adventure.

My heart was breaking; I wasn't sure how I would survive without my best friend living down the street. But it wasn't just that Jerilyn was leaving; just about everyone I knew was escaping our small town, heading off to their respective colleges and kissing the high school drama good-bye. I would be alone, if even just a phone call away.

Instead of packing up and leaving for college like my friends, I was working a full-time job, now at the Reebok Outlet, and getting in extra hours where I could. But instead of saving my money like a responsible adult, I spent it carelessly—oblivious to the fact that I was, in essence, financially supporting my unemployed boyfriend. Since I had money coming in and we couldn't just as well sit around staring at each other all the time, I paid for just about everything—gas, fast food, movies. Sometimes even his rent, which I justified since I slept at his apartment most nights, anyway.

With Jerilyn gone, it was time to introduce my parents to Nathan. I'd put it off for weeks, intuition alerting to me the fact that they probably wouldn't like him. After stressing over the impending visit for days, Nathan assured me that he would be on his best behavior and there was nothing to worry about—that moms loved him.

Whatever that meant.

When we arrived at my parents' house on Friday night, Nathan came through the door with a cocky demeanor and a smug expression on his face. He didn't bother to shake my dad's hand or compliment my mom's decor, maybe tell her that her hair looked nice. You know, things a good boyfriend would think to say when meeting his girl-friend's parents for the first time. He just simply said, "Hey, how ya doing? I'm Nathan." and then after removing his shoes, proceeded to plop his ass down on their living room couch.

The tension rippled throughout the room, and I looked on while my dad's shoulders bucked and my mom's inner conflict ensued; I had no doubt she was trying to decide whether to drag him out the door by his shirt collar.

I pretended not to notice.

I scooted in next to Nathan on the couch and let him drape his possessive arm around my shoulders and pull me in close, taking claim to something in a matter of thirty seconds that my parents had lovingly cared for the last eighteen years.

When no one could find the words to move the conversation past the awkward first impressions, I looked to my mother and said, "What's for dinner? It smells great." We sat down at the dinner table a few minutes later to a spread of pork chops, mashed potatoes and broccoli and my mother—always a quick judge of character—did her best to maintain a state of politeness.

But I could read her like a book, and it couldn't have been clearer that she wanted nothing more than to watch Nathan walk out the door and never come back.

I again carried on in faux oblivion.

Nathan scarfed his food down with poor manners, likely under the illusion that a mouthful of food meant he wouldn't have to partake in conversation—not that there was much conversation in which to partake.

I pushed the broccoli around on my plate and avoided eye contact with my parents as we ate. When I opened my mouth to speak a few minutes later, Nathan cleared his throat and said, "I could use another glass of milk." He'd eaten everything except the pork chop, which had only a bite missing, and he made a show of sawing at it with his steak knife.

"I'll grab it," I said, standing from my seat.

"Is there something wrong with the food?" Mom asked, her eyes on Nathan. She set her fork down and it clinked against her plate.

"Just thirsty."

"I see."

I reached for Nathan's glass and refilled it. Mom stood from the table and made her way to the garbage bin, stepping on the foot pedal and emptying the contents of her plate into it.

"Mom?"

"If the food's not good enough for *him*, it's not good enough for *me*," she snapped. I slumped in my chair, embarrassed not just for my mother, but for Nathan. His request for another glass of milk did little more than imply that the pork chop was dry. Mom had seen right through him.

"Honey, really, the food is great. Come sit and I'll fix you a new plate," Dad offered, rising to his feet, his hand on the small of her back.

"No, it's okay. I'm just going to...get some fresh air." Mom opened the sliding door and stepped out onto the deck. Dad, with a pained expression I couldn't quite place, followed her outside.

"That was rude," Nathan said before picking up his glass and chugging the rest of his milk.

"Are you fucking serious?" I rolled my eyes and got up from the table, pausing to watch my parents through the window. I wasn't sure whether to say goodbye before storming out or to simply walk out the door. I chose the latter, my immaturity taking the win yet again. "Let's go," I said to Nathan, swiping my purse from the back of the chair before stomping through the house.

Nathan didn't hesitate to follow.

"What's your problem?"

I clamped my mouth shut, refusing to fight in my parents' entryway. I slid my feet into my shoes and bolted out the door, momentarily debating walking back to Nathan's apartment.

I felt cheated. My parents despised every boyfriend I'd ever had, but this one stung the most. I imagine they stewed over that first impression for weeks—maybe even years—but in my state of naiveté I didn't pay it any further attention once I'd had a good night's sleep.

It would take me years to realize that my mother wasn't the one in the wrong.

———

My relationship with my parents suffered as I continued dating Nathan. I was tired of being told what to do and felt compelled to defend him instead of taking my parents' words to heart. I rebelled—as young adults often do—and spent less time at home. I believed my parents were trying to control my life, so while I often stopped at home to shower, change or do laundry, I rarely stayed to visit and tried to time my visits during the day when I knew they'd be at work.

They called. They texted. They even stopped over at Nathan's apartment once—unannounced—to check in on me. Fortunately for all of us, Nathan wasn't home when they showed up. It didn't matter, though. In the end, it did nothing more than add fuel to the fire; I was stubborn, and their butting in only pissed me off more.

A few weeks after the dinner that initiated the war between my parents and my boyfriend, I stopped over at the house again—without Nathan—to do a load of laundry and sit down for a cup of coffee. I was tired of the tension, and they'd agreed not to bring up Nathan. I managed to keep the topic of conversation off of Nathan for most of the visit, but the tension was still present.

My laundry load done, I folded my clothes and stacked them neatly in the laundry basket I'd used to haul the load, careful to hide the couple pairs of jeans and shirts of Nathan's that he'd asked me to wash. I wasn't sure my parents would appreciate being his laundromat.

"What makes you so sure this boy is right for you?" Mom asked.

My asshole puckered at the question.

She promised.

Mom stared at me from the kitchen table, sipping her

coffee like she hadn't just asked the *one* question she had agreed not to mention.

"Why are you so sure he isn't?" I countered, taking a seat across from her at the table. There wasn't a single part of me that wanted to have this conversation, but I hoped, more than anything, that we could be civil and squash the elephant in the room once and for all.

"Brynn…" She trailed off, a stony expression on her face. My mother and I stared at one another, each of us daring the other to push the issue. I didn't care to argue, it was never in my nature to do so, but I didn't want to be stonewalled either.

"Help me out here, hun," she said, looking to my father who stood at the sink washing the breakfast dishes. I looked away after a few beats, unable to swallow the disappointment on their faces.

Dad dropped his shoulders, turning to me. "We don't approve of him," he said simply. Mom sighed, her head in her hands. I stood, pushing my chair under the table and leaning over the backrest.

"I'm gonna go."

"Well, don't just leave." Mom frowned and tapped her foot against the tile floor. "Be an adult and talk about this."

I grimaced and nearly laughed out loud. "I *am* an adult, Mom. Which is exactly why you don't get a say in who I date." Her jaw clenched, and I knew she wanted to say more. It wasn't easy for her to hold back. "I don't want to argue with you and we're not going to see eye to eye on this anyway." I looked to each of my parents, all of us aware I wouldn't be by to visit for a while. "I'm sorry you don't like him." I scooped my laundry basket from the floor and made my way to the front door.

"You deserve better than him, Brynn!" my mother shouted from the kitchen. Despite my will not to, I slammed the door behind me. I wanted to un-hear her words, to get them out of my head.

They lingered there for years.

At that age, I wasn't so sure what I deserved, but I certainly didn't want to hear it from my parents.

CHAPTER SIX

NATHAN'S BEHAVIOR began to change after meeting my parents. He took issue with me any time I spent time with them, as if he had expected me to write them off as some form of punishment for not liking him.

He hated when I made plans that didn't include him. Aside from work, he guilted me into staying over at his apartment just about every night, blowing off my friends when they were in town or skipping the occasional night out with coworkers. I enjoyed our time together, yet something about it felt forced, too. Like there was some unspoken agenda behind his need to keep me away from my parents, away from my friends.

As if he didn't want me to have a life outside of him.

Despite the nagging sensation in the back of my mind, I fell in love with him. Behind closed doors, everything was perfect; it was comfortable. I knew there was more to Nathan than what he allowed me to see, and that mystery intrigued me—kept me guessing.

Physically, there was nothing amiss between us. We had a passion for one another, chemistry that was fierce and captivating. I needed attention from him just as much as he needed it from me. I needed him to want me, to show me he loved me in every physical way imaginable, and whatever we couldn't bring ourselves to say, we communicated with our bodies.

But there was still something missing.

Nathan was often quick to react, always angry about something. Always bitter and in need of affirmations. I loved Nathan. I was sure of that. I just didn't love everything *about* Nathan. And I needed more; I wasn't living my life just for the sole purpose of being his girlfriend.

One Saturday we arranged a tour of Ridgewater College in Wilmar, Minnesota. I was regretting my gap year, even though I was only a couple months into it, and since we both wanted to get our degrees—me more so than Nathan—I arranged a tour of the campus. When I mentioned my plans to Nathan, he had agreed—more or less—that it would be fun to go to the same school and live together in an apartment close to campus.

The drive up was relaxing, as fall often is in rural Minnesota, and we listened to music—albeit not my preferred choice of music—and talked about what the future may hold for us. Neither of us had a clue what we might major in, although I was leaning toward something in music or photography, but touring a campus was the first step, so that's what we did.

We parked in the campus lot, and as we walked toward the door, I reached for Nathan's hand. He pulled away, claiming it was too hot outside to be *that* close to one another. It was sixty-five degrees—unusually warm for November, sure, but certainly not 'hot.' I shrugged it off and let my arm fall to my side, taking in the sights and sounds of the campus.

A class was being conducted on the lawn; students sat

on blankets with their notepads in their laps while they soaked up the sun. I couldn't help but wish to join the group and was about to say so to Nathan, but he was several strides ahead of me, eyes forward, aimed only at the main door that would let us into the building.

I jogged to catch up, and we made our way to the administration's office, where we were introduced to our tour guide, Benjamin—who was not sore on the eyes. He had the makings of a tech nerd, but the kind you wouldn't mind going home with at the end of class. His blonde hair and blue eyes made a great addition to his surprisingly muscular build and I couldn't help but gawk at him when he spoke.

That's when I discovered Nathan's possessive side.

We were less than ten minutes into the tour and Nathan was dragging his feet, pouting like a four-year-old who had just gotten his favorite toy taken away. I ignored his behavior as best as I could, instead focusing on Benjamin as he showed us the library. But Nathan turned territorial the further we went into the tour: a hand on my lower back as we walked, an arm draped over my shoulders when we peered into a room, a random peck on the cheek. When we turned to leave the library, he smacked my ass, making a show of it and laughing when the loud clap that resulted from a palm to the ass cheek echoed down the hall.

Benjamin was clearly uncomfortable, doing his best to feign disinterest and move us further along the tour.

"And, Nathan, what major are you considering?" Benjamin asked in attempt to steer the conversation back in the right direction.

"Yeah, I really don't know," he said, making no effort to elaborate. Benjamin waited a beat and then let out an audible sigh before turning to me.

"What about you, Brynn?" I opened my mouth to speak, but Nathan jerked my arm and the words got lost in my throat.

"This place is a joke. Let's go, Brynn." I pulled my arm away from him and rubbed the area; he'd gripped it harder than he'd meant to.

"I wanted to see the Music Department."

"We're not going to school here. Let's go." He didn't wait for my response, just took off down the hall without looking back. I turned to Benjamin and shrugged my shoulders apologetically. His face was pierced with concern when I turned and headed in the same direction Nathan had gone.

"Wait," he called after me, jogging to catch up. "Are you, um…" He spoke in a hushed tone, shielding his words from the students passing in the hall. "Are you safe at home?"

"What? Of course! Why would you ask that?" I searched his face, but he clamped his mouth shut and said nothing more. I turned on my heel and jogged down the hall toward Nathan. "Sorry!" I shouted with a wave of my hand.

Nathan was waiting in the parking lot, leaning up against the trunk of my car. When he saw me, he moved to the passenger side and threw the keys in my general direction. I fumbled to catch them, but they landed on the ground at my feet. "You drive," he mumbled.

"Are you okay?" I asked, picking up the keys. "What happened back there?"

"What happened back there? Really, Brynn? You were all over that guy!" he shouted, his face wrenched in fear or anger—I couldn't quite tell. His fist was balled up at his side as if he was ready to punch something. I felt the eyes on us; the students across the yard were watching. Nathan turned and flipped them the bird and then opened the car door.

"Nathan! Stop it! You're being ridiculous, I was not. Keep your voice down."

"Fuck you!" he yelled, taking me by surprise. He climbed into the car and slammed the door. I stood motionless, unsure what to say next but knowing full well the ride home was sure to be awkward.

My nineteen-year-old boyfriend gave me the silent treatment the entire way home. It took me the length of the drive to realize that Nathan's childish behavior was his way of taking claim to me in front of Benjamin. He saw him as a threat, his actions having nothing to do with living out some librarian-themed fantasy as I had originally assumed.

I wasn't sure whether to laugh or cry.

————

"Are we going to talk about what happened earlier?" I asked Nathan later that night. We sat on separate ends of his loveseat, an uncomfortable silence hanging in the air between us. He'd been irritable since we left the college and hadn't spoken a single word that would provide me with a clue as to why he'd gotten pissed off enough to leave the way he did.

His answer would determine whether I stayed the night or went home for the first time in weeks. I wasn't sure which I preferred, but one of us needed to address the issue and I figured I'd take the liberty of doing so.

Nathan sighed and used the remote to mute the TV, turning to me and placing his hand over mine. "I'm sorry, Brynn. I just can't stand seeing you flirt with other guys." His body shifted, and his chest puffed out.

"I wasn't flirting," I argued.

"You were. And that piece-of-shit was loving it."

"Nathan, I—" He cut me off, silencing my words like he often did.

"Don't. Just, don't, okay?"

"Don't *what*?" I asked, confused. I mentally went back through the college tour in my head, retracing our steps. I may have stared at Benjamin a bit, but I certainly hadn't flirted with him. He reached out and pulled me toward him and I rested my head against his broad chest, grateful for the physical contact after hours of avoidance. His fingers stroked my hair, and he inhaled the scent of my shampoo.

"You always act like you don't see the way guys look at you. It drives me insane," he finally admitted.

"There was nothing to see, Nathan. We were touring a college. It's not like I was applying for a job in the porn industry." He laughed and the motion made my head bob against his chest.

"I'd make a porno with you any day," he teased, sliding his hand over my breast. He gave it a squeeze, and I felt him harden beneath me.

"We are definitely *not* doing that," I argued, amused and shaking my head.

"No? That's too bad. It could be fun." His other hand made its way down my arm and settled on my thigh, the hint of arousal sparking between my legs. I tilted my chin, and Nathan's lips met mine. "Will you settle for some totally private, living room sex instead?" he asked, his voice husky.

"Mm-hmm. Count me in." I agreed, nodding my head in rapid succession.

Somehow, I'd already forgotten what we'd been arguing about.

CHAPTER SEVEN

JANUARY 2004

THE WORKWEEK TRAILED by without hurry, as January in retail often does. I'd just finished my shift at Reebok and was looking forward to my first weekend off in over a month. Nathan and I were hanging out for the night, and I planned to head straight to his apartment from work. I punched out in the office and grabbed my overnight bag from my locker before heading into the changing room. Stripping out of my uniform, I slid into my favorite jeans —the ones that made my ass look good—and V-neck T-shirt, grateful to be having a good hair day despite putting in nine-hours.

Satisfied with my look, I slid my arms through my denim jacket and lifted my belongings off the bench. Exiting the dressing room, I waved goodbye to my boss, Kristina, and made my way out the door and over to my car, already warmed up thanks to a coworker who offered to start it when her shifted ended twenty minutes earlier.

I pulled into Nathan's apartment right on time and sent him a text to let him know I was waiting for him in the parking lot. He strolled outside a few minutes later, looking dapper in his CK Jeans and brown leather jacket, his hair gelled in the spiky way that I liked.

"Hey there, sexy," he said with a wide smile, opening the door. He leaned over and kissed me, lingering longer than necessary, and his kiss filled with need. "I missed you," he said when he pulled away.

"I missed you, too." His hand snaked up my thigh and tugged at the hem of my T-shirt. "Okay, okay, let's not get carried away," I teased, brushing his hand away.

"I'm sorry! You know what you do to me." He gestured toward the bulge in his jeans. I scoffed, giggling and changing the subject.

"Where should we grab dinner?" I looked at Nathan, surprised to see he was leaning back in his seat, ogling me with bedroom eyes. "Somebody's horny today."

"Very," he agreed, winking and running his tongue over his lips. He nodded toward the building and said, "Let's go upstairs."

"Now?"

"Yes, I want you. Now."

"What about dinner?" He grabbed my hand and placed it over his crotch, his erection relentless. "Nathan! Stop. Someone will see us!" Despite my embarrassment, I couldn't help but chuckle; I loved that it didn't take much to get him excited, I just wished I could get some food in my belly first. He blinked another ridiculous wink in my direction. I sighed and turned off the ignition, stuffing the keys into my purse. He leaned in to kiss me again, this time his hand tangled into my hair, holding me in place while his tongue explored my mouth. I pulled away and reached for the door handle.

"Okay, seriously. Let's go," I said, frustrated that he couldn't wait until after dinner. I'd skipped lunch and was a little on the hangry side. Stepping out of the car, I was surprised to see that Nathan had already sprinted to the building and was grinning back at me, laughing like a madman, overly excited that he was about to get laid. I chuckled and made my way over to him, kissing him once more at the door.

He took my hand and we raced up the five flights of stairs to his apartment, barging through the door and kicking it closed behind us, winded, but not wanting to waste another second. His hands were suddenly everywhere, greedy as he stripped me out of my jacket and T-shirt, dropping them to the floor before removing his own clothes in what looked like one swift motion.

"You're so sexy," he panted, pulling me to him and sliding his tongue along my ear. He nibbled on the lobe, sending a shiver down my spine and hardening my nipples. I kissed him with intensity, biting his lip and digging my fingernails into his back. He unclasped my bra with one hand and then stood back, watching in awe as I slid the straps down my arms and my breasts spilled out before him.

His hands were on my zipper in seconds, shoving my jeans to the floor while I shimmied out of them. I stood before him in nothing but my black lace panties, sucking on my swollen lip that still tasted like him.

"Bed. Now," he commanded, slapping my ass when I made no effort to move. He lifted me from the floor with little effort and tossed me onto the bed, trailing kisses along my clavicle before claiming my mouth with his, his hands roaming.

Lost in the moment, he took each of my wrists and pinned them down on the bed above my head.

"Ow, baby, that hurts," I whispered, careful not to ruin the moment. He grunted in response before releasing his grip and pushing my panties aside. He entered me abruptly and I yelped, the sudden intrusion painful and catching me off guard. I wasn't ready for him.

"Nathan, stop. That hu—"

He fucked.

And then he fucked harder, claiming me more intensely than ever before, my arms once again pinned down above my head, rendering me immobile. His mouth found my breast and he bit, sinking his teeth in deep and drawing blood.

"Nathan, please—"

He grunted again, oblivious to my pain and lost in passion. His muscles tensed and he pulsed inside me, releasing my arms, his body lax on top of me.

Oh, shit...

"Nathan!" I yelled, pushing him off me as I wriggled out from beneath him. "You didn't pull out!"

"I'm sorry, it just felt so fucking good," he sighed. I scampered off the bed and grabbed a towel from the laundry basket, shoving it between my legs. He laughed and rolled onto his side, his head resting on the palm of his hand.

"Toss me one, will ya?"

I glared at him but reached down and grabbed another towel, chucking it at his head.

"Ha! Calm down, princess, you're on the pill. It'll be fine."

I took a deep breath and sauntered off to the bathroom, making sure to shake my ass for him before crossing into the hall.

He joined me a few minutes later, standing behind me and folding his arms around me, his head on my shoulder.

"Move in with me," he said, his lips breaking into a schoolboy smile.

"Are you serious?"

"I'm *very* serious." He tucked a strand of hair behind my ear and kissed my cheek. I turned to face him, mesmerized by the gleam in his eyes.

"Okay!" I agreed. My stomach fluttered at the thought of waking up next to him every day.

"Great! We can move you in this weekend!" He smacked my ass and headed back toward the bedroom, calling out to me, "Let's grab dinner, roomie!"

I tried not to think about the pain between my legs; the blood that I'd wiped from my breast.

He didn't mean to be rough.

He had just gotten caught up in the moment.

Right?

———

I MOVED into Nathan's apartment the following weekend, having packed up my childhood bedroom while my parents sat upstairs in the living room and did their best not to come down and strangle him. We stuffed my clothes and random possessions into garbage bags and whatever boxes I'd managed to grab from Reebok's shipment that morning. Of course, my parents were less than ecstatic when I told them that I was moving out, and while they tried to reason with me—attempting to convince me that there was no possible way I was in love with Nathan—I'd already made up my mind.

A couple hours later, Nathan was carrying the last box of my stuff upstairs to our apartment. Jesse strolled in behind him, chomping on a chip, and shoving his hand into the snack-sized bag to retrieve another. The two of them had been hanging out ever since the End of Summer Shed Party, and I shouldn't have been surprised—they were kind of two peas in a pod—but I was annoyed for the simple fact that I still couldn't stand Jesse, not to mention it seemed like Nathan was ditching me for him more often than not. But Nathan needed local friends, so I did my best to bite my tongue and brush it off, to keep the peace.

I looked up to see Jesse place a hand on Nathan's shoulder and lean into his ear. "So, you excited to be able to hit *that* every day?" His head bobbed in my direction, a sly smile on his lips and a twinkle in his eye.

I dropped the box I'd been carrying and mean-mugged him; he was never one to pass up the opportunity to discuss my sex life with Nathan, even while standing right in front of me.

"You're such a pig," I spat, setting a box down next to the couch. I brushed my dusty hands off on my jeans and stuck my hands in my back pockets.

Jesse winked, flipping a hitchhiker's thumb toward Nathan, and said, "Hey, you just let me know when you've had enough of this tool. I'd be happy to go a few rounds with you myself." He patted Nathan on the chest and the two of them smirked. It bothered me that it didn't seem to bother Nathan when Jesse hit on me. I wasn't blind to the irony—he'd put up such a fit after we'd visited the college, and Benjamin's attempts at flirting were nothing compared to the brazenness that spewed from Jesse's mouth.

"You wish!" I snapped.

They chuckled and turned before making their way back out into the hall. I dropped to the couch and grabbed a bottle of water from the table, taking a sip before looking around the tiny apartment. It certainly wasn't much, but it would do for a little while until we could afford something nicer.

Nathan's cell phone rang from the kitchen counter and I popped up from my seat to answer it, hopping over the boxes that took up most of the floor. "Hello?"

"Yo, what up?"

"Umm, who is this?" I asked, not recognizing the voice.

"Roman. Where's Nate?"

Nate?

"He's busy right now. Can I take a message?" I scanned the counter for a pen and paper.

"What are you, his secretary? Nah, just tell him Roman called. I'll hit him back later." The line clicked, and I abandoned my search for paper and set the phone on the counter, looking back at the stack of boxes that needed unpacking.

Jesse's boisterous voice carried from down the hall. I rolled my eyes and made my way over to the front door, ready to kick the thing closed, when Nathan appeared in the doorway, Jesse on his heels. They reeked of weed, and I silently chastised myself for being surprised that's what they had disappeared to do.

"Some Roman guy called for you," I said to Nathan.

"You answered my phone?" He stomped into the kitchen and swiped his phone off the counter, stuffing it into his pocket.

"Yeah, I didn't think it was a big deal." I shrugged.

"I don't answer *your* calls," he barked, his eyes penetrating me.

"Okay, I...I'm sorry. It won't happen again. I just thought—"

"Just don't answer my phone!" I flinched, Nathan's anger seemingly stemming from nowhere. As if he suddenly realized he was overreacting, he stepped closer to me and lifted my head by the chin. "Look, I'm sorry to yell. I just don't like people answering my phone, okay?"

Jesse lingered in the doorway, his usual smirk still plastered on his face. "You ready to head out?" he asked Nathan, rapping his knuckles on the door frame.

"Yeah, one sec."

"Okay. I'm sorry for answering your phone. You're not going to help me unpack, though?" I whined.

"Baby, you'll be fine. Jesse and I need to run a few errands. I'll be back by dinner."

"Okay." He pulled me closer and practically jammed his tongue down my throat, his hand snaking around my waist and giving my ass an unexpected squeeze. He was showing off for Jesse; I played along since I couldn't stand the guy anyway. I wasn't against making him jealous.

"You gonna have dinner on the table when I get home?" Nathan asked, breaking away and patting me on the butt again for good measure.

I sneered. "Sure, dear."

Jesse shook his head in amusement and then backed out into the hallway. "You lucky son of a bitch…"

I guess even assholes want to be the one to get the girl.

CHAPTER EIGHT

FEBRUARY 2004

THE PINK plus sign on the E.P.T test glared back at me from the bathroom counter. I'd just pissed on the damn stick not even two minutes prior and already the thing was practically shouting its response from the rooftop.

Pregnant.

This cannot be right.

With child.

Error-proof, my ass!

Expecting.

Maybe I'll take it one more time.

So utterly fucking fucked.

I slammed my fist on the counter and swiped the pregnancy test into the trash bin, yanking out the bin liner and tying it closed to conceal the evidence of the first test I ever passed with flying colors. *So much for that birth control my mom put me on when I was fifteen.*

My heart pounded in my chest, and I felt the onset of a panic attack; how was I going to do this? My parents' dislike for Nathan was growing by the day, and while I did my best not to let their opinions influence my relationship,

I myself had grown apprehensive of the direction Nathan and I were headed.

Aside from giving my family and friends the cold shoulder, he was too buddy-buddy with Jesse, and I was increasingly tired of seeing him stoned every day. But I was bullheaded and too stubborn to do anything about it, afraid that I'd have to move back home and my parents would think they were responsible.

Not that it mattered; that pink plus sign meant I was in for the long haul, whether I liked it or not.

After bundling up and walking the trash bag containing the evil stick that changed my life forever down to the dumpster, I decided to call in sick to work and made myself a doctor's appointment for three o'clock that afternoon.

Nathan had found work with a local snow removal company and while they sported the world's dumbest slogan—"We Scoop for You!", which reminded me more of an advertisement for the latest and greatest pooper scooper—at least he was finally working. And, thanks to the unpredictable winter weather that our great state of Minnesota was often known for, we were the lucky recipients of several inches of the fluffy white crap, ensuring that Nathan wouldn't be home until well after dark and allowing me plenty of time to secretly and fearfully confirm my pregnancy with Dr. Weinstein.

She did in fact, confirm my pregnancy.

———

NATHAN CAME HOME from work just after eight o'clock that evening. He'd called as he was leaving the job site, so I threw a frozen pizza in the oven and waited for him to get home. I stopped at Target after my appointment with Dr.

Weinstein and picked up some prenatal vitamins and a copy of *What to Expect When You're Expecting*, two things she highly recommended.

Not that I had yet made any decisions about what our next steps would be, but it wouldn't hurt to read up on our situation. I was having an out of body experience, and the only thing I was sure of is that I was entirely unsure what to do, unsure what I wanted.

The timer on the oven dinged as Nathan walked through the door. I slid my hand into an oven mitt and pulled the pepperoni pizza out, setting it on top of the stove to cool. Nathan slipped out of his snow boots and shoved them, along with his wet Carhartts, on the floor by the entry closet, a puddle of slush pooling beneath them.

"Hi honey, I'm home!" he joked, pecking a kiss onto my lips.

"Have a good day?" I asked, a slight crack in my voice. My heart thudded in my chest. Nathan nodded, and I grabbed the pizza cutter from the drawer, slicing the pie and adding a couple pieces to each of our paper plates. He took a seat at the table and grabbed a slice, shoving it into his mouth and immediately spitting it back out onto the plate.

"Fuck! That's hot," he shouted. I stifled a laugh.

"Will you ever learn?" He shrugged his shoulders and picked the pizza back up, wasting no time going in for another bite.

Oh, my God, I can't do this.

"I'm pregnant," I blurted, slumping into my chair.

"You're *what?*" Confusion settled into Nathan's face—as if he were searching my eyes for a telltale sign that I was joking. He sat back in his seat and pushed his plate forward, opening his mouth to speak, but not actually saying words.

"Pregnant. Six weeks today." I folded my hands in my lap to stop them from shaking. Nathan stared at me with a blank expression.

Say something.

"How am I just hearing about this now?"

"I just found out today and—"

"Bullshit. You had to have known! Why didn't you tell me?" he shouted, pushing back from the table and rising to his feet. Of all the possible ways I imagined announcing the news of our pregnancy to Nathan, I hadn't expected his response to be anger.

"I was scared, Nathan! I wanted to wait until I went to the doctor to see what our options are."

"What do you mean, *options?*" he asked, his eyes squinted.

"About the baby. We're not ready for this."

"Of course we are. It'll be fine."

"It'll be *fine?* What kind of parents could we possibly be? We're nineteen years old, Nathan."

"Yeah, and I don't know if you realize this, but that makes us adults, Brynn. We're not in high school anymore. We have our own place..." He waved his arm around the room to make his point but trailed off, clearly having run out of examples of all the things we had going for us.

"Yeah, a one-bedroom apartment? How exactly would that work with a baby?" I asked, pinching my lips together. "I don't think I can do this."

"You're not seriously thinking I'd let you put my child up for adoption, are you?"

"No. Not adoption," I said with unnatural stillness, my eyes lowered to the floor, certain it was about to be pulled out from under me.

"Then what?" Nathan demanded, his eyes filling with

tears, another reaction I hadn't expected—I hadn't pictured Nathan as the type to cry over a baby.

"I...we...I could have an abortion," I offered nervously. He ran his hands through his hair, his fingers tugging on the strands. He paced the tiny dining room for a second and then marched into the living room to the sliding door, jammed his feet into his slippers and then stepped out onto the deck. From my seat at the table, I watched him light a cigarette and pace the roughly five-foot-wide space, his mouth moving in rapid motion as he muttered to himself and quickly smoked his Camel Light down to the filter. He flicked the spent butt over the railing, sending a tiny flare to the ground below and coming back inside. He slammed the sliding door so hard that it bounced right back open.

"No fucking way! You're not *killing* my kid!" He paced the living room, outwardly struggling to reign in his emotions and inwardly weighing our options. I pushed to my feet and crossed the room to him, my hand on his forearm, the other on his cheek. I pulled his face to me and forced him to look into my eyes.

"Nathan, I'm not ready for this. *We're* not ready for this." I spoke softly, his arms lazily wrapped around my waist.

"Then we'll get ready," he started, but I shook my head in disagreement. He pulled away and took several steps back. "There's no way in hell I'm letting you kill my fucking child."

"It's *my* body," I snapped, frustrated. Nothing about this conversation was going the way I expected.

"And *my* kid! Fuck you. No."

"That's not fair. You're not the one that has to be pregnant and carry this child. I'm not ready, and I don't want to do it."

"Get over yourself, Brynn! You sound like a child. We're keeping this baby."

"Are you nuts? We can't even afford the rent on this shit-hole half the time. How the hell are we going to afford a baby?" I folded my arms across my chest and looked at him expectantly, challenging him. I was ready to fight this battle.

"We'll figure it out."

"Oh, that's a great plan. Why didn't I think of that?"

"I said, *we'll figure it out*." He ran his hands through his hair for what felt like the hundredth time and then pulled me into his arms again, the corners of his mouth curving into a slow smile.

"Let's get married."

"What? Are you insane?" I attempted to loosen Nathan's grasp on my waist, suddenly feeling like I needed space, but he held me firmly in place.

"I'm serious!" he continued. "We're having a baby! Let's get married and start our family." He dropped to one knee and took my hand in his, smiling wildly, his eyes lit up. Happy.

Holy shit, he's actually serious.

How in the hell was I going to do this? I wasn't ready to have a baby. I wasn't even sure I wanted to stay with Nathan, let alone marry him and start a family. But I was cornered; what choice did I really have?

"Okay," I whispered, a sinking feeling in the pit of my stomach.

"Yeah?" Nathan jumped to his feet and pulled me into a hug. "Baby, this is so great! We're going to be parents!" he shouted, pulling both of our arms up over our heads in celebration and then pecking a kiss onto my lips. He stepped back and performed a deranged version of a happy dance, sheer joy on his face. I stood there motionless, watching my boyfri—fiancé—skip around our living room like a child. I laughed, despite myself.

I was supposed to register for college in the fall.

What will my parents think now?

What will Jerilyn think?

Nathan made everything seem so simple, as if we weren't about to make the biggest mistake of our lives.

And I'd just agreed to marry him.

———

WITH A CIGARETTE DANGLING from his mouth, Nathan stepped out onto the deck, flicking the lighter and igniting the tip. He exhaled the smoke from his lungs and then pressed his flip phone to his ear. He'd dialed his sister, Natalie's number—likely to share the news, even though I'd asked him not to say anything yet. I still wasn't sure how I felt about our situation and dreaded the thought of word getting back to my parents before I had a chance to talk to them myself. It was all too much to process and I felt like I needed a moment.

A baby.

"Yeah, she's right here," Nathan said, opening the sliding door. He motioned me over. "Natalie's on the phone," he announced, like it was new information. I didn't know his sister well, but we'd been spending increasingly more time with her and her daughter, Isabelle, lately.

"Hi Nat," I muttered.

"Hey! Congratulations!" she shouted, but all I could focus on was three-month-old Isabelle fussing in the background.

"Thanks."

Natalie's excitement had thrown me. I hadn't expected it and wasn't sure what to make of it. How could she be excited for us? We were much too young and still in such a new relationship; certainly not the greatest situation for welcoming a newborn.

Why am I the only one who sees that?

Nathan finished his cigarette and flicked it over the railing, stepping back inside the apartment and not bothering to kick off his shoes. "Nat, we gotta let ya go so we can celebrate," he said, winking in my direction.

"Ew, gross!" she laughed, having picked up on Nathan's hidden agenda. "Bye then!"

He clicked off the phone and made his way to the kitchen, where he poured each of us a vodka seven. He held mine out to me and I stared at it in his hand, waiting for it to click.

"What?" he asked.

"I can't drink that," I said pointing at the glass.

"Oh, fuck! Ha! I forgot." He laughed, throwing his head back and downing my drink like a shot before reaching for his own. He held up the glass and said, "Since you're eating for two now, I guess I'm drinking for two!"

Nathan double-fisted his drinks for the rest of the evening and then wondered in amazement why I wouldn't put out as we climbed into bed. He passed out next to me before we had a chance to argue about it.

I was in for a long nine months.

CHAPTER NINE

MAY 2004

"Fuck!" I grumbled as I watched a can of Campbell's soup roll down the stairs. I'd just gotten home from grocery shopping and was struggling to make my way up the five flights of stairs to our apartment. My arms were overflowing with plastic bags that I'd looped up the length of my forearms from wrist to elbow in determination to get everything up the stairs in one trip—I'd tried calling Nathan down to help carry everything up, but his phone went straight to voicemail. I looked back at the soup can that had crashed against the wall and now sat taunting me on the landing a flight below. There was no way for me to pick it up without having to set down any of the bags so, I bid adieu to my rogue can of soup and continued up the stairs, mumbling profanities under my breath.

Nathan and I had been married for three months, having obtained a marriage license and running off to the courthouse just a few weeks after his proposal and finding out we were going to be parents. He promised we'd have an actual wedding one day, but that wasn't in the cards for us anytime soon since we now had a baby to prepare for.

Not that we had the money for a formal wedding anyway—much less the support. To say that our marriage announcement hadn't gone over well with my parents would be the understatement of the century. Their approval rating of Nathan was further in the dumps than ever before; imagine their surprise when they found out we'd run off and gotten married without so much as requesting their presence in the courtroom.

And that we were expecting a baby.

So, while there was much to celebrate, there were no celebrations to be had, aside from Natalie and her husband, Seth, treating us to dinner that weekend. Nathan and I each took a half-day off from work on a Wednesday afternoon—because Judge Vesser's schedule happened to be wide open—and, dressed in simple jeans and button-down shirts, we recited the standard wedding vows and were pronounced husband and wife. Nothing had really changed other than my last name and tax filing status. We both went back to work the following day and we both came home to our crappy apartment that sat five floors above the ground where runaway cans of soup were the least of our concerns.

I reached our apartment door and was surprised to find the knob unlocked. The creaky door opened with little effort and I pushed my way inside, struggling with the bags and kicking the door shut with my foot. I flicked the dining room light on with my shoulder, my eyes landing on a wad of cash and several bottles of pills on the plastic card table that served as a dining table. All the labels were blackened out on the bottles and a dozen or so pill sorters sat next to them in a flimsy dollar store grocery bag.

I sighed and made my way into the kitchen, depositing my groceries on the counter.

"Nathan?"

"In here!" he called out from the bedroom. I abandoned my groceries for a moment and made my way down the hall, opening the door to our room. Nathan sat on the edge of the bed, staring at a dead June bug he was holding in the palm of his hand. He looked up at me, a weird expression on his face, his eyes glossy and pupils dilated. He lifted the bug in my direction. "Did you know their larvae can live in the ground for two to three years before surfacing?" he asked, a slur in his voice. "They're called June bugs because they usually don't come out until June." He eyed the bug in wonder, his face close enough to stick out his tongue and lick it. I was grateful when he didn't.

"I did know that." I hovered in the doorway, suddenly not wanting to move further into the room. Nathan stood from the bed and made his way over to me, enfolding his arms around me and kissing my cheek. I pulled away and placed a hand over his fist where he still held the dead bug. "Are you okay?"

"Oh yeah! Totally," he assured me, perkier than he'd been a moment ago, the apparent sadness over the early demise of the beetle seemingly dissipated.

"What's all that stuff on the kitchen table?" I pointed down the hall even though I wasn't sure I wanted to know the answer. But I was done talking about the bug and curiosity had piqued my interest.

"Oh, shit, I thought I put that stuff away." He flicked the dead bug into the corner of the room and darted off to the kitchen. It landed on the carpet after bouncing against the wall and I stared at it in wonder for a moment before picking it up between two fingers and carrying it with me to the kitchen.

Dropping the dead bug into the garbage bin, I watched as Nathan swiped all the pill bottles off the table and into the plastic bag that contained the sorters. He tied the bag closed and stuffed the wad of cash into the pocket of his jeans before walking back to the bedroom. I heard the closet doors swing open and then the sounds of him rummaging through something before the doors closed again.

Nathan came back into the kitchen and ran his hands through his hair—a habit I'd learned to be a telltale sign that he was anxious about something. He paced the small dining room, his eyes darting in all directions before settling on me. I paused, frozen in place with a package of yogurt in my hand. "Where's my June bug?" he asked, his face twisted with worry.

"I...it's..." I pointed to the garbage bin.

"You *killed* him? Why would you do that?" He shoved me out of the way and flipped the lid off the garbage container, digging manically through the contents and tossing it on the floor around him.

"He was dead," I said, my voice barely above a whisper.

He found the tiny beetle and picked him out from the trash, holding him up between two fingers and grinning from ear to ear. "There ya are, little buddy."

I took a few steps back and leaned against the counter, unsure what the next move would be, but fairly certain I couldn't take much more of this. My new husband had been high all week—out of work, yet again—and performing none of the duties that any normal newlywed husband and expecting father would do. Just a week earlier, I'd caught him smoking a joint in the living room when I came home from work and had to remind him why such a thing was not hospitable for an expecting mother. It'd taken me two days to get the smell out of the house, and Nathan did nothing more than patronize me for my "obsessive cleanliness".

On top of that, he made a point to again call out my inability to get on board with pot-smoking, almost as if he was trying to sell me on something that was no more harmful than a bag of candy. And sure, maybe that was the case, but it was an illegal drug and I—being the Goody Two-Shoes that I was—could not simply hop aboard the weed wagon. Call me uptight, if you must.

But as I was beginning to realize, weed wasn't Nathan's only drug of choice. A few days after finding him high as kite in our living room, I stumbled upon a small bag filled with white powder in his sock drawer while putting away laundry. I wasn't naive to its contents—although I had carefully placed the bag back in the drawer and re-covered it with the socks. I simply didn't have the energy to confront him about it.

Now there were pills and wads of cash lying out in plain sight, and I couldn't pretend I hadn't seen the evidence. Yet, the thought of addressing these issues nauseated me; no matter what I asked or how, Nathan would become defensive and it would just lead to another argument.

And another round of painful makeup sex.

"Jesse's having a party tonight," Nathan said, pushing himself up from the floor and shoving the dead bug into his pocket.

"Okay."

"Wanna come with me?" He pulled me into another hug, his hands roaming my backside. I recognized a hint of liquor on his breath and pulled away, turning back to my groceries.

"I'm not really feeling the greatest today," I lied. "Can you go without me?" His face fell into a sad expression—as if someone other than the bug in his pocket had died. I wasn't sure that my absence at a party warranted such a look, being that I rarely went with him anyway.

"My poor girl," he said, placing his hands over my belly. "Are you sure it's okay if I go without you?"

As if I have a choice.

"Yeah, it's fine, I'll probably get to bed early anyway," I brushed it off but was annoyed that he had even asked me to join him in the first place. Nathan knew I didn't like to party, especially while pregnant. Drunk people were the worst when you were stone-cold sober.

Not that I wanted him to stay home—not in his current state.

He hopped back a step and started pacing the dining room again before taking off down the hall. I pulled the gallon of milk from the grocery bag I'd been unpacking and stuffed it on an open shelf in the fridge. Nathan returned from the bedroom as I closed the fridge and turned back to the counter. He'd put on his tennis shoes and was holding the plastic bag full of pills and sorters.

I looked away, smiling nervously at him while I pulled the rest of the cereal boxes out and set them on the counter. He reached over and grabbed the box of Lucky Charms, stuffing it under his armpit. "For later," he said, offering me an unnecessary wink. "I'll be back late. Don't wait up!" He opened the front door and closed it loudly behind him.

I stood frozen in the kitchen, my face turned up in confusion as my eyes settled on the discarded trash he'd left all over the floor. I was still staring at the floor when the realization dawned on me that I'd made a mistake.

I never should have married Nathan.

CHAPTER TEN

JULY 2004

My hormones were through the roof, and at twenty-six weeks, my ankles were swollen to the size of softballs and my bladder demanded relief at all hours of the day, leaving me sleep-deprived. I was grateful the weekend had arrived so I could get in a few naps and stay off my feet, maybe kick back with a book. Nathan and I had just moved into a larger apartment, a two-bedroom complex in Albertville, a couple towns over from where I'd grown up in Buffalo. We were even on the main floor of the complex, just across from the laundry room, which would serve as a convenience once the baby arrived. But as much as I looked forward to some rest, we still needed to finish unpacking and get the nursery set up.

Nathan had been distant for several weeks and as a result, hadn't helped with much of the packing, let alone the unpacking once we were settling into our new unit. If he wasn't busy getting high with Jesse—who conveniently lived in the complex as well—he was incessantly begging me for sex or simply wasn't home—even though he'd been fired from his new landscaping job earlier in the week.

He'd lasted thirteen days with this one and hadn't even received his first paycheck before they canned him.

I was feeling lonelier by the day; my friends were all away at college and I barely saw anyone outside of Nathan, my parents and coworkers. And even then, I didn't bother to go into detail about Nathan's erratic behavior or his frequent drug use—I didn't need anyone judging him more than they already had, and I was growing tired of suggestions that "maybe he's not the right guy" for me.

Jerilyn had reached out the week of the move, asking if she could throw me a baby shower. Actually, she asked if she was *supposed* to throw me a shower. I was fairly certain she didn't *want* to, but I didn't blame her. How the hell do you throw a baby shower for your nineteen-year-old BFF when they live three hours away? Not to mention, she hadn't been overjoyed when I told her I was pregnant. Supportive? Yes. Overjoyed? Negative.

Jerilyn and Nathan had yet to grow a liking toward one another—they hadn't even seen each other but for a few times—and again, she lived three hours away and was busy making new friends at MSU. It seemed we had little in common anymore, other than the fact that we'd been friends since we were two years old. I missed her and didn't talk to her often enough.

Nonetheless, she offered to throw the shower but was let off the hook when my mom called later the same day, also offering to throw the shower and announcing that she and Dad had picked up a crib for us, which they'd dutifully dropped off that morning. While I had fully expected my parents to lose their shit when they found out I was pregnant, they had surprised me and done the opposite. They were excited to be grandparents—young ones at that—and although their feelings toward Nathan hadn't changed, for the most part, they set their differences aside in preparation for our little one.

Despite the unexpected support from my parents, the last thing I wanted was a damn baby shower. I felt like a waddling cow with hormones that often resulted in unexplainable bouts of rudeness—or as Nathan called it, 'bitchiness'—and therefore I had no interest in being around the judgmental group of women that were likely to fill out the guest list. But we needed things for the baby and with Nathan barely working, we had no way to afford a single box of diapers, let alone everything else a baby needs, if we wanted to continue making our rent every month. As much as I hated to admit it, we needed the baby shower.

"Should we put the crib together tonight?" I asked Nathan as he stepped out of the shower and toweled off. I leaned against the door frame, noticing Nathan's physique had filled out a bit, too. I'd read in the pregnancy book that it was common for expecting dads to pack on a few pounds during those months.

"I have plans later, Brynn. Jesse's having a barbeque and I said I'd stop by." He wrapped his towel around his waist and tucked the corner to hold it in place.

Nathan knew I still hated everything to do with Jesse. Harper's brother or not, he was still an asshole, and the more Nathan mentioned his name, the more I hated him. Sadly, it was my own fault for introducing them in the first place. The problem was, aside from being an arrogant prick, Jesse loved nothing more than to sit around smoking weed, playing video games and sleeping with any girl who'd willingly spread her legs for him. He was a bad influence on Nathan and always seemed to bring out the worst in him.

"You didn't tell me you had plans," I whimpered, rubbing my belly. "Why can't you hang out with me tonight? The baby will be here before we know it, and we don't really have much time left for just the two of us."

"We're together right now," he pointed out, grabbing his deodorant and rolling it under his armpits. "We've been together all morning."

"This is hardly quality time," I argued, placing my hands on my hips. Nathan had spent the morning sleeping in after binge-watching reruns of *The Fresh Prince*, while I had been up all night with Braxton-Hicks contractions, freaking out that the baby would come before we even had a chance to put the damn crib together.

"Oh? You're looking for *that* kind of quality time, huh?" he smirked and dropped his towel, stepping in close. His arms wrapped around me, his lips molding to my neck and his on-command erection jabbing me in the belly.

"That's not what I meant." I sighed and pulled his hands from my middle before turning toward the bedroom across the hall. "I'm really not in the mood."

"You're never in the mood anymore, Brynn!" He followed me—still naked—his skin glistening from his shower. "We haven't had sex in weeks. Come on, how about a quickie before I go?" He gave his hips a wiggle and his dick shimmied back and forth. I chuckled, despite my annoyance, at the unexpected and surprisingly silly gesture.

"Cute, but *ugh*. No, thanks. I've had cramps and heart-burn since last night. And I literally look like a cow."

"Then how about a blow job for me?" he pleaded, traipsing over to me in Chippendales' fashion. "I love seeing those lips wrapped around my cock." He laid a palm on my cheek and ran his thumb over my bottom lip. I stepped back until my legs found the edge of the bed and then sat down slowly, placing a hand over my belly.

"I just told you I have heartburn. So that's a no."

"And I just want to fuck my wife," he hollered back in

frustration. "Come on, you never want to anymore." He stood in front of me and put his hands in my hair, tugging and snapping my head back.

"Why do you always have to be so vulgar?" I swatted his hand away, and he stepped back and pulled a pair of boxers from the dresser, jerking them on angrily before grabbing his cargo shorts from the bottom drawer.

"Is it really so bad that I want you?" He shook his head in disbelief. "Fine. No sex. No blow job." He stepped into his shorts before pulling a black T-shirt over his head. "It's just a typical Friday night!" He chuckled bitterly to himself and left the room, slipping into his shoes and slamming the front door.

I got up from the bed and walked down the hall to the spare bedroom that would soon be Ava's. The crib leaned against the wall, still nothing more than the individual parts in the box it came in. My parents had intended to help us put it together when they'd dropped it off. My heart ached in my chest as I remembered the hurt on their faces when Nathan told them we didn't need their help and asked them to leave.

"Putting a crib together is a father's job..."

CHAPTER ELEVEN

I WAS startled awake on the couch hours later, the TV flickering in the darkness. The cable box flashed 2:24 a.m. I mumbled Nathan's name, hearing nothing in response, so I grabbed my phone from the coffee table and checked to see if he had called or texted. He hadn't—not once since he'd left for Jesse's earlier that afternoon.

I'd done nothing productive for the majority of the day, thanks to the crabbiness that had ensued following Nathan's departure. While I'd intended to start setting up the baby's room, instead I'd spent the afternoon with my nose in a book while I stuffed my face with cheese puffs—a pregnancy craving that had hit me earlier that week—in between trips to the bathroom to pee just about every half hour. We still had plenty of time to get the room set up and it wasn't like I could put the crib together by myself, anyway.

I sat up on the couch and inhaled deeply, my eyes settling on a text message from a familiar yet surprising, name in my phone: Carter Graham, my former high school lab partner who Nathan had met at the End of

Summer Shed Party. Carter's message was simple and contained a photo attachment.

Thought u deserved 2 know.

I stood, clutching my stomach, the sudden movement upsetting my stomach. The photo attached to the text was grainy and dark, but there was no denying the content in question. Nathan, sitting spread eagle on a couch, Tess *Fucking* Danielson straddling his lap with her head buried in his neck. She wore a barely-there hot pink cropped tank top and black shorts that looked more like panties, Nathan's strong hands gripping her ass cheeks like he was holding on for dear life.

What the actual fuck?

I grabbed Nathan's over-sized sweatshirt off the floor and speed-dialed his number, only to be sent to voicemail. I pulled the sweatshirt over my head and secured it snugly over my swollen belly, and then tried Nathan's cell again.

"It's Nathan. Leave a message."

Slipping my feet into my shoes, I grabbed my keys and waddled my way across the parking lot to Jesse's building as quickly as my swollen ankles would allow. Once inside the lobby, I stared blankly at the door phone, unable to recall which apartment belonged to the piece-of-shit and his deadbeat roommates. When the answer didn't come quickly enough, I forcefully pushed every apartment number's buzzer until I heard the click of the door unlocking. Pulling it open, I made my way up two flights of stairs, my ankles throbbing with each step, then down the hall to the one apartment that showed any signs of life—the Bone Thugs and Harmony song thumping just enough to tell me I'd reached the right unit.

Forgoing the courtesy of knocking, I barged my way

into the unlocked apartment and was immediately privy to the pungent smell of weed. The music was loud enough to drown out my entrance and didn't disturb the two inhabitants necking on the worn couch.

I saw her naked tits first.

Tess *Fucking* Danielson was on top of *my* husband, the co-creator of the tiny human growing inside me, her tits in his face as he sucked her nipple and cupped her ass cheeks through her shorts/possibly panties.

I'll fucking kill him.

I dropped my keys onto the linoleum floor, startling the only other people in the dark room. They stopped sucking each other's body parts and looked up at me like deer in headlights. Nathan moved first, recognition finally cutting through the fog in his brain.

"Brynn? What the fuck!" he shouted, shoving Tess from his lap. She threw her hands over her chest and scrambled to find her top.

"How could you?" I asked, my voice barely above a whisper.

"It's not what it looks like." He stumbled over to me, an obvious erection fighting for release in his unzipped cargo shorts. He fumbled with the zipper and made his way toward me, tripping over the discarded clothes strewn all over the floor.

"How fucking stupid do you think I am, Nathan?"

"What is she doing here, Nathan?" Tess asked innocently, pulling her tank top over her head.

"Shut up, Tess," he barked, taking my hands in his. I swatted him away and stomped across the room to Tess, stopping just inches from her face.

"I didn't realize you were such a fucking whore that you'd try to sleep with my *husband* while I'm pregnant with his *child*." I made sure to splatter some spit on her face as I spoke. She swiped a hand across her cheek to sop up the mess.

"*His* child?" she looked to Nathan, clearly confused by my admission.

Who the hell else's child does she think I'm carrying?

"I said shut up, Tess!" Nathan shouted through gritted teeth.

Oh, my God.

He's seeing her.

What had he told her? That we'd broken up? That I was carrying another man's child? Genuine shock spread across Tess's face. "What bullshit lies did he tell you?" I asked her, almost feeling sorry for her. She stared at me and started to speak but snapped her mouth shut, crossing her arms over her flat stomach.

"Go home, Brynn," Nathan said from behind me. He swiped my keys from the floor and held them out to me, expecting me to grab them and simply do as he said.

"Go home? That's all you have to say?"

"Yes. Go home. I'll meet you over there in a few minutes." I stepped closer and snatched the keys from his hands, annoyed that a tear was about to roll down my cheek and Tess would see me cry.

"Why are you doing this to me?" I whispered to my husband as a bedroom door opened behind us. Carter and two other guys I didn't recognize—along with two half-naked girls—stumbled out into the living room. Smoke billowed from the room behind them. Carter dropped his head, avoiding eye contact with me, and stepped back into the bedroom and out of view.

Was that guilt on his face?

I waved a hand at the thick layer of smoke as the remaining members of what I could only assume was a small orgy, stared back at me like I was an alien about to invade their homeland.

"I said go home, you're embarrassing yourself," Nathan chastised. I shoved him hard in the chest and he stepped backward, grabbing his shirt from the floor and pulling it over his head.

"No, *you're* the one embarrassing *me*, you asshole! How could you do this?" He grabbed my arm, his fingers gripping my wrist tightly, then yanked me out of the apartment and shoved me out into the hallway.

"Go the fuck home. Now." Nathan's angry pupils glared back at me; he pointed down the hall. I turned slowly and, despite my resolve, started down the hallway— tripping every dozen or so steps, a steady stream of tears clouding my vision. I unlocked the door to our apartment and stepped inside, leaning against the door.

I can't breathe.

My heart pounded in my chest as disbelief engulfed me.

My husband was having an affair.

———

NATHAN APPEARED on our patio and rapped his knuckles on the sliding door. I unlocked it—opening it enough for him to step inside—and then pulled it closed. He stood in front of me and shoved his hands into his pockets, but he said nothing, just stared at me with his usual glassy eyes while I stood there and let the tears roll down my pregnancy-rounded cheeks.

"How long have you been sleeping with her?" I finally whispered, nearly vomiting when I said the words out loud, hating the way they tasted.

"I haven't slept with her."

"I don't believe you," I said flatly.

"That's fine. I don't really care what you believe." He shoved past me and made his way to the kitchen, opening the refrigerator and grabbing a bottle of beer from the shelf. He removed the metal top from the bottle and took a long pull, draining at least half the liquid in one tilt of his head.

"Why did you want to have this baby with me?" I asked, my hands shaking and heart threatening to beat out of my chest.

"I didn't get you pregnant on purpose, Brynn." He tipped his head back and slammed the rest of his beer, a smug expression on his face, his lips pursed.

"No, but you begged me not to terminate."

"Yep. I stopped you from killing our child, that's right, Brynn! Shame on me. But you've been such a hormonal bitch that I can't stand being around you right now." He slammed his now empty beer bottle down on the counter and ran his hands through his greasy hair. I watched the empty bottle tip over and roll onto the linoleum floor with a clink.

"I...how could you say that?"

"Because it's true. I've been trying to fuck you—my *wife* —for weeks, and you turn me down every chance you get." He turned and grabbed another beer from the fridge, fumbling to remove the bottle cap and then slamming it back onto the shelf, grabbing a can instead. "You're supposed to keep me satisfied, Brynn. Do you really think you've done that?"

"Are you insane? That's not how this works, Nathan! You don't go running off to fuck some random slut just because your pregnant wife doesn't feel like sucking your dick every day!" Nathan slammed his fist onto the counter.

I flinched and took an instinctive step backward, feeling the bass of his anger in my chest.

"I'm never home because all you do is nag, and I'm so fucking sick of it, Brynn." He unbuckled his belt and pulled it from the loops of his cargo shorts, dropping it onto the floor. "Let's fuck."

"Wha…are you delusional?" I caught sight of his erection fighting for release against the fabric.

"Nope. But I'm high as shit and need to fuck, so either bend your fat ass over this counter or I'll go fuck Tess instead." He jutted his chin, unzipping his shorts and letting them fall to the floor.

He was naked underneath.

I saw him put on boxers this morning, where are they?

I had no words. No words in response to Nathan's betrayal and the subsequent threat of taking it further. And I wasn't about to let him have his way with me just to stop him from doing it.

I wondered how many other times they had been together; how long it had been going on. Vomit tickled the back of my throat, the image from Carter's grainy photo flashed in my mind.

"Yeah, I didn't think so," Nathan said patronizingly when I failed to respond to his advances. He pulled his shorts up, buttoning them as he made his way across the room and over to me, his bloodshot eyes daring me to stop him. "I'm going back over to Jesse's, and I'm going to fuck Tess," he whispered vindictively in my ear. He licked my neck and pulled me to his chest, his strong arm holding me in place while he slid his hand into the front of my sweatpants. His fingers found and spread my folds. I sucked in a sudden breath, failing to embrace his forceful intrusion. "…and after I fuck her, I'm going to sit down, smoke some more weed—maybe do another line of coke—and re-fucking-lax." He shoved two fingers inside me and then just as quickly, yanked them out and brought them to his mouth, licking each finger slowly and then bringing them to his nose. He inhaled, his eyes locked on mine. "Mmm…it's too bad, you taste so much better than her."

Nathan released his grip on me and turned quickly, opening the sliding door and stepping out onto the patio before turning back to me. "I'm staying at Jesse's tonight," he shouted nonchalantly before turning and walking off in the other direction.

"Nathan!" I called after him, but he didn't slow. "Nathan! Stop! Please don't do this!" I stumbled barefoot across the parking lot, calling out his name to no avail as he continued his leisurely pace, my pleas seemingly falling on deaf ears.

"Nathan!"

He opened the door to Jesse's building and disappeared inside without so much as a glance in my direction.

Come back.

I fell to my knees, scraping them on the pebble-filled asphalt below me. There, in the middle of the lot, I wept until I had no tears left to cry, until my voice was hoarse and snot dripped from my nose. I stared at the building and willed my husband to walk back through the door, to come back to me; to fight for us.

When he didn't, I pushed myself up from the ground and walked aimlessly back to our shit-hole apartment. I locked the door behind me and wandered down the hall to our bedroom, where I caught my reflection in the cheap full-length mirror that leaned carelessly against the wall. Streaks of mascara painted my puffy cheeks and dirt stained my sweatpants at the knees. I could suddenly understand why Nathan had taken a preference to Tess over me; pregnancy hadn't been kind to me.

Ugh, look at me.

Such…a cow.

Despite my reservations and all the warnings from those around me, I'd fallen victim to Nathan's flirtatious and playful antics, his "poor me" saga and manipulative mind games. I was hooked—and now my heart had been shattered. My husband was a conniving adulterer, a drug-abusing player who cared of no one other than himself.

And for some reason, I was surprised.

I thought Nathan loved me, that he wanted our child, our family. That's why I had agreed to marry him. I loved him, against everything in me—I fucking loved him.

Now, all I wanted was for the pain to stop, to go back to where it all started and un-meet him. To have my life back. My family. To have gone off to college with my friends.

I'd never felt as alone as I had in that moment.

When did Nathan start using cocaine?

My mind filled with images of Tess riding Nathan on that couch, pleasure playing across her gorgeous face. I placed my hand over my belly and watched in the mirror, feeling our baby move around inside her tiny home. She had been active all day.

I am nothing.

I am worthless.

Everything is broken.

My fist slammed into the center of the mirror as I let out a piercing scream. Shards of glass cracked and splintered, flying everywhere, the plastic frame bending in half and crashing to the floor. I pulled my hand from the wreckage and watched in awe at the crimson blood that flowed from my knuckle and dripped onto the carpet.

The pain delayed, my wound gaped open enough to

see bone. I gagged, suddenly feverish and certain I was about to be sick.

Oh, God. What have I done?

Panic set in and I blinked, taking in the wreckage of the mirror, my breaths coming in staccato-like spurts. I stepped over the glass and crossed the hall to the bathroom, rinsing my shredded hand under cold water and pulling out as much glass as I could. I wrapped it in paper towels before securing the make-shift bandage with athletic tape. I felt the beating of my heart pulsing in my hand, almost as if I were holding the freshly broken organ in my palm.

I wasn't usually one to self-harm, but I needed to know how it felt. I needed to be in control, to somehow exchange the invisible pain for something tangible and real. Something I could put a bandage over that proved I was actually hurting.

This is my pain.

I controlled this.

I whipped open the lid to the toilet and vomited, bile and toilet water ricocheting off the water and splashing at my feet. I pulled the handle to flush and then wet a warm washcloth and wiped my face before brushing my teeth.

Turning off the bathroom light, I stepped back into our bedroom and climbed into Nathan's side of the bed, pulling the covers firmly around my body; a body that felt so foreign, so unlike my own.

I soaked the pillow with salty tears and drifted off to sleep, my sliced-up hand bleeding through its bandaging and onto the white sheets.

I am nothing.

CHAPTER TWELVE

MY ALARM BUZZER sounded promptly at six the next morning. Not ready to harbor the weight of the prior night's
events, I groaned and threw a lazy arm over to the nightstand, yanking the cord of the demon alarm clock from the
wall and tossing the contraption to the floor. I pulled the
duvet over my head, resettled my head into the pillow and
closed my eyes; I needed a few more hours of sleep and
fooled myself into thinking it would come, but a pounding
headache already threatened at the base of my skull. And I
couldn't stop picturing Tess's slender body on Nathan's lap.

Her mouth all over him.

The look on her face when she glared at my belly.

It was all too much, too real, like a movie playing on a
loop in my mind.

I peeked an eye open and peered over to the window,
squinting as I tried to look through a gap in the sheer
curtain. Rain fell outside as the storm inside me raged on
—fitting that the gloom had followed into the morning. I
listened intently to the patter of the rain and tried to shake
the image of my cheating husband from my head.

I'd always loved the sound of the rain, the liquid pellets recoiling off the ground, reminding me that sometimes God needs a good cry too. I'm not even sure I believe in God, but I remember my mom saying that to me once. She used to say that the claps of thunder were the sounds of God bowling. "He must have bowled a strike!" she'd say when the thunder was particularly loud. I'd been afraid of storms as a little girl, and while I'd be hard-pressed to imagine Him finding time for such a leisurely activity, the sentiment of the memory nearly brought a smile to my face.

I missed my mom and almost thought to call her, but I'd never find the words to explain the hurt penetrating my heart. She wouldn't understand, she'd never been in my shoes.

And I didn't want her to hate Nathan any more than she already did.

I sighed and threw back my covers, rolling out of bed and pulling on my bathrobe, wishing for the hundredth time that large amounts of caffeine were acceptable to consume during pregnancy.

I could really go for an entire pot of coffee right now.

Broken glass was still scattered along the floor. I found my slippers and slid my feet into them before waddling to the bathroom to drain my bladder, wincing in pain at the stabbing sensation in my hand, my knuckles stiff and difficult to bend. I flushed the toilet and stood over the sink, the white ceramic tainted a light shade of pink—blood from the night before.

I managed to clean out the wounds enough to regain some mobility in my fingers, but I was fairly certain I probably should have had at least one of my knuckles stitched back together by a medical professional. I settled on a butterfly bandage and hoped for the best.

I filled a paper cup with water from the tap and grabbed the bottle of aspirin from the medicine cabinet. Popping the oblong pills into my mouth with the warm tap water, I tossed the cup into the overflowing trash can and mentally added, "clean the fucking bathroom" to my list of shit I didn't want to do today.

My stomach fluttered, and fresh bile rose in my throat. I doubled over the counter, clutching my belly as my skin grew hot and sweat beaded on my forehead. This time I didn't make it to the toilet; I filled the sink with stomach acid and then rinsed it thoroughly down the drain.

At what point during pregnancy does morning sickness shrivel up and die?

I headed into the kitchen and grabbed the teapot from the stove. Filling it with water, I reached into the cupboard and grabbed my favorite mug, selecting a bag of caffeine-free Earl Grey tea. I turned on the electric burner and waited for the water to boil, images of The Nathan and Tess Show still flashing in my mind. Her attitude and surprise when I'd barged into Jesse's apartment weighed on me. It had been evident by Tess's reaction to my "announcement" that I was carrying Nathan's baby that she had no idea Nathan and I were still together, and I wondered for the umpteenth time what he'd said to make her believe we weren't.

Nathan used to be nice, or at least I think he did—to me, anyway. There was a time he went out of his way to make me laugh and tell me I was beautiful. I hadn't heard those words from him in a long time and couldn't recall the last time he made me smile. I was starting to feel more like his mother than his wife.

Nathan had moved to Minnesota only a month before I'd met him at the Reebok Outlet in the Albertville mall. I hadn't thought to ask him why he'd moved so far from home, but he mentioned he was staying with his sister for a bit until he got a job and found a permanent place to live. For some reason that was all I thought I needed to know. When you're a naive—and probably somewhat self-centered—eighteen-year-old female, I guess sometimes the small details don't seem to matter, even when they should.

What I should have asked Nathan back then was what brought him to Minnesota. "*I had a problem with drugs and alcohol and my sister thought it would be good for me to get away from that crowd and come stay with her for a while.*" I've always been curious as to whether this information would have been significant enough for me to reconsider dating Nathan in the first place. Would it have been the information I could have used ahead of time to simply flip him the peace sign and say, "thanks, I'm not interested"?

But it wasn't just the drugs and alcohol.

I'd come to learn more of Nathan's past; that he had anger issues—a temper. He'd been arrested at least twice—that I knew of—for assault. Another time for shoplifting, apparently the concept of hard-earned money wasn't his thing; if he felt he deserved something, he went after it.

Much like he had with me.

I wished I'd known.

I had been working at the Reebok Outlet for a few months when Nathan walked into my life. It was a slow day, and in between helping the few customers that graced us with their presence, in walked Nathan—a tall, dark and handsome piece of eye candy—in his Levi's jeans and Abercrombie & Fitch sweatshirt, a big smile on his face when he approached me while I restocked shoes in the men's department.

· · ·

"Excuse me?" He leaned in. "got a second?" I detected an East Coast accent in his voice. I stuffed the shoe box into its place on the shelf and turned to him.

"Hi, thanks for stopping in today! Are you looking for something in particular?" I asked, my cheerful customer service act in full swing. We made eye contact, and his hazel eyes checked me out in my sexy uniform (which wasn't sexy at all; I wore a pair of black Reebok windbreaker pants, a cerulean blue Reebok polo and Reebok tennis shoes.)

"A job application?" he replied. YES. Please work here so I can stare at you every day from 9:00 a.m. to 5:00 p.m. Central Standard time, thank you very much! *My face fell when I remembered my boss, Kristina, had just hired two additional associates who were expected to start training the following week.*

"I'm sorry, we're actually not hiring anymore. Is the sign still in the window?" I replied, peering over to the front display window in search of the "we're hiring!" sign. For a moment I was slightly bummed that I wouldn't have an opportunity to work with this guy; I could listen to him talk with that accent all day.

He scratched his head and turned to walk out of the store, noticeably grappling with my news that there were no additional job openings. He took a few steps toward the door and then turned and walked back over to me, a puzzled expression on his face.

"Can I get your number instead?" he asked, his lips forming into a nervous smile. He tucked his hands back into his pockets, and I smiled back.

"Sure." He pulled his phone out of his pocket and handed it to me so I could enter my number.

"I'm Nathan."

"Brynnlee," I replied, smiling back at him, "but everyone calls me Brynn." I handed his phone to him, and he immediately pressed the 'send' button. My phone vibrated in the pocket of my windbreaker.

"Just making sure you didn't fake number me," he said with a crooked smile. "I'll call you tonight, Brynn."

My Only Sunshine

It took me a moment to catch my breath after I watched Nathan walk out of the store and disappear into the neighboring Adidas Outlet. It had been a while since I'd been hit on so openly, let alone been out on a date, and while I wasn't looking for a relationship, it wouldn't hurt to have someone fun to spend some time with over the rest of the summer.

Nathan called about twenty minutes after my shift ended and asked if I wanted to come over to his house to sit by the fire. When I hesitated, reluctant to head over to a strange guy's house before learning more than his first name, this was the point in the conversation where he admitted that he lived with his sister—who would also be home—and that I had nothing to worry about. I agreed to come over and we sat in the driveway of his sister's house for hours, on Adirondack chairs, with a small fire burning in a metal pit between us.

"Your feet must be tired," he said after a while, a smirk on his gorgeous face.

"My feet?" I looked down at my shoes, still the Reebok's I'd worn all day as I hadn't changed out of my work clothes.

"You've been running through my mind all day." He smiled, his cheesy pick-up line taking a moment to register on my end.

"Oh, shut up!" I said, giggling and socking him in the shoulder.

When the temperature grew chilly, Nathan offered me a flannel blanket and wrapped it around my shoulders, his hand lingering on my knee.

THE TEA KETTLE whistled and I turned off the burner, pouring the steaming water over the teabag and waiting for it to steep. I was struck with the notion that Nathan's constant need for sex—and my lack of desire for it—had somehow eliminated any chance of monogamy in our relationship. I wasn't sure what to do. Despite what happened, I wasn't ready to walk away; we had a baby coming and she deserved to have two parents living under the same roof.

I wiped a rogue tear from my cheek and then grabbed my phone from the coffee table where I'd left it to charge overnight. There were no missed calls, no text messages.

No word from my cheating husband.

I tossed the phone onto the couch, even though I wanted nothing more than to dial his number and hear the sound of his voice—to pretend last night never happened.

———

IT WAS another five days before Nathan came home. I had showered and dressed for work, forgoing breakfast again thanks to an uneasy stomach, and grabbed my purse from the counter. I heard the faint sound of snoring while I slipped into my shoes and reached for the knob to the front door. I pressed my ear to the wood and was confident that whoever was asleep in the hallway was right outside my door.

I turned the knob and pulled the squeaky door back to reveal Nathan passed out in the fetal position in the middle of the hallway. The sound of the door startled him awake and after a quick moment of disorientation, his eyes adjusted, and he struggled aimlessly to his feet. He looked like shit with rumpled, greasy hair and bags under his sunken eyes. Uneasy on his feet, he slumped into the door frame.

"Where you goin'?" he slurred.

Great, not even sobered up yet.

"To work." I pushed past him and turned to make my way down the hall.

"Brynn, wait..." he begged, reaching out and grabbing my arm. I stopped and met his bloodshot eyes. His usually taut face was puffy and sported a thicker beard than his signature stubble. He forced a crooked smile, his dumpster juice breath coming out hot and thick even though I stood a good foot in front of him. "Do you have any cash?" he asked, his hand stretched in front of him.

I shrugged my arm from his grasp and stomped off down the hallway. Five days without so much as a text or a call to let me know he was still a living, breathing human on this earth, and that's the first thing the fuck head says to me?

Of course, it is, that's why he came home.

His supply had run out.

CHAPTER THIRTEEN
OCTOBER 2004

FORGIVENESS DOESN'T CHANGE the past, but it can enhance the future. It can shed light on what are otherwise some of our darkest days. I didn't immediately decide to forgive Nathan after he slept with Tess. I honestly don't even know why I decided to forgive him in the first place; I just know that somewhere along the road I did. Or at the very least, I chose to look past it—not to allow it to affect me the way it once did.

Forgiving an unfaithful partner is a daunting task—and those words don't even do it justice. It's heartbreaking in a way that can't be explained unless you've experienced it. Some days you wonder why the hell you didn't kick them to the curb the second it happened. Other days you're convinced you were the reason the infidelity happened in the first place, that there's something wrong with you. That you're not pretty enough, thin enough or simply nothing special—easily replaceable.

I wasted a lot of days dwelling on the latter.

It was *my* fault; I neglected my wifely duties in the department of sexual satisfaction so therefore I deserved it.

I was hormonal and pregnant and therefore living with me was hard, impossible at times. I was too demanding, with high expectations that my husband would not only get a job, but help out around our home, comfort me when I was feeling down, maybe tell me I looked beautiful even though my face was swollen from pregnancy and I was overdue for a haircut. I was the difficult one, the source of all our problems—according to my husband. So, of course he would cheat on me, *of course* he would stray.

Yeah, fucking right.

It's incredible what manipulation can do to a person's mind, the things you can be convinced to believe. It took me a number of years to come to the realization that Nathan's infidelity wasn't actually my fault. Sure, I had been known to say the things that were likely to push Nathan to the limit, but none of my harmless *words* could truly justify his *physical* actions, right?

In those moments of heartache and doubt, I was convinced that I was solely the one to blame, that I was the reason he started using again, and I was the driving force in his determination to sleep with Tess. I'd let this man down because I'd lost my sex drive before either of us were even old enough to legally consume alcohol. I'd deprived him of his basic needs.

Or so I was convinced.

If I'm being honest, I had simply grown to resent him for forcing me to make decisions I wasn't ready to make. So why the fuck would I want to reward him with sexual favors that I was sure he didn't deserve?

The cold hard truth is that I had shut down the second Nathan decided we were going to keep our child. I went through the motions when we stood in front of Judge Vesser. I said our vows because that's what I felt like I was supposed to do, what was expected of me, if I was going to bring a baby into this world. But I wasn't really ready to be a wife—or a mother—and for some reason I wanted to make sure Nathan was punished for forcing me to be both.

Withholding sex was the only way I knew to do that.

Mature, I know.

Before finding out I was pregnant, I wasn't sure which side of the Roe v. Wade line I stood on. When that pink plus sign appeared on the first pregnancy test I'd ever taken, the fear set in before I had a chance to shed a tear. Panic mode engaged, and I knew I had no more than two options: fight or flight. My instincts subconsciously chose flight, and while I was pissed that Nathan ultimately made the final decision for me—for us—it's because of him that my daughter lives and breathes, and that's one of the few reasons I found the strength to forgive him.

If there's one thing Nathan did right, it was that.

I wasn't like most girls my age, or even most girls I knew growing up—I had never put on the princess dresses and dreamed about my wedding day or marrying the man of my dreams and starting a family. But once it was decided that we were, in fact, having a baby, I committed wholeheartedly.

I was having a baby.

I was going to be a mother.

I was going to give it my all.

But I was still angry, and I was still bitter. I was every one of those supplementary emotions that come into play when you feel like someone forced you to do something you didn't really want to do.

While I'd come to terms with the fact that I was going to be a mother, I think it's safe to say I had held onto that bitterness long after the decision had been made. I felt sorry for myself even before my husband cheated on me and I put my fist through a mirror. Then I got up and pretended like it never happened—as if it would be easier to live with than the glaring reality that my life had unraveled before it had really begun.

I'd be hard-pressed to claim that things got better for a while after Nathan came home that Tuesday morning in July. We argued a lot, on top of the withdrawal symptoms we had to deal with—courtesy of that white powder I'd once discovered in his sock drawer—a challenge I had not been prepared for in the least.

While I was used to Nathan's lack of contribution around our home, seeing him laid up in bed for days at a time, puking into a bucket and sweating through more clothes and bed sheets than I would've thought possible, was almost enough for me to give the guy a break, and agree he'd suffered enough.

Three months had passed and we had yet to sit down and discuss the events of the night he chose Tess over me; his withdrawal period provided the barrier we needed to allow the anger to wear off, and once he was finally feeling better, we dispassionately spent a few weeks avoiding each other in separate rooms of our small apartment. I went to work during the day and read my books at night while Nathan sat around with an Xbox controller in his hands.

The next thing we knew, it was mid-October, and my saving grace, Ava Leigh, was born.

Nathan had been attentive and helpful during the birth. He played the part and did all the things a good husband is supposed to do when his wife delivers their first child. He packed the hospital bags, finally put the crib together and sat by my bedside holding my hand in between contractions while dabbing a cold washcloth on my forehead. He breathed the he-he-hoos with me when it was time to start pushing and offered unexpected words of encouragement while I screamed profanities at him and pushed a nine-pound baby out of a ten-centimeter hole.

I'm not sure I could have survived those grueling twenty-six hours of labor without him. Nathan had been strong and supportive when I needed him most, and for some reason, that counted for something, too.

We cried together when we held our perfect creation for the first time, her ten tiny fingers wrapping around our own as she suckled her bottle and drifted off to sleep. As soon as Ava had been cleaned up, weighed and placed into my arms, Nathan had run out into the waiting room to let my parents and Natalie know that our healthy baby girl had arrived. Everyone hugged—despite their differences— and I think each of us was gifted with just a tiny shred of hope that somehow Ava would make everything better. We were so proud, smiling at our little girl and excitedly shuffling her back and forth between our family members while we took turns snapping pictures of her on my digital camera.

I hoped the worst was behind us, that we could start over.

And after a few days in the hospital, Nathan, Ava and I headed home to our apartment where Nathan's presence slowly became more tolerable. We fought less, even through the exhaustion of caring for a newborn. We ate dinners together at night while Ava napped, and although Nathan wasn't particularly helpful when it came to physically caring for Ava, he was present. He had stayed clean, and he had stopped spending time with Jesse, which was really all I'd asked of him at that point. He seemed committed to our family—to our marriage—and I think that was about the time I convinced myself that I needed to forgive him.

Ava deserved that much.

CHAPTER FOURTEEN

MAY 2005

THE SOUND of Ava crying from her bedroom at 4:22 a.m. was enough to wake the entire apartment building. I glanced over at Nathan, asleep on the other side of our bed without a care in the world. He hadn't even stirred from the piercing sound of Ava's cries—not unusual. Nathan could sleep through a World War without waking. There was no point in trying to roust him to offer a turn at comforting our little one.

I groaned, threw my covers off and slipped my feet into my slippers before trundling down the hall to Ava's room.

"Baby girl, what's the matter?" My wailing seven-month-old was sitting up in her crib, gripping the side rails like a prisoner desperate for escape, her chubby cheeks wet with tears. "Mama's here, sweetie." I scooped her up from the crib, grateful her cries had ceased. She grinned a two-toothed grin, drool dripping from her mouth and onto my nightshirt. "Does my pumpkin have some more teeth coming in?" I asked, confirming with a peek into her mouth.

I settled Ava onto my hip and backed out of the room,

making a pit stop to retrieve the teething gel from the bath-room counter. Nestling us onto the couch, I wrapped Ava in her pink blanket and squeezed some of the gel onto my finger, rubbing it along her gums before offering her the binky she loved so much. She snuggled into my chest and drifted back to sleep while I mindlessly flipped through the channels on the TV, annoyed that I wouldn't be able to fall back asleep as easily as Ava had.

Not that I wasn't tired enough to sleep; sleep just wasn't coming. Aside from tending to a newborn and doing what I could to keep our house in order, I was stressing over my husband's recent late-night activities. He'd finally landed a job—with a pole barn company that was cleverly named The Pole Barn Company—just a couple weeks after Ava was born.

I was ecstatic about the job, being that it was the best paying job he'd had since I met him. The job wasn't the problem—his coworkers were.

Outwardly Mike and Adam seemed like nice enough guys, but they had a habit of hitting up the local bars for happy hour just about every night of the week, a habit my husband didn't hesitate to pick up. Mike and Adam were single guys in their early twenties, looking to pick up women after a grueling day on the job, an exercise I didn't need my husband getting involved in.

I hoped I was just being paranoid, but given our history, I knew Nathan was capable of straying from our marriage.

Regardless of my irritation with Nathan's weeknight outings, I found evenings at home alone with Ava easier than evenings at home with Nathan *and* Ava. In spite of that, my annoyance level rose each time he texted to let me know he would be home late, those insecurities sneaking up on me again.

He hadn't climbed into bed until after midnight that morning and had lopped a lazy arm across my stomach, kissed the back of my head and was snoring within seconds, his breath smelling of stale beer and cigarettes as he breathed through his mouth.

I lay in bed and stewed in my annoyance for another several hours before finally falling back to sleep, only to be woken by Ava less than two hours later.

I knew better than to confront Nathan about his lack of involvement at home; it would just lead to yet another heated argument riddled with name-calling and makeup sex that didn't actually leave me feeling like we'd made up. I was trying to withhold less and give more, in hopes that it would prevent another Tess-like incident, but I wasn't sure how much longer I could keep up the facade.

I decided instead to start making plans of my own, and even though most of my friends were off at college, my parents still wanted to see their daughter and only grand-baby, and it was probably time I stopped declining their invitations to dinner. Not that I was avoiding *them*; I was kind of avoiding *everyone*.

I knew I'd let my parents down...the guilt I harbored for not only bringing a man like Nathan home in the first place, but for moving out in a tizzy when they'd strongly encouraged me to stop dating him and then getting preg-nant so soon afterward.

I brought my lips to Ava's cheek as she slept peacefully in my arms, suddenly understanding my parent's fears and desire to protect me from a man like Nathan.

What if it were Ava in my shoes?

"You're up early," Nathan said gruffly as he came down the hall and headed into the kitchen. He startled me but hopefully hadn't noticed.

"Shhh...Ava's asleep," I whispered, carefully standing

from the couch with her still in my arms. I walked us back to her room, laid her gently in the crib and closed the door. She was likely to sleep for another hour or so now that the teething medicine had kicked in, and I hoped that would allow me time for a quick shower.

I joined Nathan in the kitchen where he had taken a seat at the table, a bowl of cereal in front of him. He looked at me expectantly and then motioned toward the coffee pot. "No coffee?"

I turned my back to him, rolling my eyes at the wall, and grabbed the carafe, taking it to the sink and filling it with water.

"Plans today?" I asked, scooping the ground coffee into the filter.

"Work, why?" he replied with a mouthful of cereal. That was an answer I hadn't expected. Nathan was barely able to drag himself out of bed to make it to work during the week, let alone over the weekend.

"On a Saturday?"

"That a problem?" he asked, looking up from his cereal. I pushed the brew button on the coffee pot and then joined him at the table, reaching for the cereal box.

"No, not a problem."

"Should you be eating that?" Nathan scolded as I popped a few of the sugary cinnamon squares into my mouth. Chewing slowly, I placed the box back onto the table, sat back in my chair and adjusted my nightshirt, a sudden wave of self-consciousness rolling over me. "What are you and Ava doing today?"

"Just cleaning the apartment for the most part. I'll probably take her to my parent's house for dinner later."

"Why?"

"Because I miss them and haven't seen them in a while," I admitted, unsure why Nathan took issue with my plans, considering he very likely wouldn't be home in time for dinner as it was. I'd have to call my dad and ask him to pick Ava and me up, since Nathan would apparently have the car. We were down to one vehicle thanks to a blown engine in the beat-up Bronco Nathan had been driving for the last few months.

"Whatever. Don't expect me to join you."

You weren't invited.

He lifted his cereal bowl and drank the residual milk from it and then set it down on the table. "I'll be home late," he stood and pecked a kiss on top of my head before stuffing his wallet and keys into his pocket. "Is the coffee ready?" he asked, leaning against the door and putting his tennis shoes on. He was perfectly capable of pouring his own coffee, but still I rose from my seat and performed the task for him like a good wife.

Those don't look like work boots.

I handed the tumbler to Nathan just as Ava started crying from her bedroom.

"That's my cue!" Nathan announced, a smug smile spreading across his face. He turned and left the apartment, not bothering to stop the door from slamming behind him.

So much for that shower.

CHAPTER FIFTEEN
JANUARY 2006

AFTER MATERNITY LEAVE ENDED I took a temp position with Regions Marketing, a small agency where I was trying to make a name for myself and start a career. I was grateful, as well, for the insurance benefits and 401K that came with it after I was hired on permanently a few months later, despite my lack of a college degree.

I loved the job—I even liked my coworkers—and happened to be a natural in my client services role.

Not only was my foot in the proverbial door, I was also bringing in more money per bi-weekly pay period than any of my previous jobs combined, which was something we desperately needed. We'd recently moved out of the shit-hole apartment complex—away from Jesse—and into a three-bedroom townhouse on the other side of town that my friend Elle, from the agency, told me about.

I made it through the first half of the workday managing to keep my head down and focus on the emails that had piled up in my inbox. It was a cold Friday after-noon in the dead of a Minnesota winter, and that meant I wouldn't be leaving the office for lunch. The report I'd been working on for the last two hours in preparation for the upcoming quarterly sales meeting was finally finished, just as my stomach growled and I realized I had yet to eat anything.

I locked my computer and grabbed my purse from the bottom drawer of my desk, having decided to pick up lunch from the cafeteria we shared with the other business suites in the building. I stopped by Elle's desk, and she popped up from her chair, quickly inviting herself to join me, just as I'd hoped she would.

While I hadn't known Elle for long, she quickly became a close friend and I'd opened up to her about my rocky relationship with Nathan. She was easy to talk to and always seemed to know when to listen without offering advice. While she'd never actually been in my shoes—most people in my life hadn't—Elle had a way of offering support in ways I couldn't explain. She was someone I needed in my life and just so happened to come into it at a time when I needed her most.

"How are things at home?" She asked as we set our lunch trays down on the table and slipped into the bench seats across from each other. The lunchroom was busier than usual, and it seemed we weren't the only ones avoiding the sub-zero temperatures.

"They're...good, actually," I admitted, surprising even myself. "We're having date night tonight." Nathan was still working at The Pole Barn Company and we were excited to finally be catching up on overdue bills, and even more excited to be able to afford a dinner outside of our own kitchen.

"Sounds dirty," she joked with a quick wink in my direction before taking a bite of her turkey burger.

"There's nothing dirty about a husband and wife going on a date, Elle."

"Well, there is if it goes well!" We laughed and the subject shifted elsewhere while we finished up our meals. Lunch over, we parted ways from the elevator, Elle offering me a lascivious look and a quick shimmy to wish me luck on the date before returning to her cubicle. I chuckled and made my way back to mine, realizing that for the first time in what seemed like forever, I was looking forward to going home to my husband.

———

I PICKED Ava up from daycare on my way home. She was chatty and giggly, singing the *Dora the Explorer* theme song while kicking the back of my seat. She was officially walking, crawling, running and jumping—essentially terrorizing our living room every chance she got. While she was a busy-bodied fifteen-month-old, she was also a sweet, loving and happy little girl that loved to play and snuggle. But Mommy and Daddy were tired and ready for a much-needed night off, and while I had to stifle the guilt of leaving her for the evening, I was relieved she'd at least be able to bond more with her grandparents, and they'd been more than ecstatic when I asked if they'd take her for the evening.

Nathan's daily happy hour trips with Mike and Adam had dwindled a bit, thankfully, and he was spending at least a few nights a week at home with us. He was even attentive after Ava was tucked in for the night and we'd find ourselves enjoying a drink—Nathan with a beer in a chilled mug because it was fancier than a can, and me with a glass of Riesling—while sitting together on the couch and watching a movie. On a few occasions, we'd even managed to enjoy each other's company without the distraction of the TV, when we'd reminisce about our early days together, laughing over stupid shit that was never actually funny.

I was surprised to see a vase of red roses on the kitchen counter when I got back from dropping Ava off with her grandparents. A note was folded and lay propped against the vase of the flowers, a tiny heart drawn on the outside of the page. I set my purse down and reached for the note, leaning over to sniff the roses.

I've never been more excited for a date!
I'll pick you up at 7:00!
Love, Nathan.

Since we hadn't had a night out in months, Nathan had gotten ready while I dropped Ava off across town and then headed over to Mike's house to borrow his Lincoln Navigator for the evening. He'd wanted to drive us around in style and get dressed up for a nice dinner and Mike had been generous enough to let us trade him my Pontiac Sunfire—purchased used and for cheap after Ava was born—for the Navigator; kind of like a Cinderella story, except we wouldn't be turning back into pumpkins until roughly eight o'clock the following morning.

I placed the card back down on the counter and then headed upstairs to take a quick shower, making sure to shave my legs twice so they were extra smooth. I toweled off, applied some lotion and then put on my matching red lace bra and panties before pulling my brand new little black dress over my head.

Feeling sexy for the first time in months—thanks to finally having dropped a good thirty pounds of baby weight—I sauntered over to the vanity where I sang along to Mariah Carey's "Fantasy" at the top of my lungs and applied thick black mascara to my lashes, and a soft powder blush to my cheeks.

I dried and curled my long blonde hair, letting it fall loosely across my shoulders and drape halfway down my back. Nathan always preferred that I made an effort with my appearance, especially on date night, so after taking a second look in the mirror I decided to add a touch of red lipstick to complete my look. I smushed a wet kiss onto Nathan's side of the bathroom mirror and drew a 'xoxo' underneath it for good measure.

Nathan arrived back home promptly at seven o'clock and pulled the Navigator up to the curb in front of our house. He jogged his way through the crunchy snow and up to our front door, ringing the bell just as I opened it.

"Wow..." he stammered, "you look...beautiful." I smiled and offered him a lazy curtsy before pulling on my black leather jacket, a Christmas gift from Nathan a month before.

"Thank you, Mr. Reeves," I smiled, kissing his cheek. He pulled the door closed behind me and locked it while I waited on the step for him to lead the way to the Navigator.

"My darling," he said, offering his arm to me. I took hold of him and stepped onto the icy sidewalk. Temperatures had cooled again overnight, leaving a thick layer of ice on the pavement. I held onto Nathan for dear life, and we made our way to the Navigator and even though chivalry had been dead for decades, Nathan pulled open the passenger door for me and then helped me into the seat. He paused for a moment to look at me longingly and licked his lips before closing the door and jogging over to the driver's side, managing to narrowly avoid a face full of icy pavement when he slipped on a patch of ice.

NATHAN and I had originally planned to see a movie but opted for a nice steakhouse dinner instead. We were offered a small table in the back of the restaurant, complete with ambient lighting and a candle in the center of it, fancy by our standards.

We were seated by the hostess, who filled our drinking glasses with ice water and placed a set of menus on the corner of the table. Nathan reached for my hand and smiled. "I can't get over how beautiful you look tonight," he said once she'd left. I dipped my head, suddenly bashful, and squeezed his hand. Quieter, and accompanied by one of his signature winks, he said, "I can't wait to get you back home and throw that dress on the floor."

"You're such a horn ball."

"You love it," he said with a smirk and opened his menu, his eyes scanning the pages. I reached for mine and did the same, settling a few minutes later on barbecue chicken breast, steamed veggies and a side salad, while Nathan opted for baby back ribs. I set our menus on the edge of the table and Nathan motioned for the waiter, who took our order and headed back to the kitchen.

"Do you think Ava's doing okay with my parents?" I asked while Nathan fiddled with his phone.

"I'm sure she's fine," he said, a hint of annoyance in his voice. "Let's focus on our kid-free evening, hmm?" I relaxed in my chair, realizing he was probably right, and silently reprimanded myself for worrying.

"Do we have plans next weekend?" Nathan asked, looking up from his phone. I crossed my legs under the table and buried my hands in between my thighs, goosebumps snaking up my legs. My little black dress wasn't the most appropriate for January in the upper Midwest, but its effect on Nathan had been worth my discomfort.

"I don't think so," I answered. Nathan noticed me shivering and set his phone on the table. He stood from his chair and draped his jacket across my lap.

"Poor baby, you're cold," he said, leaning over and kissing the top of my head. My heart skipped a beat at the gesture. He sat back down across from me and reached his hand across the table. I fed my fingers through his. "Mike has some side work for me on Saturday. Think you can survive the day without me?"

"What kind of work?"

"Just some snow removal at his dad's farm." He shrugged. "Said he'll pay me a couple hundred bucks." I pulled my hand back and reached for my water glass, taking a cold sip and then setting it back onto the coaster.

"Sure, that's fine," I said, secretly wishing he'd stay home for the weekend. He tapped out a text response to Mike and then shoved his phone into the pocket of his jeans. He looked up at me and smiled, his eyes shimmering from the glow of the candle.

"I can't wait to bury my face in that cleavage," he said, his voice husky. He tipped his head and gestured toward my chest. Instinctively, I almost covered it up with the jacket but decided instead to accept the attention I desperately needed.

"Oh? This cleavage?" I leaned further over the table. Nathan licked his lips and offered a sly smile just as the waiter cleared his throat and hovered over the table with our entrees. We laughed genuinely and made space for him to set our meals on the table.

We struggled to keep our hands off each other through the rest of dinner.

———

SINCE WE HAD the Navigator until morning, Nathan parked it safely in the garage where we wouldn't risk another slippery patch of ice. He threw the SUV into park and turned off the ignition and then leaned over the center console and pulled me over to him for a kiss, his hand running up my thigh and under my dress, teasing me through my panties.

I sighed and kissed him harder than I had in months, my hunger for him more intense than I had anticipated. I'd missed this version of Nathan more than I cared to admit. I reached a hand over to his side of the car and rubbed my palm tauntingly over the bulge in his jeans. He groaned and shifted in his seat and then pulled away abruptly. "What's wrong?" I asked, licking my lips while I leaned back in my seat and parted my legs, offering him a peek at my red lace panties.

"Not here," he managed, his voice raspy. He made a move to open his door and then turned back to face me, his hands quickly sliding underneath me as he lifted me from the seat and clumsily pulled me over to his lap. My ass pressed against the steering wheel and the horn blasted, echoing through the confinement of the concrete garage and effectively scaring the shit out of us.

"Oh, my God, Nathan!" I screamed as we laughed together and quickly climbed out of the car. He wrapped his arms around me, pulling me tightly against him and pressing himself against me. I lifted my leg and wrapped it around him, our tongues exploring each other. We slowly made our way into the house, Nathan grabbing my hand in an effort to lead me upstairs to our bedroom. But I had other plans in mind and instead pulled him into the living room, kicking off my stiletto heels along the way. I guided him to the couch and seductively pushed him down onto the cushion.

"Brynn?"

"Yes?"

"What are you doing to me, baby?" he pleaded.

"Teasing you..." I momentarily questioned my abilities in the art of seduction. This was a new play for me, and Nathan was just as aware of that fact as I was.

"Come here," he demanded softly. I placed myself in front of him, spreading his legs with my foot as I hiked up my little black dress and watched a crooked smile spread across his face. I climbed onto his lap and straddled him, leaning down and laying a heavy kiss on his lips, my hair falling around our molded faces, his hands moving from my back to my ass cheeks, squeezing greedily.

I arched my back and locked eyes with Nathan while he pulled down the straps of my dress and unhooked my bra, my full breasts falling gracefully in front of his face. He soaked in the view and tossed my bra to the floor.

Tess Fucking Danielson ain't got shit on these.

"I love you," he said, quickly colliding his lips with mine.

Where did that come from?

I parted my lips, grateful not to have to return the sentiment, and accepted his kiss in a way I hadn't allowed myself to for so long. He tasted of after-dinner mints and still smelled of aftershave, a scent that almost always lit the fire between my thighs.

I knew in that moment that I was desperate to reclaim what had been stolen from me the night I'd caught Nathan with Tess. I wanted to remind Nathan that I could seduce him better than any other woman, simply because I knew exactly what he liked. He wanted to be needed; to be craved and desired. More than any other man I'd ever known, Nathan needed me to worship him.

And worship him, I did.

———

"I'M SO SORRY," Nathan whispered when we lay together in bed hours later, our bodies turned toward one another while our eyes searched back and forth—desperate to know what the other was thinking.

"I know." I looked away, not wanting to be reminded of the past.

"I mean it." he assured me, placing a hand under my chin and gently turning me back toward him. "Look at me...I know I've owed you an apology for a long time. I never should have done what I did to you. You deserve so much better, and I promise I'm doing what I can to make it up to you."

He reached his hand over again and laid a palm on my cheek. I leaned into it, closing my eyes and finding the comfort I hadn't known I'd needed in his words. I'd longed to hear them for so long and had come to terms with the fact that they likely were never coming. So much had gone unspoken between us, and even though it felt like Nathan was finally giving me what I needed, I wasn't sure I would ever be able to say the things I felt I needed to say back to him.

Sometimes when you're focused on moving forward, it's simply too painful to turn and look back.

CHAPTER SIXTEEN

FEBRUARY 2006

"HEY, LADY!" Jerilyn chirped through the speakerphone. She rarely called in between classes anymore, but I was grateful for the distraction from the dishes I'd been scrubbing and had quickly punched the speaker button with a dirty fork so I wouldn't miss her call. I dried my hands on a towel and pulled the phone to my ear, making my way over to the couch. Ava had gone down for her afternoon nap less than an hour ago, and I was giddy at the chance to talk to my best friend after weeks of radio silence.

"Hey! Wow, it's nice to hear your voice!"

"How's Ava?" she asked, aware that I'd taken a few sick days to nurse Ava through a double ear infection.

"She's doing better today. How's school?" I settled into the couch and muted the game show that played in the background.

"School's good! It's so much fun. I'm meeting so many new people this year and the parties are *insane*," she offered. I could hear voices in the background and pictured Jerilyn walking across the quad—because that's what college kids do in movies, right?—and waving to all her friends while she headed to class. "Oh! Do you remember Evan from high school?"

"Of course," I managed, shocked at the sudden mention of the familiar name. How could I forget Evan? Jerilyn and I had met him at one of The Shed parties shortly after we graduated high school. He'd gone to school in the neighboring town of Monticello and was pulled into The Shed party crew through a mutual friend. It was well known to most of our group at the time that he had a bit of a crush on me. What was less known is that the feelings were mutual. But I had met Nathan a few weeks after meeting Evan and, well...

"Anyway, Evan was at this frat party we went to last night!" Jerilyn continued. "He was asking about you..."

"He was?"

He was?

"Yeah, he asked for your number but I wasn't sure if I should give it to him, so he gave me his instead. Said to give it to you if you'd be up for talking."

"Oh. Um. Yeah, actually, that would be nice," I decided.

"Okay, I'll text it to you. I gotta run though, I'm just heading into class. Miss you!"

We hung up and I headed back to the kitchen to the dishes. As I finished up and wiped down the countertops, my phone dinged with a message from Jerilyn, Evan's phone number attached. I stared down at the phone, trying to make sense of my emotions. The mention of Evan's name had caused a flutter in my chest; I hadn't thought about him in a long time and couldn't help but smile.

"So do you have a boyfriend or do I actually have a chance with a beautiful girl such as yourself?" Evan asked. We sat on the tailgate of

his pickup truck, our feet dangling over the edge. He took a sip of his Mountain Dew, and I picked at the tab on my Coke can. We were sober cabs for the evening, bonding over our soft drinks as our inebriated friends hooted and hollered around us.

"I don't have a boyfriend," I admitted, unable to make eye contact.

"Hmm, that surprises me." He smiled, flashing his white teeth in the glow of the bonfire in front of us. Evan reached over and placed his hand on my knee, rubbing it through my jeans with his thumb. I looked up and met his brown eyes, the curly mop on the top of his head blowing slightly in the breeze.

"Why does that surprise you?" I asked, tucking a loose curl behind my ear.

"You're just too much of a catch to be single." He stated like it was obvious. "But you're in luck, because I'm kind of a catch, too," he teased, winking in my direction. He leaned closer and reached a hand up to my cheek, re-tucking the curl that had already gone astray again. I leaned my face into the palm of his hand and our foreheads touched. I could feel his breath on my lips, the sweet scent of his Mountain Dew wafting across my face. He placed his hand under my chin and tipped my mouth up to his, softly brushing his lips against mine.

"Get a room!" someone shouted from across the grass. Evan and I broke apart, smiling sheepishly when Harper and Jerilyn made their way over to us.

I snapped out of my reverie when Ava's cries came from down the hall. I abandoned my phone on the counter and made my way to her room, trying to shake off the wave of sadness that had unexpectedly settled over me.

———

THE REST of the afternoon had gone smoothly. Ava seemed to be overcoming her ear infections and, after eating some oatmeal and toast, went down for bedtime without a fuss. I'd just popped a bowl of popcorn and sat down to watch *Sweet Home Alabama* when Nathan texted to say he'd be a little late getting home.

You were a "little late" over two hours ago, dear, but sure, no problem.

It was just after 11:15 p.m., and Nathan already sounded like he'd had several beers as it was; I didn't anticipate seeing him until morning.

When he had stopped home to shower and change clothes after work, I asked him not to leave, not to spend another night in a dirty bar drinking with his new friends while I sat at home alone with our daughter.

"She sleeps most of the time, anyway, Brynn. Quit being so dramatic. I'm the one going out and working my ass off every day."

"Really, Nathan?"

"What?"

"You don't think staying home with a sick child is *work?* Not to mention, I have a job, too! And who do you think does the grocery shopping and cleans the apartment— certainly not *you!*"

He mocked applause, frantically clapping his hands together in a celebratory manner as he laughed in my face. "Congratulations, honey, you're a housewife!"

"Oh, fuck you!"

"Don't fucking talk to me like that!" he roared, suddenly in my face and angry. He shoved me hard, palm to chest, knocking me backward against the wall.

I stared at him in shock.

He'd never hit me like that before.

123

His face pierced with regret, he softened his tone and said, "Baby…I didn't mean to do that. I'm so—"

"Just go." I whispered.

He reached for my face and I batted his hand away, the contact unwanted. I refused to look at him. He turned, walking away and closed the door behind him without another word.

Ignoring the memory, I recalled my conversation with Jerilyn earlier, and I flipped to my text messages, grabbing Evan's phone number. I programmed it into my phone and sent him a text with my number, my heart pounding in my chest.

Evan! Hey, it's Brynn!

He replied almost immediately, even at the late hour.

Hey girl! HUB?

HUB? I stared at my phone for a few minutes before I finally gave up and asked Evan for a definition of the word that I'd only known to date as a description for the central part of a wheel.

Hey! Sorry, I'm not hip with the lingo. What's HUB?

Evan's response came quickly, and I swore under my breath as I realized it should've been a no-brainer.

how u been

I typed back:

Oh, wow, silly me! I'm good. You?

I hoped he'd find my cluelessness endearing, perhaps even cute, as opposed to the latter.

Not bad. Miss u

He misses me?

You do?

of course! drinks soon?

umm...I don't know. I don't really drink and I have the baby...

I sat in wait for a response that never came, from someone I shouldn't have been talking to in the first place. As much as I wished for my old life back, I had Ava to think about, which meant I needed to be careful. Even though it was tempting to find a sitter and grab that drink with Evan, I knew it would be wrong. I was married. I'd said my vows.

I sighed and flipped my phone closed before setting it on the coffee table and resuming my movie. I'd have to settle for living vicariously through Reese Witherspoon instead.

Sometimes I wished I had it in me to be the heartless one.

CHAPTER SEVENTEEN
MARCH 2006

I THINK if you were to ask any battered woman, she would be able to recall the exact moment when her partner first crossed the line between abuse to assault. Most likely, she wishes she could forget that moment but more importantly, she wishes it never happened. It's a defining moment in her life, one she knows will leave her with no more than two options: stay or go.

Live or die.

I've always been pretty accustomed to yelling. My mother is a veteran of the Navy and she raised her voice plenty, especially during my teen years, considering I had a problem with mouthing off. I think it's common for a service member to be a yeller, though—it's how they were trained—so I could never really fault her for it. Not that she yelled all the time, but there's a difference between someone who never yells and someone who yells when they're passionate about their point. They aren't yelling because they're angry or mad at you; I mean sometimes they are, but not always. Sometimes they just *mean it* and raising their voice is the only way to get that point across.

I used to be a yeller.

I don't raise my voice much anymore, but I used to. Nathan and my mother were two people who had a talent for getting a rise out of me. So, I yelled. And that meant I could also take it in return. You see, when you're a yeller, you have to accept that at some point the other person is going to yell back at you. I could stand directly in front of a yeller, and it didn't matter who it was or how much residual spit landed on my face while they did it, I could take it and barely flinch. That's how you know you're a yeller. It simply doesn't scare you when someone yells back. I didn't flinch when Nathan put his hands on me for the first time; I think it's because I'm a yeller.

Also, I had no fucking idea it was coming.

I'd just wrapped up a busy work week and was headed home to snuggle Ava before kicking back on the couch with a cup of tea and several episodes of *Friends*. Elle had just sent me home with the complete boxed set on DVD.

We'd had lunch together that afternoon, and she introduced me to Caribou Coffee's Turtle Mocha—for which I will be eternally grateful—and even though I only indulged in a few shared sips from hers, I was very likely still experiencing a caffeine high when I finally walked through the front door that evening.

Nathan was in between jobs, as usual, having been fired from The Pole Barn Company after failing to show up and not bothering to call in for three days straight. He didn't admit it to me until a couple days earlier, and I found his admission especially interesting, considering he'd gotten up and "left for work" every one of those mornings.

Nevertheless, since he wasn't working, we decided that Ava would stay home with him during the day while I was at work; we didn't have the extra money for unnecessary daycare and needed the cash for groceries. And despite the frequent yelling that echoed throughout our home, Ava loved her dad and couldn't withhold her excitement when we told her she'd be staying home with him.

"Daddy, can we color?" she asked, tugging on Nathan's arm. His face was buried in his phone, his attention elsewhere. He shrugged and shook his arm loose from her grasp.

"Sure, baby girl," he said nonchalantly, his eyes still glued to his phone.

"Daddy, *look*!" she tugged again, and I watched Nathan's expression shift from simple annoyance to pure anger. Ava scooped the coloring supplies up from the table, on a mission to win Nathan's attention.

I knew better than to think she'd manage to do so.

I knelt to her level and held her hand in mine. "Ava, sweetie, let's show Daddy the coloring stuff later. Do you want to come with me to change the laundry? You can help me put the socks into the dryer."

"Okay!" She dropped the coloring book onto the table and skipped down the hall to the laundry room, her auburn curls bouncing in step. I stood and dared to glance over at Nathan, but he was still too preoccupied to notice, his head buried in his phone, tapping out another text message.

Maybe staying home with Dad isn't the greatest idea, after all.

———

WORK the next day had been nuts; I was exhausted by the time I finally parked my Sunfire in the garage. I entered the house through the connecting garage entrance off the kitchen, setting my keys and purse on the kitchen counter. Parched, I opened the refrigerator to retrieve a bottle of water and twisted the cap off, taking a long, cold sip.

That's when I caught sight of it.

I crossed the kitchen and stared down at a sandwich-sized Ziploc bag stuffed to the brim with weed; a younger me would have assumed it was nothing more than a cooking herb, but I'd learned a bit during my days with Nathan. Without a second thought, I swiped the bag from the counter and marched up the stairs toward our bedroom to confront my husband, stopping quickly by Ava's room. I knew Nathan and I were about to head into battle, and I wanted to set her up with a pair of head-phones and the portable DVD player before throwing any punches.

I reached the landing and sucked in a breath, pushing open the door that had been left cracked open. But my daughter was not in her bedroom. Her toys and blankets were scattered everywhere, as if a small tornado had blown through. I called out for her, checking the closet and under the bed.

Where the fuck is Ava?

My heart thudded in my chest; I called out for her again, running across the hallway to the master bedroom and whipping the door open. Nathan was asleep on our bed, sprawled out as if he'd passed out unexpectedly.

Ava wasn't in there with him.

"Ava!" I called out, shaking Nathan's shoulders. He jolted awake and stared at me like I was crazy.

"Where's Ava?" I shouted again, my voice frantic.

"Relax, *psycho*. She's at daycare," he replied groggily, as if that information had previously been shared and should have been obvious.

"Why is she at daycare?"

"I needed to get some sleep."

"So, you sent her to daycare?"

"Yep." He pulled the duvet over his head in attempt to shut me out, the conversation far from over.

Now that my daughter was safe, I slammed the bag of weed down onto the bed and pulled the comforter away from Nathan. "Where did you get this?" I demanded, "and why the hell was it sitting on our kitchen counter where Ava could have easily gotten into it?"

"What the fuck, Brynn!" Nathan yelled, still half asleep but already pissed as hell. I'd woken the beast, but I didn't care. He promised he wouldn't do this anymore. "I'm fucking sleeping. Get out," he grumbled, sitting up lazily.

I folded my arms across my chest. "Answer the question!"

I yelled.

"Fuck you." He rolled back over, taking the covers with him and pulling them over his head. I yanked them away and pulled the duvet off the bed, shoving it onto the floor, the bag of weed tumbling down with it.

"Really? That's all you have to say?"

"Get over yourself. It's not even mine." He pulled himself from the bed and grabbed his wallet from the nightstand, jamming it into the pocket of his sweatpants.

"Bull-fucking-shit!"

I yelled again.

"It's not like you have a history of drug use or anything." I picked the bag up from the floor, determined to fight this time, not to be a pushover.

"Fuck off. I don't need this shit." Nathan snatched the plastic bag from my hands and then grabbed a rumpled T-shirt off the floor and pulled it over his head.

"No! You don't get to take it with you." I yanked the bag back and headed toward the bathroom. Despite having been rudely awakened, Nathan was quicker than I had anticipated, beating me to the door and blocking the entrance with his body. I stood in front of him and he held out his hand in expectation.

"Give it to me."

That stare.

That flush-my-weed-down-the-toilet-and-I'll-fucking-kill-you stare. As if a sandwich bag full of weed was worth such a thing.

"You promised me you were done," I whispered, the fight in me dissipating.

He nodded and swiped the bag from me, waving it in my face. "I *am* done. With *you*. I'm done with your petty fucking bullshit and nagging me over stupid shit that doesn't even matter. If being married to me is such a problem, why don't you just give *Evan* another call?"

Evan?

Tears threatened my eyes. I hated that I was about to fucking cry. I wanted to be strong, to stand up to Nathan. I wanted to prove that his words meant nothing, that he couldn't hurt me with them anymore.

The usual doubt crept into my stupid brain. It's just weed. What's the real harm? It's not like he left a dusty line of coke on the coffee table or a used needle in the bathroom sink. What's the harm in smoking a little weed?

The harm in smoking a little weed is that he promised he wouldn't.

"You're not leaving," I said, intending to sound confident, but my words came out more like a plea.

"You know, if you weren't such a controlling lunatic, we wouldn't have so many problems in our relationship. Maybe *you* should smoke some of this," he patronized, stabbing his index finger into my chest. "It'll probably calm your hyper ass down." He chuckled to himself, likely at the thought of me smoking a joint. "Get it through your thick head," he mocked, pulling his finger to his temple, "you're not my fucking mother." He shoved past me, clipping my shoulder and knocking me backward into the wall as he moved to retrieve his car keys from the dresser. I pushed off the wall and stood firmly in front of Nathan, my feet planted firmly to the floor, my arms crossed over my chest.

"If you weren't such a *junkie* we wouldn't have *any* problems!"

Nathan's fist slammed into the wall next to my head, the drywall crumbling into tiny pieces on the floor around me, a perfect fist-shaped hole left in its place. I drew in a sharp breath but stood tall.

"Fuck you, Brynn! You don't know shit. I quit all the other stuff months ago, but you're too fucking stupid to notice. Not even a "thank you" or a "hey, I'm proud of you for getting clean" It's bullshit!" He waved the bag of weed in my face again. "*This* shit keeps me calm enough not to bash your fucking head into this wall!"

Silence.

"What's the matter? Cat got your tongue?" He shook the drywall remnants from his hand, and I stared at him through the tears that flooded my eyes.

There was so much anger in his face.

"I hate you," I whispered. Without a second thought, I snatched the bag out of his hand and stormed into the bathroom, flipping the toilet seat open and tearing the plastic bag open before dropping in the contents and pulling the handle. In the split second that I stood there watching what was likely several hundred dollars' worth of marijuana swirl down our toilet bowl, I wondered where he'd gotten the money for it to begin with.

I never got the chance to ask.

Enraged hands grabbed hold of my hair and pulled me backward. I landed hard on the tile floor, a sharp pain shooting through my lower back as I hit the floor with a thud.

"YOU FUCKING BITCH!" The bass that reverberated from the voice behind me rang loud, deafening. I flinched, his words echoing in the confines of the small space, stumbling as he dragged me out of the bathroom. I kicked and dug my fingernails into the skin on his hands, trying to pry my hair loose from his grip.

He shoved me down to the floor next to the bed, my scalp on fire. A clump of hair dangled between his fingers. When he finally unclenched his fist, a yelp escaped from my lips and I curled into the fetal position. He thrashed around the room, smashing everything in sight and throwing things in every direction, screaming expletives louder than I've ever heard him scream before. He grabbed a picture frame and pitched it into the wall, shattering it to pieces.

Panicked, I held a hand to the back of my throbbing head and reached up to the nightstand with the other, my fingers trembling while they wrapped around the telephone receiver. I pulled it from its cradle, dialing three numbers on the keypad.

But Nathan charged toward me, and he was too fast.

He ripped the receiver from my hand, the jack flying from the wall. "Fuck you!" he screamed, grabbing the base of the phone and barreling it against the wall. It crashed to the floor as more bits of the wall fell like snow and sprinkled across the worn carpet. With the plastic phone cord still in his hand, Nathan grabbed me by the arm and pulled me up from the floor, holding me just inches from his face, his breath hot and labored as a terrorizing smile played across his lips.

Tauntingly, he wrapped the cord once—then twice—around my neck.

And then he pulled.

I gagged and tried to scream, but couldn't get enough air to make a sound.

He wouldn't.

I clawed at the cord while he held my gaze, his eyes crazed, sweat dripping from his forehead.

I needed air.

Ava.

"Nath-a-n...plea-se...s-t-o-p," I choked out. Thick tears slipped down my cheeks, and I realized for the first time that this was the reason I never fought back before, the reason I never stood up to my husband.

Somehow, deep down, I always knew my husband was capable of taking my life.

"What's the matter?" he mocked. "Don't want to fight anymore?" He smiled a deviant smile and then ran his tongue along the length of my cheek, mopping up the salty tears that had fallen against my will.

Then he winked at me.

I was lightheaded, about to pass out at any moment, and when I nearly choked on the bile that snaked up my throat, something flashed in his eyes.

He let go of the cord and I fell to the floor, sliding against the wall and bringing my hands to my neck. I coughed violently, gagging as I tried to catch my breath.

Nathan headed for the door before stopping and looking around at the aftermath of the storm that brewed inside him. "Clean this shit up. I have to track down Mike to get another bag since you just flushed the fucking stash I was supposed to sell. When I get back, you'll be a good wife and apologize by sucking my dick," he commanded, nodding to himself as if satisfied with the punishment he'd assigned.

He shoved his arms into his jacket and stomped down

the stairs. From the hallway, he shouted, "I grabbed the fifty from your purse!"

He was supposed to sell that stash?

When did my husband become a drug dealer?

I brought my hands to my stomach and rubbed the tiny pouch that had been forming for the past few months. I hadn't gotten a chance to tell Nathan we were expecting another baby.

CHAPTER EIGHTEEN

I LAY on the floor of our bedroom, staring at the popcorn ceiling, for more than an hour after Nathan left. My head pulsed at the base of my skull and every muscle in my body ached, as if I'd collided with a Mack truck.

I wanted a nap.

I wanted to sleep for a week and forget everything about this day, to erase it all. The hollowness I felt inside was unbearable, debilitating and leaving me uncomfortably numb.

How did we get here?

I forced myself up from the floor, the fog in my head leaving me unsteady on my feet. I went downstairs to retrieve a garbage bag from under the kitchen sink. I needed to get the bedroom cleaned up before picking Ava up from daycare.

The garbage bag in hand, I headed back upstairs, pausing at the door to our bedroom, and taking in the scene as if for the first time. My breath caught in my throat. Three fist-shaped holes receded from as many different walls, and a lamp lay shattered by my side of the bed. The busted picture frame, chipped paint and specks of drywall littered the carpet. I crouched to my knees and scooped the picture frame up from the floor, swiping at a tear. It was a photo of Ava, Nathan and me smiling widely at the camera—the only family picture we had.

We had attended Jerilyn's birthday party a month earlier, making an appearance for my best friend's sake, but staying only long enough to say hello, grab a bite and leave. Nathan had been anxious; we didn't stay longer than necessary. We faked a happy marriage long enough to have the photo snapped while we sat at a picnic table and nibbled on walking tacos.

Jerilyn sent me a copy of the photo in the mail a couple weeks later with a sticky note attached that said, "thanks for coming." She had no idea of my husband's battle with addiction and abuse, but had been intuitive enough to know how much of a piece-of-shit he was. Her instincts had been spot-on that first night she met him.

I shoved the photo and what was left of the frame into the garbage bag, tossing shards of glass in behind it. I grabbed the vacuum from its place in the hall closet, plugged it in and vacuumed the carpet, having to go over it three times to get all the drywall particles. I dusted the furniture and covered one of the holes in the wall near the bathroom with a canvas print I had stored in the closet. My mom had given it to me for Christmas the year prior. Nathan had said it was horrendous, and the next day it had been removed from its place on the wall and shoved into the back of our closet. "It's not like she ever comes over anyway, she won't even know it's missing," Nathan had said.

After I finished cleaning up the bedroom, I showered and brushed my teeth. I rinsed the toothpaste from my mouth and caught a glimpse of myself in the mirror; two red lines circled the center of my neck, shades of purple already forming alongside them as the bruises formed. I gasped and brought my fingers to my neck.

Fuck.

I grabbed my makeup bag and pulled out my compact, dabbing and distributing it over the thin lines. It didn't seem to do the trick.

Turtleneck it is.

I finished applying my makeup, adding some black mascara to my eyelashes and then quickly blow-dried my long hair. Pulling a gray turtleneck sweater over my head, I made sure the marks on my neck weren't visible and headed out of the bathroom.

I moved down the stairs slowly, still lightheaded, scooped my car keys off the kitchen counter and threw my purse over my aching shoulder. I would be late picking up Ava from daycare and hadn't had a chance to call to let the center know, which meant we'd be hit with another late pick-up fee as well.

And Nathan just took my fifty to buy more drugs.

———

I was startled awake several hours later to the sound of the garage door closing. I steadied my breathing and faked sleep as best as I could in hopes that Nathan had forgotten about his earlier threat and would just fall into bed. I heard him place his keys on the kitchen counter, then the thud of his boots coming up the stairs.

He entered our bedroom and sat down next to me on our bed, stroking my hair and running his fingers along my cheek. I wanted to hate it—to hate him for what he had done to me. But it felt nice; my heart a double agent, the romantic gesture causing a flutter in my stomach. Nathan pulled the covers from my body, rubbing my breasts through my tank top, giving my nipple a pinch through the thin fabric. He kissed me gently on my mouth as he toyed with my sensitive nipple; it hardened and sent a shiver coursing through my body despite my willing it to shut the fuck up.

"Brynn...I'm so sorry," Nathan whispered, kissing on my neck.

"I know."

"Let me make it up to you, baby," he brushed a loose strand of hair from my face and pressed his lips to mine. His tongue forced its way into my mouth, exploring while he slid a hand underneath me and cupped my ass. He tasted like whiskey and stunk of weed.

"Nathan, I...I can't." I pushed him away and climbed out of bed. He stood, unzipping his jeans, and then grabbed my hand and planted it over the bulge. "Come on, I'm ready for you," he pleaded.

"No." I removed my hand and turned away from him.

"Sex or weed, Brynn. You decide. One way or another, you owe me for earlier. So which is it?"

"Weed," I decided quickly. Nathan's arms wrapped around me from behind. He rubbed his erection against my backside and brought his fingers to my neck, soft at first and then slowly tightening his grip.

My breath caught in my throat.

He turned me around to face him, pulling the straps of my tank top down and exposing my breasts, slapping at them while I winced.

"I'd rather have you," he admitted, pecking kisses on my neck, down to the tops of my breasts. His cock was hard, fighting for release in his pants and pressing against my inner thighs.

Resist, goddamn it.

I grew warm in my middle, my body responding to his advances while my mind fought to push him away. The kisses ceased, and Nathan's hands grew rough again. He grabbed me by the neck and shoved me to the floor.

I stumbled onto the floor in front of him.

He let out a throaty laugh.

"You weren't very nice to me today," he mused, pulling his jeans and boxers the rest of the way down before stepping out of them. He grabbed me by the hair and forced me to my knees. "It's not polite to flush some-one's stash down the toilet. You're lucky Mike was willing to forgive you." He stroked the length of his cock, dangling it in my face before he slapped it against my cheek.

I flinched in surprise, the tip of him suddenly forcing my lips apart, invading my mouth. With a moan, he said, "Now, apologize."

I tried to pull away, pushing his legs in hopes that he might lose his balance and stumble backward, but strong hands held my head in place.

He bucked his hips, fucking my mouth.

He slapped at my breasts, leaving welts behind.

With each thrust into my throat, I gagged and coughed and scratched at his thighs, digging my fingernails into his skin. Spit pooled and dripped from my lips, my breaths erratic.

My eyes watered, and warm tears landed on my breasts. I unwillingly sucked his length, careful not to graze it with my teeth when it passed in and out of my mouth.

"You're *mine*, just remember that," he growled. "These fucking tits are *mine*," he reached down and palmed between my legs, making me wince from the unexpected invasion. "This pussy is *mine*." He yanked himself from my mouth, his hands rough, his fingers pinching my chin, tilting my head and forcing me to look at him. "No one else will ever want you."

Dead eyes glared back at me.

"See, Brynn, you're *my* wife. *My* fucking property. Don't forget that. If you *ever* fucking text Evan—or any other guy —again, I swear to God, I'll fucking kill you."

"How...how did you know?" I whimpered, a lump forming in my throat while I caught my breath.

"I said don't fucking text him again!" he screamed. "Now, you're going to stop crying and start sucking my cock like you actually enjoy it. And then you're going to climb onto the bed and bend over so I can fuck *my wife*. Got it?"

I nodded, slowly.

He let go of my chin and shoved his dick back between my lips. I wrapped my hand around his shaft, stroking it, another moan sounding from his lips. "Good, baby, just like that..."

Stop crying.

Suck his cock.

Let him fuck me.

How romantic.

———

WHEN HE FINISHED, Nathan went into the bathroom and turned on the shower, too much of a coward to look me in the eye while I watched him walk away. I grabbed his crumpled T-shirt from the floor, pulled it over my head and ran to the bathroom on the lower level, where I vomited until my insides were empty.

My throat burning and my jaw sore, I popped a few aspirin and splashed cold water on my face. The upstairs shower still running, I found myself standing outside the door to Ava's room. I turned the knob, tiptoeing across the room. She was beautiful in sleep, her arm above her head, her fingers closed in a tiny fist.

I reached for the music box on the nightstand, winding it before lifting my daughter from the mattress and clutching her to my chest, her body instinctively curling into mine. I lowered us to the rocking chair and sang to her softly, along with the melody that played:

You are my sunshine, my only sunshine,
You make me happy when skies are gray.
You'll never know, dear, how much I love you,
Please don't take my sunshine away.

CHAPTER NINETEEN
OCTOBER 2003

"Wow....Nathan, look! It's so beautiful..." I pointed to the tranquil sunset, the swirling of the brilliant reds, yellows and oranges against the crystal-clear blue sky. I'd always been enamored by sunsets, their ability to somehow provide synchrony to nature.

To set a mood.

To send a message.

"I wish I had my camera," I stared down at my cheap flip phone that would do little justice to the radiance displayed above.

Nathan looked over at me from the driver's seat of my LeBaron, a half-cocked smile on his face. He shifted the car into drive and pulled back onto the road. We'd had a PG-13 make-out session in the middle of nowhere, having found ourselves on a secluded dirt road, driving around and listening to music while talking about our childhoods.

Nathan's had been rough, his dad having passed from cancer when he was just nine years old. A significant age gap separated him and Natalie, and with his mom grief-stricken over the loss of her husband, Nathan had often felt like an only child, something that afforded him more freedom than a child of single digits should have.

He smoked pot for the first time that year and shortly after, fell into a bad crowd and started drinking—all before he reached puberty.

My heart ached for him, and I longed to absorb some of his pain. To comfort him and let him know things would be different now. That I'd be there.

"Where are we going?" I asked, buckling my seatbelt.

"You'll see." He winked at me and slid his fingers between mine. I sat back, a smile spreading across my face while I watched the glow of the sunset against the changing trees.

Once we hit the main road, Nathan signaled a left turn and I looked away from my view out the window to see we had pulled into the Tom Thumb gas station. He threw the car into park and let go of my hand. "I'll be right back," he said, opening his door and jogging inside.

I reached for the dial on the radio and turned it up, Justin Timberlake's, "Rock Your Body" blasting through the speakers. My hand slipped a bit on the dial and JT crooned a little louder than intended, causing a couple gas station customers to turn and glare at me and my rattling trunk, thanks to the cheap subwoofers I'd picked up a couple years back.

I was halfway through the song when Nathan popped out of the gas station and jogged back to the car. He didn't get back in though, just stood expectantly next to my passenger side door, staring at me with a weird grin on his face. I offered him a puzzled look in return. "What are you doing?" I asked, reaching over and turning the radio down.

"Come here." He opened my door and held out his hand to me. I took it and got out of the car. He closed the door with his hip and produced an odd-shaped Tom Thumb bag, whatever was inside wrapped in the plastic. "They didn't have wrapping paper." He shrugged. I wasn't sure what I expected to find in that bag—or what kind of gift he could have possibly gotten me from a rundown gas station—but I took a mental picture of that moment and tucked it away for another time; the look on his face too tender to forget.

I took the bag from Nathan and opened it slowly, savoring the moment. I brought my hand to my mouth, my eyes swelling with tears. I held the plastic disposable camera in my hands, and for a moment, found myself at a loss for words.

I leaped into Nathan's arms and pressed a quick kiss onto his lips. He grabbed the bag from my hand and tossed it into the car through the open window before taking my hand.

We ran off, hand in hand, to capture a picture of the sunset.

————

IT TOOK a couple weeks to get the disposable prints back from Walgreen's, and even though it wasn't a high-quality photo, I framed that sunset and kept it displayed on my nightstand for several years. Today it sits in a storage box in the garage; I can't bring myself to part with it.

CHAPTER TWENTY

MARCH 2006

THE FIRST TIME I left Nathan was three days after he tried to strangle me. My decision to do so wasn't made lightly. The fact that my husband had raped me hadn't set in yet; we were married, so in my mind what he'd done to me wasn't rape. I wasn't privy to that fact until I showed up at the Rivers of Hope center in Monticello, clutching Ava's hand as we trudged through the melting snow and crossed the parking lot. I stood outside the entrance, staring at the sign on the door, trying to convince myself that I shouldn't be there, that I didn't belong.

Nathan was gone before I woke up that morning.

A note from him sat unread on the kitchen counter; I didn't give a shit what he had to say.

Ava had a scheduled play date with her friend Calli from daycare, and I dropped her off that afternoon, having hidden the red marks and purple bruises on my neck with the same turtleneck sweater I had put on the night before. When Calli's mother invited me in for a cup of coffee, I thanked her politely and said I was on my way to meet a friend for lunch.

I went home to an empty house and fought the urge to call someone—maybe my mom or Jerilyn—settling instead on watching six mindless hours of *Friends* on DVD.

Not even Ross's leather pants could force a laugh out of me.

I cried at least once during every episode and was grateful Ava wasn't home to witness it, even though I felt guilty for shipping her off in the first place—one of the many reasons for my relentless stream of tears.

Was my daughter suffering at the hands of my husband, too?

By the second day, Sunday, my tear ducts had dried up, and although I was exhausted, I hadn't slept well in days. Ava and I spent the day doing arts and crafts. After we'd colored more than a dozen terrible *My Little Pony* pictures, we bundled up in our snow gear and went outside to play in the fresh powder that had fallen the night before. We made snow angels and caught the snowflakes on our tongues.

Even that didn't bring a genuine smile to my face.

We ate microwaved chicken nuggets for dinner, and after Ava's bath, I tucked her into bed, pulling the covers around her before winding up her music box and humming along to the melody.

"Mama sad?" her little voice asked under the blankets.

"Yes, sweetie." I knelt beside Ava's bed and brushed the curls out of her face. "Mama's just tired."

"Me too," she managed through an exaggerated yawn.

I kissed her forehead and said, "Goodnight, baby girl," before backing out of her room and making my way downstairs to the couch. I debated a few more episodes of *Friends*, but I'd already started crying again. I did little more than wrap a blanket around myself and let the tears fall in silence, unable to scare away the thoughts in my head.

It was on the third morning—Monday—after dodging calls from Andi and Jerilyn, that I decided to call into work and pack a few boxes of Nathan's things. I kept Ava home from daycare, and while she napped that afternoon, sent a text message to Nathan telling him that I changed the locks on the house and that if he showed up I'd call the police. I hadn't actually changed the locks—I couldn't afford to—but I had managed to sneak his copy of the house key off his key ring. I expected him to argue, maybe rattle off some hurtful words or call half a dozen times demanding I open the door and let him in.

But that never happened.

All he said in response was, "okay."

One lousy word uttered in a simple text message was apparently all I deserved—not an apology. Not an explanation.

After lunch, I buckled Ava into her car seat and drove over to Natalie's. I knew she'd be at work; I wasn't going there to talk. I parked at the curb and sat in the car for a moment, mentally convincing myself I was doing the right thing. I unloaded the boxes from the car and left them at her door, Ava in the backseat humming Christmas songs, even though it was the middle of March and Christmas had already come and gone.

———

I INHALED the winter air and pulled the door to the crisis center open. I was desperate to escape from the trauma that would inevitably divide my life into two parts: before and after.

Before my husband wrapped a telephone cord around

my neck and pulled just enough that the lights went out for a second.

After my husband wrapped a telephone cord around my neck and pulled just enough that the lights went out for a second.

I wasn't sure what had taken place in between those two moments.

There was just the before, and there was just the after.

Ava and I were greeted by a couple of friendly faces inside, all women. I wondered what thoughts went through their minds as they watched us standing at the door.

How many women had walked in before me? Were their stories like mine? Did anyone believe them? Would anyone believe me?

I didn't feel important enough to be there, to take up their time. But I didn't know where else to go; I couldn't find the strength to tell my story to anyone other than a stranger.

"Hi, I'm Lacy. I'm glad you came in today," the dark-haired woman said, offering her hand and looking down at Ava. "And who is this little one?"

"I'm Ava!" my daughter announced, blissfully unaware of her surroundings.

"Hi, Ava, it's nice to meet you." Suddenly bashful, Ava wrapped her arms around my leg and tucked her head against my thigh.

"Brynn," I offered.

"Would you like to come back and talk?" I expected to see some form of pity in Lacy's eyes, but couldn't find any. I appreciated that and felt some of the tension drain from my body.

"Sure, thank you," I replied, my eyes drawn to an inspirational quote framed on the wall.

I am a survivor, not a victim.

Lacy knelt in front of Ava and offered her a hand. "Do you like to color, Ava?"

"Yes!" She took Lacy's hand and let her lead her to the children's table, where a curly-haired blonde about my height sat with another little girl, slightly older than Ava, coloring a picture of Cinderella.

"Is it okay if your mom and I go sit over there and talk for a little bit?" Lacy asked Ava while pointing to a desk down the hall. Ava nodded, taking a seat next to the blonde and picking up a crayon.

I walked down the hall with Lacy, suddenly anxious about being alone with her and subjecting myself to her questions.

I shouldn't be here.

She pulled out a chair and sat down, motioning for me to take the seat across from her. Reluctantly, I did, placing my purse on my lap and glancing over at Ava. She smiled and waved before turning her attention back to the pretty princesses she was coloring with the nice lady. I was grateful not to have to let her out of my sight.

Lacy slid a pamphlet across the table and then pulled out a notebook and pen, scribbling the date at the top of the page.

"What can I do to help you today, Brynn?" she asked, offering me a slight smile.

"Um, I don't really know. I've never been here before," I admitted. She flipped the page on the pamphlet and slid it closer to me.

"How about I start. I can tell you a bit about the services we offer and then maybe you can tell me a little bit about what you brought you here today. Does that sound okay?" I nodded, and she reached for the pamphlet.

———

AFTER AN HOUR of recalling the events that led me to Rivers of Hope, Lacy helped me fill out an Order for Protection form, an order that would be filed with the court requesting protection from my abuser.

My abuser.

My husband, who strangled me, and then raped me so I could apologize for making him mad.

It seemed silly, filling out a piece of paper with the notion that it could somehow protect me. As if a recycled sheet of paper that produced no more harm than a paper cut could be used as a weapon.

I wasn't convinced, but I went through the motions anyway.

"So, we'll file this with the Wright County Courthouse right away, and then the judge will typically read the order and make an immediate ruling. That ruling will determine whether the order will be put in place for a temporary ten-day period. After the ten days, you'll have a hearing where the judge will review the case and offer your husband a chance to speak on his own behalf. If the judge rules the order necessary, it'll be put in place for thirty days and then reviewed again for a longer-term."

I nodded.

"What if he comes home?"

"Do you have somewhere you and Ava can stay for a while?"

Yes. But no.

"Brynn, considering everything you've told me, I think it would be best for you not to go home. We have a shelter available if you and—"

"No. I...I have somewhere we can go."

Home.

THE ORDER for Protection was signed the following morning by Judge Vesser, the same judge whose chambers Nathan and I stood in when we vowed to love each other in sickness and in health, until death do us part.

I couldn't help but stifle a laugh at the irony.

CHAPTER TWENTY-ONE

APRIL 2006

I CALLED in sick to work the rest of the week. I figured it'd be best to keep the days consecutive so it would only count as one unexcused absence. I still brought Ava to daycare—which felt wrong, but necessary—even though my dwindling bank account would take a hit.

I couldn't sleep.

Other than playing with Ava in the evenings and forcing myself to eat a few times a day, I couldn't seem to muster the energy to focus on anything. I was supposed to be gaining weight, being four months pregnant, but instead, I'd lost five pounds.

My brain wouldn't shut off. I lay in bed awake for hours every night, afraid Nathan would come home in the middle of the night, that he'd find a way to get into the house. We hadn't spoken, though he'd called several times, even after he didn't show up in court and the protection order was put in place.

· · ·

Four weeks passed since that night, and I slept with a wooden baseball bat at my side. I still couldn't comprehend how a slip of paper would protect me in the event I actually needed protection. It reminded me of that Jennifer Lopez movie, *Enough*, where JLo's character, Slim, finally goes to the police for help, and all they do is suggest she file a restraining order. *"And what am I supposed to do with that? Throw it at him?"*

Slim had to fight back in that movie; she had no other choice. I wasn't necessarily planning to fight my husband, but I learned how to swing a baseball bat at a young age, and that gave me peace of mind in case using it was warranted.

During the day I kept the bat leaning up against the entrance by the garage or on days I was feeling particularly jumpy—after a night of little sleep, which was just about every night—I carried it around with me from room to room.

I was able to breathe a little easier when Natalie called to let me know she received his box of things. Her voice was somber, and I could tell she wanted to say more but didn't know how to.

"Is there anything I can do?" she asked.

"No."

"Are you going to leave him?" I felt the hitch in her voice, the fear that I would divorce her brother and no longer be her sister-in-law or Isabelle's aunt.

I didn't blame Natalie for asking the inevitable question, yet I wasn't ready to hear it. I didn't know what I wanted anymore, what was best for me, Ava and my unborn child. I just knew something had to change and I needed the screaming in my head to stop.

"I don't know, Nat," I said finally.

"He loves you, you know."

"If only that were enough."

The line grew quiet and I knew there was nothing more to say. Natalie would give me space, but it would be difficult for her. I would miss seeing her and Isabelle, but it was time for me to distance myself—and my kids—from my husband and his family. Natalie meant well, but her intentions would always favor that of her flesh and blood.

Things had otherwise been quiet at home, and while I often caught myself missing Nathan, I was relieved he hadn't tried to come home. I was never skilled in the art of turning him away, his manipulation tactics too advanced for me. I didn't know where he'd been living, although Natalie confirmed he had asked if he could stay with her. She said no on account of Isabelle, coupled with Nathan's unpredictability. I hoped he wasn't sleeping on the street or under a bridge somewhere.

Or in someone else's bed.

On the fifth week, I called Nathan to tell him about the baby. I dialed his number, unsure if it was even in service, and was surprised when he answered on the first ring.

"Brynn? Baby?"

"It's me."

"Baby, thank God. I miss you so much." His voice shook, and I sat down on the edge of the couch in our living room staring blankly at the wall.

"I'm pregnant," I blurted, much like I had the last time I'd shared that news with him.

"What? *Again?*"

"I think it happened on date night. We didn't use a condom."

"We're having another baby? Are you sure?" I heard a twitch of excitement in his voice and immediately regretted calling; he would find a way to convince me that another baby could save our marriage.

That he could change.

"Yes, I'm sure. I just thought you should know."

"Brynn—wait!" I stayed on but said nothing, just listened to the sound of Nathan's breathing on the other end. "Is...is the baby okay?" he asked, stifling tears, the catch in his voice almost unbearable.

"Yes," I whispered.

"Baby, I'm so..." His words caught in his throat as the tears fought for release. "...So fucking sorry."

"I have to go, Nathan." I pressed "end" to disconnect the call, and threw the phone across the room, watching as it bounced against the wall and landed with a thud.

Sorry would never erase the damage that had been done.

———

I CONTINUED to pass the time. After calling in the first week that the protection order was put in place, I went back to work. The bruises on my neck had faded, and I covered what was left of the faint imperfections with makeup. None of my coworkers batted an eye, except for Elle, who was concerned and peppered me with questions about why I'd missed so much work. She didn't know—I told her Ava and I had come down with the flu.

The dust settled and week after week, I showed up to work and Ava went to daycare. On the weekends we'd play and snuggle and make each other laugh by practicing our goofy faces in the mirror. Most nights she'd fall asleep on my lap or climb into my bed with me in the middle of the night, her little body pressed up against my hip, providing comfort and warmth when I needed it most.

But when it was just me, by myself and lost in my own thoughts, it felt strange to just *be*.

I found myself growing fond of the quiet, taking more time to appreciate the silence. And while I liked my job, I'd grown to like the quiet more. The fact that I'd been written up for my attendance at work the week I returned was just another reminder of how fucked up my life had become. I was good at my job. Really good. But I was no longer dependable, and that just wouldn't cut it.

I came to terms with the fact that things were never going to be the same. And that was a good thing; I could breathe again. I was regularly talking to and seeing my parents, even though I couldn't bring myself to tell them much of anything about what was actually going on; they knew Nathan and I were separated, and the reasons why didn't really matter. I spent time catching up with Jerilyn and Andi, albeit over the phone, and even grew closer to Elle, finding strength from the inner circle that I trusted more than anything.

And just when I started feeling overwhelmed with the terrifying thought of being a single mother to two children under the age of two, my high school friend, Meg, who I'd kept in touch with and knew that Nathan had moved out, asked if I'd be interested in taking in a roommate. I jumped at the chance, knowing that Meg would be able to help keep me sane and grateful I could help out a friend at the same time.

I couldn't have been more relieved the day she walked through the door, her belongings in tow, her arms stretched open wide in acceptance.

CHAPTER TWENTY-TWO

MAY 2006

A LOUD NOISE sounded from the front of the house; someone was out there. Muting the TV, I zoned in on the footsteps that approached the front door. I powered off the TV, swiped my cell from the table and shuffled over to the kitchen. Out of view from the front window, I pressed myself against the wall, my hands shaking. Meg was out for the night, so it was just Ava and me at home. And Ava was all the way upstairs, asleep in her bed.

How the hell do I get to her?

"Brynn, let me in!" Nathan shouted, his fist pounding on the door. His voice was frantic, almost terrified. My heart leaped from my chest, suddenly on high alert as I remembered that the protection order had expired a week earlier. I tightened my grip on the phone in my hand, prepared to call for help at any second.

"BRYNN! OPEN THE FUCKING DOOR!"

Thump. Thump. Thump.

What the fuck do I do?

"BRYNN! Hurry, they're coming!"

Who's coming?

"Please, sweetie, let me in..."

Is he...crying?

I grabbed the wooden baseball bat and walked slowly to the front door, peering cautiously through the window. Nathan had slid down to the ground, his knees tucked up to his chin and head in his hands, his body lax against the door. I pressed the "send call" button on my phone and slid it into the pocket of my hooded sweatshirt. Sweat beading on my forehead, I gripped the bat tight and tapped on the window. Nathan turned and looked up at me, streaks of tears covering his blotchy cheeks.

I hadn't seen him cry since Ava was born.

He jumped to his feet, his hand on the doorknob and forehead pressed against the window. There was a longing in his eyes when he spoke.

"Brynn? Baby?"

"Nathan, what's wrong?" I was reluctant to open the door, but the imminent threat seemed to have dissipated. I reached up and unlocked the deadbolt in slow motion, unsure of my actions and willing some higher power—any higher power—to tell me what the fuck to do.

"I need you, Brynn...please...open the door." I heard the caller on the other end shouting out to me, asking if I was in danger. I sent him a silent plea not to hang up. Tightening my grip on the handle of the bat, I undid the final lock on the door with my left hand and pulled it open. Nathan rushed in, pulling me into his arms before slamming the door and manically re-securing the locks.

At close range, it was easier for me to get a good look at him. His eyes were bloodshot and dilated, and he was sweating, almost profusely. It looked like he hadn't showered or eaten in days.

I broke him.

This is my fault.

"What happened?" I asked again. Nathan grabbed me by the arm and dragged me over to the kitchen, away from the front windows. I glanced out the sliding door to the backyard, the night dark, the rest of the neighborhood seemingly tucked in for the night.

What the hell is he running from?

"They're after me, Brynn. All of 'em!" he announced, running his hands through his greasy hair. He walked quickly to the fridge, opened it with urgency and grabbed the milk from the shelf. Removing the cap, he brought the half-full gallon jug to his lips and threw his head back as he drank.

"Who's after you, Nathan?" I fingered the cell phone in my pocket, no longer able to hear the voice on the other end, not knowing if he'd hung up. "Who are you running from?"

He kept drinking the milk.

"Nathan?" I placed my hand on his forearm, hoping to recapture his attention. He stopped drinking suddenly and slammed the nearly empty jug onto the counter. I took an instinctive step back and watched the jug fall to the floor, the leftover milk splattering out of it.

"All the fucking assholes are after me again, Brynn. All of them! Every fucking one of them. I can't fucking think." He paced the length of the kitchen and then made his way over to the pantry, rummaging through the snack bin and settling on a handful of Oatmeal Cream Pies. He tore the cellophane package open with his teeth before shoving the entire thing into his mouth and chewing it like a cow. "You know," he said with his mouth full, "I miss these fucking things." A chunk of cream dangled from the corner of his mouth. "I forgot how good they are."

I stared at my estranged husband. What kind of response had he expected to such an idiotic comment under the circumstances? "Are you okay?" I asked again.

"No, I'm not fucking okay!"

"Can you tell me what's going on? Who's after you, Nathan?" *Always make sure to state the name of your attacker.*

"What?" He glared at me, as if I were the one who asked the stupid question. *Find a natural way to state your location.*

"Well, you show up here at my house in the middle of the night, screaming that someone's after you, and when I finally let you inside, you drink all my milk and start gorging on cream pies...care to tell me why?" *Keep your attacker talking, keep them distracted.*

Nathan scratched his head and looked down at the floor. I maneuvered so that the bat stayed behind me and took another cautious step backward. The half bathroom was less than ten feet from me. *Separate yourself from the attacker and find a phone to call for help.* "What's behind your back?" Nathan asked, his eyes wide.

"Nothing." He held my gaze and I watched the fear settle back into his eyes as they grew wide and then fell into a glare.

"I said what the *fuck* is behind your back? You're one of them, aren't you? You're in on it, too?" He turned his head, talking to no one as he said, "I told you!"

"In on what, Nathan? I don't know what the fuck you're talking about!" The urgency rose in my voice, and my heart rate picked back up. I was terrified that Ava would wake up and come downstairs to witness Nathan's manic state. I shot a glance over to the stairs by the front door to make sure she wasn't there, and when I turned back around Nathan was charging at me.

He tackled me to the ground and easily wrestled the

bat from my grip. I covered my belly with my arms, maternal instinct kicking in, and tried to shield my unborn son from the blows I had expected that never actually came. I felt myself scream, the vibrato shaking my chest, as I closed my eyes and folded into the fetal position.

Please! No!

But I heard Nathan take a step back.

...and heavy boots on the linoleum floor.

Shouting.

Glass breaking.

Handcuffs.

Ava crying.

"Hands behind your head!" an officer shouted, barging through the side door off the kitchen.

He didn't hang up.

I opened my eyes to see Nathan on his knees in front of me, his hands behind his head, fear in his eyes. "Did you...I..." he stammered.

I let out the breath I was holding and pressed my hand to my stomach, thankful to feel movement within my womb. I accepted the hand that was offered to me and allowed myself to be pulled to my feet as my father wrapped his arms tightly around me and my mother ran to Ava, who now stood on the staircase landing, clutching her blanket and crying out for me. Not only had they answered my call, but they'd stayed on the line and even thought to bring backup.

"It's okay, baby, Grammy's here," Mom assured her.

"Are you all right?" Dad asked.

I nodded. "I'm okay."

I'm so sorry.

"You thought...I was going to...hit you with it?" Nathan asked while one of the officers walked him out the door in handcuffs.

The pain in his face was too much to bear.

———

IT WASN'T until just over a week later that I found out that Nathan had been hallucinating on mushrooms. I never did have the heart to tell Meg why the backdoor was broken.

CHAPTER TWENTY-THREE
AUGUST 2006

"YAHTZEE!" Meg shouted, throwing her arms in the air in celebration. I huffed and tossed my pen at her; the snot had already gotten two Yahtzee's to my none and there was likely no coming back for me, the game a bust.

"I quit!" I conceded with a huff. "No fair!"

"Awww, I'm sorry, I didn't realize we had seats for the sore losers at the table," she teased. We laughed and she reached for the iPod Nano on the table and cranked it up as The Backstreet Boys blared from the tiny speaker. We leaped from our chairs and broke into an early 2000's choreographed dance to "Everybody (Backstreet's Back)".

When the song ended, I plopped back down in my chair, winded from the half-assed dance performance, my baby bump having hindered the true spirit I intended to bring to the dance.

Two months to go.

"All right lady, I'm about ready to call it a night," I admitted.

"No worries, I need to be up early anyway. We have a floor change to get out before opening. You need anything before I head up?" Meg asked, packing the contents of the game into the box. She set it on the shelf in the living room, a sign that we'd play again tomorrow.

"Nope, I'm good, but thanks."

"Night, bitch!" she hollered and made her way up the stairs, waving in Paris Hilton fashion. I chuckled and waved back, relieved to have kept my mind off Nathan for the evening.

I'd given Meg the master bedroom when she moved in; I couldn't stand to sleep in that room without Nathan and needed a change of scenery. Plus, it made sense for her to have the bigger room with an en-suite bath and walk-in closet. My new room was smaller, but it connected with Ava's through a Jack and Jill bathroom.

And it didn't smell like Nathan.

Meg worked in retail, at *OshKosh B'gosh* in the outlet mall across the freeway. She not only loved her job, but also received a healthy discount on store merchandise— that she couldn't use, being that she was a twenty-one-year-old single woman with no kids—which made me the lucky, and very grateful, recipient of brand new kids' clothes that I otherwise couldn't afford. She'd come home with another handful of outfits earlier that day, excited to show me what she'd picked out for my son.

She had been living with Ava and me for nearly four months, and already it felt like we'd lived together forever. Meg brought sunlight to every room she entered; that's just who she was. During the week she helped take care of Ava, even though there was never an expectation for her to do so, and sometimes she'd even bring her to daycare for me or pick her up in the evenings. I wasn't used to that kind of live-in help; Nathan certainly had never been that helpful with Ava, and she was his daughter. Earlier in the week, I'd come home to a clean and folded basket of laundry sitting on my bed. Meg had the day off work and was kind enough to do the wash.

As much as I could, I made sure the favors went both ways. I was the better cook, so I often made dinner, and Meg took her place as my sous chef most nights, alongside Ava—who served as our taste tester.

But what I appreciated most about Meg's presence during those months was that she gave me hope. I smiled, every single day.

I laughed.

Sometimes we cried together, too, but most days she just made me feel normal again. But I was about to let her down; I was about to disappoint her.

Nathan called.

He'd spent the last four months back home in West Virginia. He claimed he'd been clean, that he wanted to come home for our son's birth. I didn't say yes right off the bat.

My head and my heart were torn.

Do I say no and keep attempting to function without my estranged husband? Or do I tell him to come home and uphold the vows I'd made?

Those fucking vows hung over my head for years. I didn't know divorce; I was the product of two parents who made marriage work, and I was convinced that meant I was supposed to do the same. I wasn't supposed to keep contributing to statistics and throw in the towel just because things got too hard. I was supposed to keep my head in the game, to keep trying.

What I was too naive to understand at the time is that there's a difference between making marriage work because you genuinely loved and respected one another and making marriage work because a piece of paper and a guilty conscience told you that you were supposed to. What

I kept forgetting was that Nathan hadn't held up his end of the bargain. He'd had affairs, one-night stands. He didn't love, honor and cherish me.

He abused me.

He belittled me and put his hands on me in ways that no husband ever should. Nathan made me feel like so small of a person that some days I barely managed to get out of bed.

But he was my husband.

He was the father of my children; didn't that count for something?

Nathan's call wasn't quite out of the blue; I allowed him to call once a week to talk to Ava. I found myself at a loss for words when he called again hours later that night, after he had already spoken to Ava hours ago and she was sound asleep in her bed. At the sound of my ring tone, a panic sensation came over me, and I settled on the assumption that something must be wrong—he never called more than once.

When I answered, Nathan's voice came in clear. He spoke with determination and purpose, like he'd had time to change, to put his family first. I laid in bed listening to the sound of his voice, the low rumble providing comfort that I desperately needed.

"Do you remember when we went to Quarry Park?" he asked. I could hear the smile in his voice, and my heart fluttered in protest to my mind.

"I remember," I whispered.

We had made the roughly two-hour drive to Mora, Minnesota on a hot day in June the year we first met. I was pregnant with Ava, and we were tired of sweating our asses off in our apartment. Nathan hadn't yet slept with Tess, and my heart hadn't yet been ripped to shreds. We were still mostly happy, just two young idiots in love.

"I wish we could go back to that day…"

"Mmm…" I said, not agreeing with him, but not disagreeing either.

After swimming, we grabbed our towels and sat on the rocks in the quarry, our feet dangling in the water as we ate sandwiches from our picnic basket and picked out a name for Ava. I think it was the last time I remember being genuinely happy with Nathan. Life had seemed so much simpler then.

I hadn't yet been broken.

————

It was less than a week later that Nathan boarded a Grey-hound bus back to Minnesota. The evening he knocked on my front door—his duffle bag at his feet and a sheepish grin on his face—a wave of sadness washed over me. I could see the regret in his eyes, the tears soaking his cheeks as he took in the sight of my pregnant belly—evidence of the time he had lost and could never get back.

Ava was asleep upstairs, and Meg was out with friends for the evening, so despite my reservations, I not only opened the door, but invited him inside. After months of no physical contact, of sleeping alone, my tears soaking the pillow night after night, I couldn't turn my husband away.

His hands reached for my belly, cupping it as he leaned down and kissed the bump.

"Nathan, I don't think—"

"Shh, baby, please. Let me have this." He tucked a strand of hair behind my ear, his palm resting on my cheek, our foreheads touching. His arms embraced me. His lips met mine, tender, reserved.

I pulled away, took a step back.

"I don't know if you should be here." I whispered,

unconvinced of the validity in my words. His face fell, and his eyes dropped to the floor.

"I don't have anywhere else to go." He shrugged and stuffed his hands into the pockets of his jeans. "Is Meg home?"

"No."

"Maybe I could just stay tonight, then?"

"I…"

"Baby, please. Let me hold you." He reached for me again, pulling me to him, his body pressed to mine. "We don't have to figure this out tonight. Just let me have this."

I nodded, reaching around him to lock the deadbolt on the door.

One night.

I could do *one* night.

———

Before Meg came home the following morning, I asked Nathan to leave so she and I could talk. I gave him the keys to my car, and he left to visit Natalie and Isabelle, instructing me to call her house when it was time for him to come home.

Home.

It wasn't a question, but a statement—the idea of "just one night" snowballing in a matter of hours. My resolve punctured at the mention of a few more empty promises, a few more assurances that things would be different.

That he would love me.

That he would protect me, protect our children.

That I would forgive him.

I was the emotional wreck caught between my husband and my friend. She wouldn't stay, and I knew that the moment I saw Nathan standing at my doorstep. I thought I was doing the right thing, keeping my family together…

———

MEG MOVED out that afternoon before Nathan returned. I wasn't sure our friendship would ever be the same, or if I'd managed to break that, too.

CHAPTER TWENTY-FOUR
SEPTEMBER 2006

Continued from Chapter One

ONCE NATHAN WAS CONSIDERED stable for transport, he was taken straight to the Hazelden rehabilitation center from the hospital. He was admitted as a voluntary check-in, but considering he had nearly died, the admissions staff highly recommended direct transport to prevent any opportunities for relapse. He had been clean for about twenty-four hours and sending him straight to rehab a couple days early was considered a necessary precaution.

After the ambulance and Officer Randall left, I called Natalie. I could barely find the words to explain just how bad things had gotten with Nathan, but she seemed to have had a good idea. Her brother desperately needed help, and she knew him well enough to know that staying sober would never come easy for him. He'd been dependent on drugs and alcohol for so much of his life that he simply didn't know how to function without it.

As if by default, Natalie was that one person in my life who had any inkling of what took place behind the closed doors of our home. Not only had she come to the rescue a few times, but she also lived close, and because of that I found myself rushing Ava to her more times than I care to admit. I like to think she just wanted the best for all of us and hoped we'd find a way to make it work.

I was relieved when she offered to keep Ava overnight. The world had felt so loud for so long, and I needed to turn down the noise. I couldn't keep giving tiny parts of myself in hopes that I'd one day feel whole—that Nathan could be the person I thought I'd seen when I met him. I don't know why, but I was convinced I could fix him. I knew he was broken that first night I sat with him by the fire in Natalie's driveway.

I knew he needed someone to love him, to take care of him.

At the time, I didn't know much about him, other than that he was living with his sister and trying to get a fresh start. But there was something about him that drew me to him, like a bad car crash that you just can't look away from no matter how hard you try. That's what Nathan did to me—he sucked me in. He was good at finding little ways to get to me, to make me feel just sorry enough for him that I couldn't walk away.

I had never imagined I'd find myself in a relationship with an addict. Sometimes the fact that I did surprises me more than the fact that he was physically abusive. I was so naive at that age, so unaware of what was happening around me, of the severity and abnormality of it. Here I was, married to a guy I met by way of a cheesy pick-up line, and even though I saw red flags on that first night, I just kept coming back for more simply because he'd shown interest in me. Because he'd pursued me and made me feel special. It makes me wonder if Nathan wasn't the only one with an addiction—maybe I had one too.

Focused on taking care of Ava and not going into early labor, I had to avoid the worst of Nathan's withdrawals this time around, so I decided to wait a few more days before visiting him at Hazelden.

I didn't really want to visit him at all.

As his wife, I felt obligated to. But as his *pregnant* wife, who was less than a month shy of her due date, I didn't feel like I should have to.

Nathan called on Thursday night, a couple days after he'd been admitted to Hazelden. The first thing he said was that he was feeling like shit and wasn't sleeping well.

Welcome to the club.

I half-listened as I sliced vegetables for a salad.

"I'm going insane here, baby. These people are fucking *junkies*."

"Well, what did you expect?" I asked, slicing a tomato in half.

"Not this! All they talk about in here is God and forgiveness. They keep shoving the Bible in my damn face."

I put my chef's knife down and dried my hands on a towel before going into the other room to check on Ava. I rounded the corner and poked my head into the living room. She was conked out on her mini couch and I took a mental picture, wishing more than anything that I could lay down beside her for a nap.

"You there?" Nathan asked.

"Yeah."

"Will you come see me tomorrow?"

"I can't, I have to work." I headed back to the kitchen and stirred the chicken breast that was browning on the stove.

"Call in sick."

"Nathan, you know I can't do that. I've missed so much time already."

"Can't? Or won't?" he snapped. *Sigh*.

"I told you I'll be there in a couple days. Just follow the program and stay focused." He exhaled into the phone, frustrated with me yet again.

"I miss you," he admitted, the line going quiet. "Brynn?"

"Listen, I have to go." I ended the call before Nathan's response came through the line; he hadn't bothered to say the two words I needed to hear more than anything.

In that moment I felt nothing but shame. I stabbed my knife into the wooden cutting board and slid down to the floor, my head in my hands as the tears rained down my cheeks.

I am nothing.

My husband was in rehab while I was at home waiting on the birth of our second child, trying to figure out how the fuck to keep it together. I was so embarrassed, so angry. So hurt.

I am worthless.

Looking back, I realize a lot of that shame I felt stemmed from nothing more than pure regret. I had vowed to love my husband in sickness and in health but all I could think about was how badly I just wanted to take every one of those fucking words back.

I didn't want to be the wife of an addict.

I didn't want to be *his* wife anymore.

Everything is broken.

How could I leave this man when he was at his lowest? My husband needed me; he needed our daughter. We had to show him that he was loved, didn't we? How could I kick him while he was down?

The weight of my heart in my chest was excruciating. I

didn't know what to do, what to think. There was no one I could talk to, no one who would understand the torment I was going through. Surely they would judge me for my decisions, for staying with Nathan and continuing through this never-ending cycle of abuse. But I was carrying another child, one we made together out of love. How would leaving be fair to our unborn son? To our daughter who lay beside me snuggled up to my hip on the nights when her daddy didn't come home? What had I done to deserve this life, other than love a broken man?

Nathan's harsh words echoed in the back of my mind: *"No one else will ever want you."*

He was right. I was a broken woman now, too. Could I let my husband down at a time when he needed me the most?

Could I abandon him again?

Abandon our family?

I can't.

CHAPTER TWENTY-FIVE

OCTOBER 2006

ON SATURDAY MORNING I dressed in comfortable leggings and a gray sweater and then dropped Ava off with my parents, leaving them with the assumption that I was seeing a movie with Jerilyn. They were aware that Nathan was in rehab, but I wasn't sure how they would feel about me going to visit him there in my current state.

I'm sure deep down they knew where I was going.

Despite the dread of seeing my husband in rehab, the roughly hour-long drive had been relaxing. There was something about the open highway, the colors on the trees as the season changed from summer to fall—the reds, oranges and browns mixing cohesively in the foliage of the trees that stood tall beyond the open road. I'd nearly forgotten where I was headed.

I would have rather been on my way to get my wisdom teeth pulled again, but Nathan needed clothes and toiletries, so I went. I felt dirty the second I walked in the door, even though the place was relatively clean.

I waddled my way alongside the addiction counselor I'd been scheduled to meet with—who was walking much too quickly for my pregnant body to keep up with—as we went down several long corridors that led to the pod in the men's wing where Nathan was living. I was almost surprised by the normalcy of it—the pod reminding me of a college dorm with its shared living space equipped with couches, a television, a shelf filled with movies and books and a kitchenette stocked with water, a coffeemaker, tea and snacks.

The Twelve Steps of Narcotics Anonymous were displayed over inspirational portraits that framed the walls. *We admitted that we were powerless over our addiction; that our lives had become unmanageable.*

Nathan's room was to the left of the living space. He was in between roommates so he had a fairly large room to himself. His twin-sized bed sat unmade, the hospital issued blankets crumpled and piled up at the foot of the bed. He stood up from the worn chair he'd been sitting in and set his blue copy of the Narcotics Anonymous book on the nightstand but didn't make an effort to approach me. His face fell and his eyes landed at my swollen feet. *We came to believe that a Power greater than ourselves could restore us to sanity.*

"Hi," I managed, suddenly self-conscious. I'd left the house in somewhat of a hurry, having fed and dressed Ava quickly before rushing her off to my parents, and hadn't had time to do my hair; it sat in a chignon on the top of my head, still wet from my shower.

"You came."

"I brought you some things," I said, handing him the backpack I'd stuffed with clothes, shampoo, body wash, deodorant and a toothbrush. It had been rummaged through by the security clerk when I arrived and for some reason, none of its contents fit back in the same as they had come out and the zipper wouldn't close.

"Thank you." He still hadn't moved and made no

effort to take the bag from me. I set it down on the bed and rested my nervous hands on my belly. The addiction counselor stood in the doorway, observing our conversation since we weren't allowed to be alone. *We made a decision to turn our will and our lives over to the care of God as we understood Him.*

"Are you…okay?" he asked.

"I'm fine," I admitted. While I hated that Nathan was in rehab, I found an odd comfort in knowing not just where he was, but also what he wasn't able to do while he was there—no sex, no drugs. *No abuse.* He was getting help and despite the devil on my shoulder, I was trying to be supportive. *We made a searching and fearless moral inventory of ourselves.*

"Can we sit? My feet are killing me."

Nathan's head lifted and a smile spread across his face, but not the kind that tells you someone's happy—more like the kind that's filled with regret. "That must be because you've been running through my mind all day," he said.

My mouth curved into a smile, the sentiment so touching, and I watched a single tear roll down Nathan's cheek. I stepped forward and wiped it away with my thumb, letting my hand rest on his face a little longer than necessary. *We admitted to God, to ourselves, and to another human being the exact nature of our wrongs.*

Nathan wrapped his arms around me and buried his face in my neck as if he were holding on for dear life.

Maybe he was.

"I'm so sorry, Brynn," he managed, his body shaking as the sobs took over. I held him, rubbing his back while the already broken pieces of my heart shattered into another million broken pieces. *We were entirely ready to have God remove all these defects of character.*

I didn't stay at the center for long, and I was grateful Nathan didn't fault me for it. I was far too pregnant, far too exhausted and far too uncomfortable. I wanted to be somewhere, anywhere else. *We humbly asked Him to remove our shortcomings.*

Nathan and I hugged goodbye, and he passed me a folded sheet of notebook paper. "Read it when you get home," he said, kissing my cheek. *We made a list of all persons we had harmed, and became willing to make amends to them all.*

I stuffed the note into my purse and held my hand out to Nathan. He took it, squeezing it as if he thought it might be the last time. "I want to be proud of you," I whispered, my voice catching in my throat as I struggled to say the words he needed to hear. *We made direct amends to such people wherever possible, except when to do so would injure them or others.*

He pressed his lips to mine, despite the "ahem" from the counselor who still hovered at the door, and then kissed the tip of my nose. I pulled away, unsure if it really was goodbye. Unsure when I'd see him again. *We continued to take personal inventory and when we were wrong promptly admitted it.*

"I love you, Brynn," he confided, his eyes glistening with fresh tears. I wanted to stay. I wanted to go. I wanted so much more than what we had left. *We sought through prayer and meditation to improve our conscious contact with God as we understood Him, praying only for knowledge of His will for us and the power to carry that out.*

I gave Nathan's hand one last squeeze and then made my way out of the room. The addiction counselor walked me back through the long corridors to the front desk and watched while I signed my name on the visitor's log. I zipped my jacket, put my sunglasses back on my face and walked through the door, the scent of the cheap bar soap Nathan had been using lingering in my nostrils as I took a deep breath of the crisp autumn air.

I didn't want to go home yet.

I just wanted to be.

In my car, I pulled the note from Nathan out of my purse, my breath catching in my throat as I read the crooked scribble he'd left on the page.

> *It's okay to let me go. I will never stop loving you.*
> *Nathan*

I crumpled the note and stuffed it back into my purse, wishing I hadn't bothered to open it. I slid my Mariah Carey *Charmbracelet* CD into the disc player and pushed the skip button until I reached the thirteenth song, then cranked the dial until I could no longer hear myself think. My head leaned back against the seat, I closed my eyes.

And started to sing.

> *You got the best of me*
> *Whoa, can't you see?*
> *You're bringin' on the heartbreak*
> *Bringin' on the heartache*

I couldn't remember the last time I sang at the top of my lungs. I didn't even care that I was a very pregnant young woman—sitting in a beat-up car in the Hazelden parking lot—singing off-key, cheeks soaked from the tears of a thousand cries.

I just needed to breathe.

Having had a spiritual awakening as the result of these steps, we tried to carry this message to addicts, and to practice these principles in all our affairs.

————

NATHAN SHOWED up at the house one week later. He said he didn't believe in God, so there was no point in working the twelve steps.

PART TWO

I see you—
and all your beautiful scars

CHAPTER TWENTY-SIX

SEPTEMBER 2008

"Higher, Papa!" Ava yelled, dipping her head back and pumping her feet. She loved to watch the clouds fly by and would swing every day if she could. My dad gave her another push before turning back to Hayden, who was busy throwing Wiffle balls at him and giggling every time he managed to hit him with one. It was an unusually warm afternoon in September so, like many Minnesotans, we took advantage and walked the mile from my parent's house down to Sturges Park at Buffalo Lake.

"Grammy, watch!" Hayden said, spinning around in a circle. He made himself dizzy and dropped to the ground, landing hard on his bottom. I watched as my mom scooped him up and brushed the dirt off his pants. He quickly took off running in the other direction, daring her to chase him, the sound of his laughter carrying across the park and bringing a smile to my face.

I sat on a bench down the hill from the playground and closed my eyes, the gentle breeze brushing across my face. It was hard to believe my son was already about to turn two, Ava four. It'd been a little over a year since the three of us had moved in with my parents, and while it wasn't a decision I made lightly, I was grateful for their willingness to take us in.

To love us.

To forgive me.

But that's what parents do; they pick us up when we fall down, just as I'd watched my mom do for Hayden.

Hayden James had graced us with his presence shortly after midnight the day Nathan came home unexpectedly from Hazelden. I'd gone into labor early that morning, and while I was disappointed that he'd come home early—bailing on the help he desperately needed—I was relieved he'd be there for the birth of our son. Like he had with Ava, I knew I could count on my husband to support me through it. He somehow made me feel safe in those moments, like we were in it together. If there's one thing I'll always look back on fondly, it's that I didn't have to bring our children into this world alone.

We'd dropped Ava off with my parents, and while they were reluctant to watch Nathan and I go off alone, we promised to call them once the baby came and they'd agreed to meet us at the hospital later.

But Hayden didn't come easy.

I'd been in labor for hours, having tried everything imaginable to speed things along. Eventually, we made our way to the hospital, and after less than an hour of checking my cervix and eating ice chips while my uterus contracted, were discharged. The maternity ward was full, and I wasn't progressing quickly enough. So, we went home.

Back at home, after trying tirelessly to sleep, to eat, to walk, Nathan finally drew me a hot bath and helped lower me into the tub. I tried to remember to breathe through the contractions while Nathan held my hand and asked me a hundred times if it was time to go back to the hospital yet. Finally, four hours after we'd been sent away, I took his hands and he pulled me up from the tub and dried me off with a towel. He helped me into a pair of his sweatpants and an oversized sweatshirt and then looped my hair into a crooked bun on the top of my head. The bags already in the car, I sent my mom a quick text and back to the hospital we went.

"Oh, fuck! Fuck! Fuck!" I shouted through gritted teeth as I doubled over in the passenger seat. Nathan pressed on the gas pedal in an attempt to get the piece-of-shit Flintstone car moving a little faster.

"Do you think we waited too long?" he asked, panic spreading across his face.

"OBVIOUSLY!"

We made it to the hospital with just enough time for me to climb onto the bed and throw my feet up into the dreaded stirrups. It was much too late for an epidural, and it was time to push.

I bore down as hard as I could, screamed profanities at every person in the room and in less than nine minutes, my eight-pound-five-ounce beautiful son, Hayden James, was placed in my arms. I didn't even have an IV in yet.

"He's so handsome," Nathan said when he climbed into the bed with us. I was nursing Hayden, his tiny head pressed up against my breast as he suckled and drifted off to sleep. Nathan laid his head on my shoulder and softly ran his fingers along Hayden's chubby cheek. "We made that," he said, full of pride, a wide grin on his face. "I'm so proud of you."

I smiled and closed my eyes, laying my head back against the pillow, my body sore from the trauma it'd undergone.

I can't believe I just did that.

I wasn't sure what the future held for us, but I left the

hospital a couple days later with more than just my newborn son—I left with hope. Hope that Nathan could stay clean, that we could somehow figure out how to make our marriage work for the sake of the kids.

But as my mother always used to say, "You can hope in one hand and shit in the other and see which one fills up faster."

I think it's safe to say my hand filled with shit long before the other filled with hope, but I suppose that's the sentiment of the phrase.

CHAPTER TWENTY-SEVEN

FEBRUARY 2007

THE SOUND of my cell phone ringing on the coffee table jolted me from the land of make-believe. I set down the book I'd been reading and grabbed my phone, unsure who would call at the late hour. "Unknown" flashed across the screen, and without hesitation, I flipped the phone open.

"Hello?"

"You have a collect call from NATHAN. Press one to accept the charges."

I rolled my eyes and pressed one as my pulse began to race.

What now?

Nathan's muddled voice greeted me on the other end of the line. "Brynn, it's Nathan."

"You're in *jail?*"

"Yeah, fuckers pulled me over on the way home from Jesse's," he mumbled, nonchalant. He had told me he'd planned to stay the night there, so I hadn't expected to hear from him until morning.

"Were you drinking?" *Or high?*

"Yeah, but I only had a couple. Cop said I failed the

sobriety test, but it's bullshit. I had two fucking beers and these assholes want five-hundred dollars for bail. Can you come get me out?"

"Nathan, it's almost midnight. The kids are asleep."

"Well, wake 'em up. I'm not staying in this shit-hole all night." He sighed and I couldn't help but feel sorry. Not for him, for myself. My own husband only ever called me when he needed something and even then, he couldn't be bothered to ask nicely.

"We don't have five-hundred dollars," I pointed out, annoyed that he assumed I could pull the money out of my ass.

"I know, call Natalie. She'll pay it," he spat, his words slurred together.

"Right now? It's late." I looked at the clock on the wall, surprised to find it was later than I had thought. I'd been lost in my book ever since the kids had gone to bed several hours ago.

"I don't care how fucking late it is, Brynn. Get me out of here." I heard a voice in the background tell Nathan it was time to wrap it up. "I have to go. Call Natalie."

The line went dead. I snapped my phone shut and stared at it in my hand, unable to wrap my head around Nathan's insistence that I not only call his sister in the middle of the night, but wake up our children and drag them down to the county jail.

I got up from the couch and walked into the kitchen, set my phone on the counter and plugged it in to charge before I sat down at the kitchen table. Even if Natalie helped cover the cost of Nathan's bail, with the impound fees on the car, there was no way we were going to make rent for the month. I opened my laptop and navigated to my budget spreadsheet. The stack of bills that sat in front of me taunted me as I made a mental list of which ones would have to go unpaid. I'd gotten good at alternating the ones to pay late each month, but this would set us back significantly.

And Nathan was in between jobs again.

———

I SLEPT on the couch in the living room, if you could call it sleeping. I'd laid down a half hour or so after my call with Nathan, but I knew he'd be upset that I didn't pick him up and he had to stay in jail overnight. To say I was on edge would be an understatement.

I called Natalie from the car after dropping the kids off at daycare and calling into work. While she had been reluctant to lend us the money—she seemed certain we hadn't paid her back from the last time we had borrowed money from her—she agreed to help. "You have to pay it back by Friday this time," she'd said, a nervousness to her voice.

"Oh, we will, I promise." I'd said. But that wasn't likely; we'd be lucky to pay her back over the next ten Fridays. Of course, I couldn't tell her that, though.

I pulled into a parking space at the Wright County Courthouse. It was the last place I wanted to be. I leaned back in the seat and took a few deep breaths as I watched a snow plow clear the snow from the lot across the street. It'd snowed again overnight, another few inches, and I'd used the excuse to get out of work for the day.

I grabbed my purse and stuffed the keys inside and then got out of the car, having shut the door a little harder than intended. My boots sloshed through the wet snow, and I made my way to the jail entrance.

I stepped inside and stomped my feet on the rug, unaware of the noise I was making. Someone cleared their throat to get my attention, and I looked up from the floor to find several sets of eyes upon me. I mumbled a quick apology and then made my way over to the security desk.

"Can I help you?" the desk clerk asked. He was a brawny man in his late fifties who looked like he'd rather be somewhere else, too.

"I'm here to bail my husband out of jail," I said, unsure of the proper way to state such a request.

"What's the inmate's name?"

"Nathan Reeves." He typed something into the desktop computer and stared at the screen for a moment before he clicked a few keys on the keyboard.

"Bail is five-hundred dollars. How would you like to pay?"

"Um, cash." I reached for my wallet, pulled out the crisp bills from Natalie and handed them to him.

"Photo identification, please," he stated, setting the cash aside. I pulled out my driver's license and slid it over to him. He picked it up and looked at it, then back at me.

"Do you have any warrants out for your arrest, Mrs. Reeves?" he asked.

"Me? No…"

"Any drugs or alcohol in your system?"

I stared at him, a blank expression on my face.

"We can't release inmates to someone who's under the influence," he advised, having picked up on my state of confusion. "It's standard procedure for a Book and Release."

Oh.

"No, sir, I'm not under the influence," I answered after regaining my composure. He slid a piece of paper to me and handed me a pen before he pulled out a small black device and stepped away from the desk. He pressed a buzzer to release the lock on the security door and stepped over to me.

"Sign here," he said, pointing to the form. I picked up the pen and scribbled my name on the signature line. He held up the device, and I realized it was a breathalyzer; I'd never taken one before.

"Blow until the beeping stops," he instructed. I placed my lips around the mouthpiece and blew while it beeped.

"You'll need to blow harder than that," he chuckled. "You must be a first-timer?"

I nodded, the device still in my mouth. I sucked in a breath and then blew again, harder this time, like when I had to blow up balloons for Ava's first birthday. The machine finally stopped beeping, and the officer looked at it for a moment and then scanned his security badge to reopen the door.

"All right," he started, back at the desk, "I'll put in the release order and he should be out in a bit. Have a seat." He gestured to the lobby behind me, handing back my driver's license. I stuffed it into my purse and then made my way over to a worn leather chair in the corner of the lobby, waiting for the wrath of my husband.

———

"NATALIE NEEDS the money paid back by next Friday," I told Nathan while he stuffed the final bite of his second peanut butter sandwich into his mouth. We'd been home for less than twenty minutes and he'd already eaten two sandwiches, a snack-sized bag of chips and two ho-hos. Apparently, the food in the county jail wasn't much to write home about.

"Not happening. We won't have it," he said, chomping on the sticky sandwich.

"I know, but what was I supposed to do?" I folded my arms across my chest and sat back in my chair.

"Did you tell her we can't do that?" he raised a brow and looked at me expectantly.

"No."

"So I have to be the one to tell her? That's bullshit!" he threw his hands in the air, frustrated that I hadn't figured out a way to eradicate his problem.

"What was I supposed to do, Nathan?"

"Use your fucking head! You could have called your mom or taken an advance on your paycheck." He paced the dining room.

"My mom would never loan us money." *Again*, I should have said. The last time my parents had helped us out financially, Nathan found the cash in my wallet before I'd even had a chance to deposit it at the bank. When I asked where the money had gone, he couldn't even remember what he had spent it on, and I over drafted in my account.

"She would if you didn't tell her what it was for," he declared, confident in his statement.

"I can't lie to her, Nathan. I'm not like *you*."

"You're such a pussy, you know that? And why the hell didn't you come get me until today? You made me sit in that dump all fucking night."

"It was late—"

"Bullshit! You're a selfish bitch," he said, in attempt to rile me further. I sat at the table in silence, not caring to further instigate the argument. Nathan took a drink from his Mountain Dew, pressing buttons on his phone.

"We need to go pick up the car from the impound."

"How much will that cost?" I pulled up our budget spreadsheet again and searched for miracle money to pull from somewhere.

There was none to be found.

"I don't know, a few hundred probably," he replied. I watched him smirk at his phone and then punch some keys in response to yet another text message. He'd barely set his phone down since we'd gotten home.

"We don't have three hundred to spare," I told him, my eyes locked on the computer screen. "I already have to pay a few bills la—"

"Then get the fucking money," Nathan barked, cutting me off. His arm flew across the table, clearing the remnants of his lunch onto the floor. The yellow soda dripped from the wall and pooled on the linoleum, the empty can tipped upside down. I scooted back in my seat, he continued yelling. "This is such fucking bullshit! What the hell did you spend all our money on?"

I slammed my hand down on the table. "*Me*? You're the one going off getting arrested and having your car impounded! I haven't bought a damn thing other than food. When was the last time I got something for myself? Or for either of the kids, other than clothes and diapers?"

"Don't get attitude with me, Brynn," he snarled.

"You blew all our money on booze and drugs, Nathan. Again! And who knows what else? You have no problem spending money, but you don't ever bother to help *make* any of it!"

I recoiled in disgust as Nathan's spit hit my face and ran down my cheek. I reached up to swipe it away, surprised by his brazen action, but he was looming over my chair and held me down into the chair. His fingers dug into my skin as he pressed hard and leaned further into me. "You don't know shit," he said, taunting me.

"Get off me," I said through gritted teeth. I reached up and shoved Nathan, palms to chest, somehow sending him flying backward. He stumbled into the dining room wall and knocked over a chair, his face laced with shock.

"You fucking bitch!" he hissed, jumping to his feet and charging at me. We collided and fell to the floor, the chair tipping on its side. I tried to crawl away, but with little effort, he rolled me onto my back and straddled me, his strong legs flexing into my hips and rendering me immobile.

I heard the crack across my cheek before I even realized he hit me.

The searing pain of a second crack knocked my head into the floor.

The metallic taste of blood pooled in my mouth, and I kicked and screamed for Nathan to get off, to stop hitting me. The blows stopped, but just as I started to pull myself up from the floor, Nathan's hands were on me again, tearing at my clothes.

"Nathan, please," I begged.

His eyes were dark, angry, his dick impossibly hard and pressed against my middle through the fabric of his sweatpants. He held me down with muscles I didn't know he had, using his other arm to shove his sweatpants and boxers down to his ankles. Sweat beaded across his forehead and dripped from his face onto mine, mixing with my tears.

He tore viciously at my blouse, ripping it open, the buttons flying and scattering across the floor. He yanked on my bra with both hands, shoving it down and exposing my breasts, slapping at them before moving down the length of my body and unbuttoning my jeans. I did everything I could to crawl away, to shove him off me.

I couldn't move; he was too strong.

"Don't do this," I pleaded. He said nothing, just panted as he fought me. I didn't have the strength to stop him, to free myself from the weight of his body.

There was no other option but to wait.

To let it happen.

Despite my resolve, I relaxed beneath him.

Like an animal, he tore my jeans from my body, leaving claw marks on my thighs as he pulled them down and slid my panties to the side.

Still, I wasn't prepared for his intrusion.

I hadn't expected it, not again.

So…invasive—so primal.

"Nathan—" I pleaded, almost in a whisper. He pushed into me with one hard shove, his erection stiff and deep. I felt my insides tear and screamed out in pain, tears soaking my cheeks. He pumped rapidly, biting and pecking at my breasts and neck while holding my arms down.

A guttural moan escaped his lips; he fucked, finishing quickly, and unloading into me, laying his body on top of me and panting as he caught his breath. He pulled out abruptly but backed away slowly.

I curled into the fetal position, my hands over my face. My stomach cramped, my entire body on fire. I felt the bile rise up in my throat and swallowed it back down.

I refused to let him see me get sick.

Nathan got to his feet and stood on the other side of the room, pulling his pants up. He wiped his face with the bottom of his T-shirt and slid down against the wall to the floor.

He said nothing as he placed his head in his hands and cried.

CHAPTER TWENTY-EIGHT

I STRIPPED off what was left of my torn clothes and tossed them to the floor. The shower ran, filling the bathroom with steam, and I was grateful when the mirror fogged up enough to blur my reflection. I didn't care to see it. Everything hurt; my muscles ached and I could already feel the bruises developing on my face, the cut on my lip tender.

I stepped into the shower and stood under the water with my arms wrapped around myself. Flashes of pink mixed into the water at my feet and I watched it snake down the drain.

How could he do this again?

I couldn't help but feel like a fool; Nathan had betrayed me. I knew he would be upset when I picked him up from jail, but just like the first time, I hadn't expected the physical abuse that accompanied his anger. He'd changed after our son was born; he'd become attentive, almost caring.

He'd been sober.

Until Jesse came back into the picture.

I was convinced he'd relapsed within a week of their reconnection. The late nights, the drinking, the constant attention he paid to his cell phone. No good ever came from their friendship. Nathan was an entirely different person when it came to Jesse.

I read a self-help book while Nathan was in rehab—I can't recall its title—but in it, the author explained that we, as humans, tend to turn into the people we associate with most often. That we are subject to their influence, their mannerisms and ideals. Their bad habits, their good ones. I relayed that to Nathan, but he laughed it off and said I was an idiot if I believed it even a little bit.

I believed every word of it.

Once out of the shower, I dressed in baggy sweats and a hooded sweatshirt and then threw my wet hair into a messy bun on the top of my head. I didn't bother to put on makeup; it wouldn't cover the bruising on my face even if I caked on ten layers of it.

Jerilyn had agreed to pick the kids up from daycare, even though I hadn't told her why I had asked her to in the first place. I stood in the doorway to my room and glanced at the pile of suitcases I'd brought up from the basement after Nathan left. He hadn't said anything when he grabbed his wallet and keys and walked out the door.

He'd be back, though—he always came back.

So, it was time for me to leave.

I watched from the window as Jerilyn and her boyfriend, Jackson, parked in the driveway and pulled Ava and Hayden from the backseat of his Chevy Silverado. Ava skipped to the front door and stepped inside, her curious eyes scanning the room for me. "Mama?" she called.

"Brynn?" Jerilyn came in behind her, Hayden's car seat hanging from the crook of her arm. Jackson carried their bags and set them on the floor before helping Ava get her shoes off.

"I'm up here," I said from the top of the stairs, the

words catching in my throat. I'd pulled the hood of my sweatshirt over my head in hopes that it would shadow my injuries, but knew she'd see them the second she got close enough. "Can you settle the kids in the living room, please?" Jerilyn looked up, confused, but she did as I asked and left Jackson with the kids. He gave a nod to let her know it was okay, and I mentally thanked him for being there.

"Brynn, what's going on?" she asked, making her way upstairs to my bedroom. I sat on the edge of the bed, looking down at the floor, reluctant to meet her eyes; I knew doing so would reveal the dark purple bruises that were settling on my cheek. Jerilyn knelt in front of me and brought her hands to her mouth, gasping.

"Fuck, Brynnie, what happened? Are you okay?" I couldn't speak; couldn't bear to see the hurt and anger in my best friend's eyes. "Did Nathan do this?" She placed a hand on my cheek and I nodded into her palm, unable to bring an audible voice to the admission. "Oh, honey…" she whispered, pulling me into a hug. I winced from the pressure on my abdomen, certain I had a broken rib or two.

Jerilyn stood and looked around the room, spotting the suitcases on the bed. "You and the kids are coming to stay with me," she decided. She made her way to my closet, where she grabbed a stack of clean clothes from a laundry basket and stuffed them into one of the suitcases.

Having graduated the summer before, Jerilyn had moved home with her parents for a while before landing a job at the Plymouth YMCA and renting an apartment closer to work. It was a decent-sized one bedroom, and I was riddled with guilt at the thought of putting her out. But it would be easier than lowering my head in defeat and knocking on my parent's door.

"Jer?" I said, my voice barely above a whisper. She stopped abruptly and made her way over to me.

"What is it?" I looked at my friend and watched her heart break.

"I'm sorry I ruined your trip."

"No, no, you didn't ruin anything, hun. We can go to Brainerd anytime. I promise." She grabbed my hand and gave it a squeeze. "Let me go talk to Jackson quick and then I'll come help you pack. Why don't you try to pull together some of your bathroom stuff, okay?" She offered me a sad smile and handed me a travel bag for my toiletries.

I pushed myself up from the bed, wincing at the sharp pain in my ribs, and headed to the bathroom. I gathered my toiletries and stuffed them into the bag and then into the suitcase. Jerilyn came back into the room a few minutes later, her arms filled with Ava's clothes and a few toys. We locked eyes and both of us shrugged as we shared despondent smiles.

We finished packing up the clothes and carried the stuffed suitcases downstairs, setting them by the front door. Jackson sat with Ava on the living room floor, playing with her dollhouse and watching a show on **PBS Kids**. Hayden still slept in his car seat across from them, and Jackson rocked it with his foot every couple minutes.

I headed to the kitchen and grabbed a canvas bag from the pantry. Jerilyn and I filled it with snacks, canned goods and juice boxes; there was no sense in letting food go to waste. As we finished up in the kitchen, Jackson came in and whispered something to Jerilyn before they both looked at me with a twinge of fear in their eyes.

"Is he here?" I asked.

"He just pulled up," Jackson confirmed. "I have 9-1-1 on speed dial," he assured us. Nathan barged through the front door a moment later and froze in his tracks when he spotted Jerilyn and Jackson.

"Daddy!" Ava exclaimed. She threw her arms up and ran to Nathan, but Jackson pulled her back, catching her mid-launch and handed her over to Jerilyn, who tried to distract her with a toy.

"Who the fuck are you, and what the hell are you doing in my house?" Nathan barked to Jackson.

"Nathan, Brynn and the kids are going to come stay with us for a few days. There's no reason to get upset; we'll be out of here in just a minute."

"You're not taking my family," Nathan said, his eyes meeting mine. No longer did I see anger, but fear. "Brynn, don't go. Please."

Jackson held up his cell phone. "We don't want any trouble," he said.

"Fuck you," Nathan spat before turning to me. He stepped forward, but Jackson was closer, throwing a protective arm over my chest. Nathan's eyes darted back to me, his face suddenly stoic. He winked, the cocky demeanor returning.

"You'll be back," he taunted.

He's higher than a kite.

I opened the door and backed out slowly, Ava at my side, as Jackson grabbed our bags and Jerilyn picked up Hayden and his car seat. Nathan stood on the front steps, glaring at us as we rushed outside to load the bags into the bed of the truck. I buckled Ava into her booster seat as Jerilyn strapped in Hayden and Jackson loaded the luggage. Climbing into the back seat next to the kids, I closed the door and leaned my head against the headrest. Jerilyn reached back and grabbed my hand from the front seat.

Jackson started the truck and threw it into gear, and

Ava watched her father from the window. "Isn't Daddy coming too, Mama?" she asked, innocently.

"No, baby, not today..." I trailed off.

"It's going to be okay," Jerilyn assured me as we pulled away from the curb.

It'll never be okay.

———

JERILYN TOOK me to see a doctor the next morning. "It's not an option," she'd said when I tried to argue. We dropped the kids off at daycare—Jerilyn having been the one to bring them inside—and then drove to the urgent care center of the hospital.

In addition to several lacerations and bruises on my face and forearms, I had two broken ribs and a first-degree tear in my vagina. After suggesting I file a police report and press charges, the doctor recommended the name of a family counselor and then gave me a brochure for the Rivers of Hope crisis center.

I didn't bother to tell her that I'd been there before.

Back in the car, Jerilyn turned to me and asked, "Are you okay?"

"I will be." I fumbled with the hospital paperwork in my hands. "Why do people waste so much money on printing? Half this stuff probably goes directly into the garbage bin," I said.

"What are you going to do?" Jerilyn asked, ignoring my attempt at small talk. She turned the key in the ignition and let the engine idle to warm it up, the heat blasting from the air vent.

"I don't know." I stared out the window at a lady walking her dog on the sidewalk. Jerilyn sighed and placed a hand on my forearm.

"Brynn, you know you can't go back to him, right?"

"I…he's their dad, Jer—"

"Fuck that! He's hurting you, Brynn! How is that okay?"

"He's my husband…I—"

Was that enough?

Nathan was my husband, the father of my kids. But was that enough for me to stay? To put my life in the hands of someone who had, by all accounts, become a monster? Someone who relied more on drugs and alcohol than he did his own wife?

"You and the kids can stay with me as long as you like," Jerilyn offered. I knew she meant it, but there was only so long four people could share a one-bedroom apartment.

"Thank you. It really means a lot," I said, meeting her eyes. "We'll figure things out."

"You can't go back to him, Brynn. You just can't."

"It's not that easy…" I trailed off, my head and my heart in battle once again.

Jerilyn put the car in reverse and backed out of the parking space, her hands shaking on the steering wheel. "He'll do this again, you know. One day he'll kill you." She swiped a tear from her cheek, anger settling on her face as she pulled out onto the road.

I broke her, too.

CHAPTER TWENTY-NINE
APRIL 2007

THERE ARE ONLY two guarantees in life: that we will live and we will die. We can't always predict what will happen in between those moments, whether or not we will find our purest strength and rise above the storm to see the sunshine reappear through the clouds. It is during our darkest moments that we often see the light, that we find the answers in the silence that surrounds us.

I saw the darkness in the early hours of that morning in April, felt the silence closing in around me, attempting to suffocate me. My heart ached as it broke into a million little pieces and my world caved in around me.

My husband had taken his final breath.

Nathan lost his life on a Monday, sometime between one and four in the morning, as confirmed by the Wright County medical examiner.

He was gone.

I was asked to go down to the morgue to identify Nathan's body. I'd never actually considered what it might be like to set foot in a morgue. It made total sense, if I thought of it in terms of a movie or read its descriptions in a book, but when it's real life and you're the one asked to identify the body of your dead spouse, it adds an unfathomable weight to what is otherwise a simple one-syllable word. You want to pause that movie and never come back to it, or close that book, maybe set it on fire and watch it burn.

Identifying a body may be a logical first step in laying a loved one to rest, but the certainty of it—the finality of it—weighed heavily on me. Nathan had been reduced to remains, a body, a corpse. A capsule consisting of non-functioning organs, skin and bones. No longer was blood flowing through his veins or oxygen diffusing in his lungs.

Dead.

No longer of the living.

No longer able to hurt me.

"Mrs. Reeves?" The coroner's voice echoed through the phone. I snapped back to our conversation, focused on my breathing and the sound of her voice. I turned to look out the window in the kitchen where I'd been preparing breakfast for Ava. The scrambled eggs were burning, but I couldn't seem to move to pick the spatula up from the counter. I'd need to wake the kids up within a few minutes if there was any chance of us getting out the door on time.

Not that it mattered—we could be late now.

"Yes, I'm here...sorry, I..."

"It's okay, take all the time you need."

Time.

Something Nathan no longer had; something we no longer had. Not together as a family of four anyway. You know that phrase people say as they get older, develop wrinkles and fight tirelessly to prevent the inevitable gray hairs from sprouting? "It all goes by too quickly!" they say. It's weird though; I don't think of my time with Nathan as going by too quickly. It's always felt more like the minutes, the hours, the days...they all dragged on in slow motion. One day felt like two. One week felt like one month.

I'd arranged to meet the medical examiner at the morgue at 9:00 a.m. That gave me roughly forty-two minutes to get the kids fed, dressed and dropped off at daycare. I finished scrambling Ava's eggs, after dumping the first batch in the trash, scooped them onto a plastic plate and placed it on the kitchen table. I dried my hands on the dishtowel and then went upstairs to Ava's room, my body on auto-pilot as I went through the motions.

She was awake, and sitting in the corner of the room playing with her Little People set. My heart rate increased, my breathing heavy and sporadic as the reality sunk in that I'd have to tell my daughter her daddy was never coming home.

That I'd have to raise my son with no father at all.

He won't even remember him.

"Mama, fruit snacks?" Ava had gotten up from the floor and tugged on my maxi dress, her tiny green eyes looking up at me expectantly as she sucked on her pacifier. Nathan had said she was too old for the paci, but I couldn't bring myself to take it from her yet. She dragged her Winnie the Pooh blanket across the carpet, her footie pajamas wrinkled and half unzipped. She grabbed my hand and led me from the room.

"Sure, sweetie," I patted her head and followed her down the stairs to the kitchen where her plate of eggs sat on the table.

"Tanks, Mama." She climbed into the chair, reached for her fork, and scooped a bite full of eggs into her mouth. I retrieved a pack of fruit snacks from the snack bowl and dumped them next to the eggs on her plate. She plucked up a strawberry one and plopped it into her mouth, humming a tune from a PBS show I couldn't place, just as

Hayden's tiny cries came through the baby monitor. I couldn't help but feel the weight of his cries in my chest.

I took a breath, never more grateful to feel the air in my lungs. Nathan may not have survived the storm, but I would. The sunshine would find me—us—one way or another.

———

AFTER DROPPING the kids off at daycare, barely saying a word to anyone at the center, I drove down to the hospital where Nathan's body awaited. I'd spoken with the police and learned that Nathan had arrived in the ER after being picked up by an ambulance. He'd been partying with a group of friends who were all high on cocaine—and whatever else they greedily snorted, smoked or shot into their veins—so when they noticed Nathan slumped over on the couch, they didn't think much of it. It wasn't until one of them got up hours later to use the bathroom and turned on the hall light that he noticed Nathan still slumped over in the same position on the couch, his skin an odd shade of gray, his body lifeless.

His chest unmoving.

I had missed the first call from Nathan's phone at 2:13 a.m., along with four additional calls that had come in before I had turned my phone on later that morning. No one at the party wanted to take the fall for Nathan's overdose. They didn't want to risk jail time, so they'd called me. I'm not sure which one of them finally grew a pair and made the 9-1-1 call, but the only person other than Nathan who was in that apartment when the ambulance arrived was the girl whose name was on the lease: Tess *Fucking* Danielson.

The very last time I spoke to Nathan, we had an argument about the fact that he was, yet again, choosing drugs and alcohol over his family. I'd let him come home, I'd let him back into our family, and I tried so fucking hard to forgive him.

Yet, Tess got to be the last woman ever to kiss his lips; the last woman to feel the warmth of his body before all the blood was drained from it. I adjusted the silver wedding band on my left ring finger, the tiny .25 carat diamond twinkling in the sunlight reflected in the window.

I always hated that ring.

The morgue was unreasonably cold and smelled strongly of formaldehyde, like frog dissection day back in high school. The pungent aroma of death was sure to waft through any person's nostrils whether welcomed or not. I nearly vomited in the hallway. It felt lifeless, creepy. And there was so much metal—walls of metal doors—where they stored the dead bodies. The floor was hard, a simple layer of vinyl over concrete.

How could someone work in here all day?

What I assumed was a body laid face up on a high metal table with a white sheet covering it presumably, from head to toe. I stepped to the side of the table as the medical examiner looked to me for approval to remove the sheet. I nodded apprehensively. She folded the corners of the sheet back to reveal the lifeless face of my husband. I drew a sharp breath—something Nathan could no longer do—certain I was about to pass out.

It was him.

Until death do us part...

I COLLECTED NATHAN'S THINGS, everything having fit into one plastic bag—like one of those laundry bags you get at a hotel. It contained nothing more than his cell phone, car keys, wallet and the clothes he had been wearing. That's what was left of my husband's earthly possessions in that sterile room; a few random necessities that he'd carried in his pocket and the outfit he'd nonchalantly selected that morning.

I signed some forms, and the medical examiner explained how to file the death claim and obtain Nathan's death certificate. Zombie-like, I thanked her—although I wasn't exactly sure what I was thanking her for—clutched my purse to my chest and left the room. I walked the long corridor to the elevator, pressed P for the parking garage and walked to my car. I got in, set my purse and Nathan's belongings on the passenger seat and stuck the key in the ignition.

With my heart hammering in my chest, I placed my hands on the steering wheel, gripped it tightly and dropped my head as my entire body convulsed, the emotions taking over and pouring out from every inch of me.

He was gone.

I would never see him again.

I'm so sorry!

I couldn't save him.

I hate you!

I love you.

I was free.

CHAPTER THIRTY

MAY 2007

SOMETIMES I THINK MAYBE Nathan didn't die by accident. Maybe he did it as an easy out, like some fucked-up form of suicide that tricks everyone into thinking that even though he wanted to die, he didn't kill himself on purpose. I realize how that sounds...but I had cause for such suspicion. About a month before he died, Nathan threatened to kill himself.

I'd asked for a divorce.

I had failed him. I had proven that the *one* person who had promised to love him forever had changed her mind.

What I hadn't realized at the time was how much Nathan actually needed me. While he had a funny way of showing it, he needed me to love him more than anything. He needed me to believe in him, to accept him. No one really ever had. Any time I'd given him even a slight indication that I no longer did, he always found a way to make sure I knew I'd hurt him without actually saying so. He exchanged emotional pain for physical and took it out on me. As book smart as I thought I was, these are things I never realized until it was too late.

The pain I felt when my husband died did nothing but confuse me.

I felt guilty for the relief I felt.

I didn't have to run again. I didn't have to hide. But I didn't want him to die, either; I just wanted to get away.

After Nathan wrapped that telephone cord around my neck and tried to strangle me, I was terrified in the days that followed, especially when he'd been using or drinking; he was always the angriest then. I convinced myself that I could somehow control the situation on the days that he was normal, that I could keep him away from Ava or give myself to him willingly so that he wouldn't have to rape me. I behaved. I played the role of a good wife when I needed to. Not that it mattered.

For the life of me, I couldn't figure out why I could breathe easier knowing he was gone.

So many others had gone through what I did; did their abusive partners die, too? Did they ever get to breathe that sigh of relief knowing they would never be able to hurt them again? Did they feel guilty about it, too?

The day I'd asked for a divorce Nathan told me that if I ever actually tried to divorce him, he would kill himself and do it in a way that guaranteed I would be the one to find his body. That he'd hang himself from a rope strung through the rafters in the garage or sit in the car with the engine running, the windows down and the garage door closed while he waited for the carbon monoxide from the gas fumes to suck the oxygen from his lungs.

"But don't worry," he'd said, "I'll leave a note for you."
Wink.

He hadn't left a note the morning he overdosed for the last time, but if he had I don't imagine it would've said anything more than "fuck you."

After that first suicide threat, I parked my car outside in

the driveway every night so that I'd never have to open the garage door again.

———

A FEW WEEKS after his death I finally mustered up the energy to wash his dirty clothes so I could donate them to Goodwill. I pulled the wet garments out of the top-loading washer and chucked them into the open dryer, hearing a clink as something plastic fell back into the well of the washer. Leaning over, I peered into the machine. A clear pen with an orange cap sat in the bottom so I reached in to scoop it up, pulling back suddenly as I realized it wasn't a pen.

Dammit, Nathan.

I grabbed an empty cereal box from the recycling bin and then carefully plucked the hypodermic needle from the bottom of the well and placed it inside the box. I secured the flaps with scotch tape I'd grabbed from the supply cupboard and then walked the box out to the garbage bin that sat in the driveway, tossing it in angrily and slamming down the lid.

Reminders of Nathan's shortcomings were all around me, constantly pulling me deeper into the funk I'd been marinating in. Thunder rumbled in the sky above as a heavy breeze settled in the air. I took a deep breath and closed my eyes, a cool rain drop landing on my cheek. I swiped it away along with the unwelcome tears that had fallen.

I missed Nathan.

I wasn't sure why, but I missed him. I fell to my knees in front of the garbage can, a hole tearing in my leggings as my knee scraped the asphalt, my heart pounding in my chest. I took a deep breath, hoping the panic attack would subside but feeling little relief.

Lightning flashed in the sky, and a crack of thunder boomed and rattled my chest. The rain poured down in thick drops that pelted my face. I tipped my head back and looked up to the sky.

I can't breathe.

"Why?" I shouted to no one, the storm silencing my pleas. "Why me?"

Strong arms wrapped around me, lifting me from the ground and onto my feet. They pulled me into a hug, and a familiar aftershave settled in my nostrils. My wet hair clung to my face, my body trembling as I cried.

He held me.

He let me weep in the rain.

"Let's go inside," Dad said softly. I could barely hear him over the storm. I hadn't even heard him pull into the driveway or noticed the headlights from his car. He put an arm around my shoulders and led me through the still-open garage and into the house. I stood at the door and watched the rainwater pool at my feet. Dad made his way to the laundry room, his tennis shoes squeaking on the floor.

He had grabbed a couple clean towels and handed me one and then removed his glasses, cleaning the lenses on the end of the towel before wiping the water from his forehead. I met his eyes, and my heart dropped at the sorrow on his face.

I broke him; I broke Mom.

I broke everything.

"What are you doing here?" I asked finally, my voice scratchy.

"Mom tried calling a few times. You weren't answering your phone," he said with a shrug. "Are you okay?"

"Yes. No. I don't know…" I dried my hands on the

towel and stepped out of my flip-flops, kicking them to the side and then drying my feet.

"Where are the kids?" Dad asked, looking around. The house was quiet, not a radio or TV to drown out my pain. I'd lost the cable again.

"Daycare," I admitted.

Yes, even though I'm not at work.

"Do you want me to pick them up?" he asked. I nodded, appreciative of the offer. Dad's phone rang and he gestured to it before flipping it open and answering. "It's Mom," he said, though I already knew. He answered and let her know he was going to pick up the kids before handing the phone over to me.

"Brynn? Is that you?" Mom asked, her tone riddled with worry.

"It's me, Mom," I said, my words caught in my throat at the sound of her voice as tear rolled down my face.

"Is everything okay?" I pictured her holding me like she used to when I was a young girl, my head in her lap, the smell of her perfume lingering on my clothes. I longed to recapture those carefree days when the world had felt so simple, so magical. I was tired of the darkness I'd been living in.

"Mom?"

"I'm here, sweetie," she assured. She was crying too.

"I can't do this…" I whispered.

"Come home, honey…Dad and I can fix up downstairs for you and the kids," she offered sincerely. I realized in that moment that I didn't need to think about it. I was in no position to take care of myself, let alone Ava and Hayden. As much as I didn't want to wave the white flag, I needed my mom; and I needed my dad.

After I hung up with Mom, Dad and I packed a few bags for the kids and me. He left to pick them up from daycare, and we agreed to meet back at their house. Alone again, I moved around my townhouse, unplugging elec- tronics and making sure all the doors and windows were locked. I stood in my bedroom for a few minutes just looking at the comforter draped over the bed that I hadn't slept in since Nathan died.

It still smelled like him.

———

I MOVED BACK HOME with my parents the following Satur- day. While we brought all the kids' things, I'd opted to store most of my furniture, even though I'd probably end up selling it later. I'd still need to pay rent on the townhouse for another month, but I couldn't stay there anymore.

Dorothy was right, there's no place like home.

CHAPTER THIRTY-ONE

JULY 2007

I BOLTED UPRIGHT, screaming, throwing the comforter from my body as if it were on fire. I'd sweat through my clothes again, my tank top clinging to my chest. The nightmare had been intense, frantic.

I climbed out of the queen-sized bed I'd been sleeping on in my parent's guest room and slid my feet into my slippers, groggily making my way upstairs for a bottle of water. I navigated up the creaky steps and tiptoed into the kitchen, using the light from the ice maker on the fridge to guide the way through the dark. It was just after midnight, and I didn't want to wake anyone.

Not ready to go back to sleep and risk another nightmare, I unlocked the sliding door off the dining room and stepped out onto the deck. The humidity in the air was thick, and a soft breeze blew against the trees. I leaned over the railing and watched the branches of the willow sway in the wind as images of my nightmare played like a movie in my mind.

I clutched a sleeping Ava to my chest, struggling to carry my thirty-pound toddler, purse and diaper bag while fumbling with the key in the lock on the front door. Hayden was asleep in his car seat that I'd set on the concrete landing by my feet. I managed to get the door open and deposited my bags on the floor, setting them down gently so I wouldn't wake either of the kids.

"Uh, oh yes! Fuck me, Big Daddy. Pound it, harder!"

What the fuck?

I covered Ava's ears as best as I could and started up the steps.

"Yes, choke me harder!"

Thankful Ava was asleep, I picked up the pace and trotted up the stairs to her bedroom, placing her on the bed and covering her with her favorite blanket. I ran downstairs to grab Hayden and set him, still in his car seat, in the room with Ava. I kissed each of their foreheads and then backed out of the room, closing the door behind me.

Flashbacks of Nathan and Tess played in my mind. Not again. It was one thing to know of your husband's frequent infidelities, but catching him in the physical act left scars that not even the best of doctors could fix. Reluctantly I tiptoed across the hall and opened the door to our bedroom.

I had expected to see a naked woman on our bed, Nathan's hand around her throat as he pumped into her. But it was just Nathan— clad in nothing but his boxer shorts, a bottle of baby oil and a hand towel on the nightstand. His dick in his hand, he pumped ferociously, licking his lips and staring penetratingly at the porno that played on the TV across the room.

He hadn't even noticed me yet.

I considered backing out of the room to offer him the privacy he assumed he had, but the audible sigh I let out at the relief of the lack of female presence in the room gave me away.

"Oh fuck, Brynn! You scared the shit out of me!" He reached for the remote with his free hand and turned down the volume on the TV but didn't turn it off. I glanced over at the screen where a blonde with fake tits was offering us a close up of her crotch. I looked back to Nathan, who hadn't stopped stroking himself even after discovering I was in the room.

An anxiousness rumbled in my belly; I knew I would have to finish him off.

Nathan's eyes penetrated me deeper than the STD-riddled penis that Blondie was enjoying. "Come here," he commanded hoarsely.

I stepped further into the bedroom and closed the door, securing the lock with a click.

"Take off your clothes."

I paused for a second, unsure how to respond. Nathan raised a brow and motioned for me to hurry up. I pulled my blouse over my head and dropped it to the floor, kicking it to the side. He watched with anticipation. I reached behind me and unhooked my bra, letting it fall to the floor, my nipples immediately tightening from the chill in the air. "Mmm," Nathan groaned, stroking himself.

I unbuttoned my jeans and slid them down my legs, stepping out of them and standing in front of Nathan in nothing but my panties—hoping he would get too excited and accidentally finish himself off on his own.

"Like her," he said, pointing at Blondie on the TV. She was on all fours, her ass in the air while a tattooed biker took her from behind. I exhaled and crawled onto the bed, looking to Nathan, silently pleading with him not to be too rough. He grabbed the bottle of baby oil from the nightstand and squeezed some into his palm. Rubbing his hands together he licked his lips and then massaged the oil onto his cock before moving to his knees behind me.

I looked away and shoved my face down into the mattress, hoping he would finish quickly and then disappear for the rest of the night. I felt the cold oil hit my backside and then slide into the crevice. He used his fingers to spread it around, pausing on my clit and rubbing for a moment. A soft moan betrayed me.

Nathan pushed into me and immediately pulled out. This was how he liked to start things off—there was rarely any foreplay anymore—no opportunity for me to prepare for my body for his intrusion. Three more times he did this, shoving himself deep within the walls of my body as he watched the biker do the same to Blondie.

I bit down on the comforter. The grunting and moaning from the porn grew louder as Nathan turned up the volume on the TV. My head snapped back; he took a chunk of my hair in his fist and pulled. He slapped my ass and then his fingers wrapped slowly around my neck. I mumbled something inaudible, and he pulled his hand away quickly.

"Tell me you love me," he commanded between breaths, pulling back and then slamming into me again. My body jerked from the momentum, and he pulled me back to him by my hip. "Tell me you fucking love me!" he shouted.

"I love you," I whispered.

He cupped and squeezed my dangling breast, thrusting one last time and then pulling out, the sticky warm semen splattering across my back. He groaned violently, slapping his dick on my ass cheek before climbed off the bed and going straight to the shower.

I remained on all fours for a moment while I collected my breath and listened to the slapping sounds coming from the TV. I watched Blondie take a load in her mouth and swallow it gratefully. As she wiped her mouth with her hand, I pushed myself from the mattress and pressed the power button on the remote, muttering a quick "fuck you."

I got to my feet and grabbed the towel from the nightstand, wiping the mess from my back. I wanted to soak in a hot bath more than anything but didn't care to join Nathan in the bathroom. I bent over and grabbed my clothes from the floor, scooping them up and placing them on the bed. A piercing cramp tightened in my abdomen. I doubled over the bed, a thick stream of blood sliding down my inner thigh.

A DOG BARKED and snapped me back to reality. I shivered and took a sip of the water I'd grabbed from the fridge and then made my way back inside. I locked the sliding door and grabbed a bag of chips from the pantry, taking it back to my room with me.

Climbing back into the bed, I wrapped the comforter around me and then pressed the power button on the TV remote. I flipped to an episode of *Friends* and settled back against the headboard, chips in hand.

There was no way in hell I'd be getting back to sleep.

CHAPTER THIRTY-TWO
NOVEMBER 2008

I FINISHED the edits on the short story I'd been working on, at long last pleased with the draft and anxious to ascertain some feedback on it. I'd dabbled in writing ever since I was a young girl—focused mainly on short stories, poetry and lyrics—but it had been years since I'd written anything more than a grocery list, and I'd forgotten how much I needed it, how much it nurtured my soul.

After Nathan died, I craved an outlet—something to help me cope not only with his death, but with the abuse I'd endured during the course of our relationship. So, I resumed writing, focused instead on honing my journaling abilities, and did everything I could to get my innumerable thoughts onto the page.

Some days it was still all too much, the memories raining down and drowning my will to move forward. I'd catch myself over-thinking everything and often wondered if I could have done more to save Nathan. I wasn't sure who I was without him. My thoughts drifted back to the day he had pulled off the dirt road and bought me that disposable camera just so I could capture a picture of the sunset. I was happy then. But it had been so long ago, and I was so far removed from who Nathan and I had become. It felt nearly impossible to find myself again.

I'd done a poor job of opening up to anyone. I had yet to admit to my parents or anyone else—other than Jerilyn —what I'd been through. I guess that's what happens when you make assumptions that people won't understand; that they can't relate and because of that, that they will judge your decisions, your actions. I certainly would have, had it happened to someone else and I was the one who stood on the outside. But that's the thing about life—you'll never truly understand someone unless you walk in their shoes, and that's simply not feasible.

I snapped back to reality, my mouse hovering over the save button. A quick left click officially stored my most private thoughts, a start to my story, to the confines of my computer, and I was grateful I'd had the wherewithal to get up early and work on it before the kids woke for the day. My parents had left the night before for a weeklong trip to visit with some friends in Surprise, Arizona so the kids and I had the house to ourselves for a few days.

It was eerily quiet.

I was used to morning coffee in the kitchen with my parents and wasn't sure how I felt about the silence around me. But, as I flipped my laptop closed, the door to the kids' room opened, and Ava stood in the doorway. Her pajamas were wrinkled and her hair a mess as she rubbed the sleep from her eyes. She spotted me at my desk and came over to climb up onto my lap.

"Good morning, sweetie." I enveloped her in my arms and gave her a squeeze.

"Owwy, Mama," she said as she giggled and tried to squirm away.

"Sorry, baby girl. Did you sleep well?"

"I didn't have no accident," she said, her face illuminated with pride.

"Good girl! Mama's proud of you." I brushed the tangled hair from her eyes and kissed her freckled forehead. "Do you want some breakfast?"

"Mmm-hmm. Yucky Charms!"

"All right, peanut, Lucky Charms it is." She climbed down from my lap and ran toward the stairs. "Hold on a second, I'm going to see if your brother is awake," I said.

"He is!" she announced with glee before skipping away and running up the stairs toward the kitchen.

I laughed and shook my head, detouring to the kids' room where Hayden sat playing with a Buzz Lightyear toy.

"Hey bubba," I cooed. Hayden looked up and his mouth formed into a wide smile. He tossed Buzz down onto the bed and threw his arms up toward me. I scooped him up and secured him on my hip and made my way upstairs to prepare breakfast.

———

THE REST of the morning flew by. Between breakfast, baths and coloring, you'd think I'd have worn the kids out enough for a nap, but Ava and Hayden had worked up a good amount of energy and we had no choice but to burn it off outside. So, the three of us walked across the street to the park—a playground I'd practically grown up in—and as we made our way over the kids ran straight for the swings. I snapped a few pictures of them on my digital camera as Ava climbed onto the tire swing.

"Hayden, watch this!" she shouted with glee, spinning around on the giant tire. She leaned her head back and held on tight while it spun in circles. Hayden giggled and ran in the other direction toward the plastic curly slide, stopping for a moment to pick up a handful of pebble rocks. He looked over at me and I gave him the don't-you-dare-throw-those look, and he dumped them back onto the ground and made his way to the ladder.

After I helped Hayden with a few trips down the slide, my phone rang, and I dug it out of my pocket to find it was Natalie. I hadn't spoken to her in months, and I sent the call to voicemail just as I had so many times before. She called often, checking in on us and begging to get together. But I'll be the first to admit that I struggled with the thought. Natalie was still heartbroken over Nathan's death, still so shocked and in disbelief that his life had ended the way it did.

She had no perception of the hell her brother had put me through. And the worst part was that I could never tell her; she wouldn't have been able to comprehend the magnitude of such knowledge. As much as Natalie had been there for me, I couldn't bring myself to say these words to her—to tarnish her brother's memory more than it already was. But I couldn't go on pretending it never happened either.

To Natalie, Nathan was simply an addict who never found his way. She hadn't even been privy to the extent of his addiction, that it had controlled every aspect of his life. I stopped taking her calls a few months after the funeral, and while I harbored some guilt over that decision—in addition to my continued stubbornness—I couldn't move forward with the constant reminder of the past.

I snuck a look over to the house as a car pulled into my parents' driveway. I hadn't been expecting company and couldn't recall making any plans for the weekend. My cell rang again, still in my hand, and I looked at the screen but didn't recognize the number.

Please don't be Natalie.

"Hello?"

"Brynn? It's me," the voice said.

"Meg?" My heart skipped a beat in my chest, and I looked back over at the car across the street in our driveway.

"Yeah…" she sniffled.

"I…how are you?" I asked. Ava tugged on my wrist and I looked down at her, her face twisted in concern.

"I have to go potty."

"Okay, sweetie, let's get home." I scooped Hayden up from the rocks where he'd been digging and grabbed hold of Ava's hand. My phone balanced on my shoulder, I said, "Meg, I'm so sorry, can I call you back in a few minutes?" The driver's side door opened across the street, and I watched as Meg stepped out of the car, her phone still held at her ear. I stopped in my tracks, my breath caught in my throat.

"Let me help you," she said. Ava let go of my hand and ran toward Meg.

"Waggy!" she exclaimed and jumped into Meg's arms.

"Hey, squirt!"

"Heads up, she has to pee and doesn't have a pull up on," I warned.

"Yikes!" Meg said to Ava, who giggled. We made our way to the front door, and I tried to make sense of the expression I'd seen on Meg's face.

Was she sad?

Had she been crying?

Meg took Hayden from me so I could tend to Ava and get her to the bathroom. I flipped on the light and she swatted at my hand. "I can do it myself, Mama." She shooed me further out of the bathroom and closed the door.

"Make sure you wash your hands," I chided through

the door. Meg sat with Hayden in the entryway where they played patty cake, Hayden cackling every time she made a goofy face at him.

She looked up when she noticed me watching them from the hallway. "I'm sorry to just drop by," she said.

"No, it's okay. Want some coffee?"

"I'd love some," she smiled and stepped out of her flip-flops, and we headed upstairs to the kitchen.

I had prepared the coffee maker for afternoon coffee after breakfast earlier, so I pressed the brew button and then pulled the step-stool up to the sink, waving Hayden over to wash the dirt off his hands.

"Have a seat," I said to Meg. She pulled out a chair and sat at the table.

"You look good," she said. I furrowed my brow and looked at her in disbelief.

"You must need your eyes checked!" I helped Hayden dry his hands on the towel.

"Oh stop, you really do!"

Hayden stepped down from the stool and ran off to the living room, where he rescued a previously discarded Buzz from the floor before climbing onto the couch.

I grabbed two mugs from the cupboard, added my signature sweet cream to each of them and then poured the fresh coffee. I walked them carefully to the table and handed one to Meg.

"Thanks," she said, taking the mug from me. She slurped a quick sip and said, "Ahhh," elongating the word and closing her eyes like it was the greatest thing she'd ever tasted. "You always make the best coffee."

"Thanks," I said, sitting down across from her. "So, what brings you by?"

"I miss you," she blurted. She reached her hand across

the table and placed it over mine, her eyes welling up with tears.

I relaxed and said, "I miss you, too."

"I just…I can't do this anymore. I need you in my life, and I feel so terrible knowing you've been going through so much on your own. You don't deserve that, Brynn. I'm so sorry."

"Hey, it's not your fault," I assured her. "You know that, right?"

"I do. But I wasn't a good friend to you. I walked away when you needed me the most and—"

"Stop," I said, cutting her off. "We just move forward," I said simply.

"It's *that* easy?"

"It's *that* easy," I confirmed with a smile. Meg popped up from her seat, a tear running down her cheek, and pulled me into what was likely the best hug I've ever received in my life. I couldn't help but cry with her, grateful she'd mustered the courage to do what I couldn't.

"Mama, cry?" Hayden asked, pointing at us. We ended our embrace, each of us sniffling and wiping our tears. I looked to Hayden and smiled.

"Yeah buddy, Mama cry. They're happy tears, though," I said. But he'd already lost interest and had run back to the living room where he plopped back down next to Ava. Meg shrugged and winked at me.

"Yahtzee?" I asked with a raised brow.

"Oh, hell yes!" she said.

And just like that, we were back.

CHAPTER THIRTY-THREE
APRIL 2009

TWO YEARS HAD PASSED, and still his voice haunted me —*suffocated* me at times. It was hard to breathe—hard to function—without the fear that he'd find a way to come back and put me through it all over again, even though I knew that wasn't possible. Yet, I still found myself missing him, too. Wishing he were here, that he was sober and I could watch him with pride as he played catch with our son and took our daughter to Daddy and Me dance classes. A moment later, the anger would resurface, and I would recall all the fucked-up shit he put me through.

That's anxiety for you—irrational and unwelcomed thoughts jumbled from too many years of mixed emotions, of the ups and downs of domestic abuse.

I hated him, but I loved him, too.

Then the nightmares had started. Too real, movie-like reminders of the life I felt I'd been suckered into, even though I was fully aware that the decisions I'd made were my own. It was as if I were constantly reliving it all over again.

I wasn't sure how many more nights I could take.

The looks from Nathan's family and friends as his coffin was lowered into the ground—I knew they blamed me, as if it were my fault he was gone. I, the wife who could not save her husband from his untimely demise.

The lies he'd told likely still danced in their ears—they believed them, despite my efforts to set them straight. I'd given up trying and decided instead to move on, to wash my hands of them and focus on raising my kids, on being a good mother even though the odds were stacked against us.

I felt so alone.

Even with the support of my parents those two years after I'd packed up my life and my children to move back home, I didn't feel whole. They didn't need to hear about the abuse I had endured at the hands of my husband. It would break them all over again. It would probably break me, too. I harbored so much guilt by not telling them the truth, by suffocating those secrets deep within.

Depression set in and decided to stay a while. For some reason, I hadn't expected it, hadn't anticipated the sinking feeling in my chest every time I walked into the grocery store or the movie theater, my kids in tow, without a ring on my finger. Were people judging? Forming their opinions of the young mom with two young kids and no father in the picture? Did they assume my kids had different fathers? That I couldn't hold a job and therefore lived off the system?

I didn't want to be a statistic.

But I was.

Ava and Hayden were, too.

———

To say that I was in denial about my lack of mental wellness was an understatement. I'd gotten fairly good at pretending everything was okay when I needed to, that I didn't need help. Holding everything in wouldn't kill me, I'd proven that, and I could fake a smile like the best of them—for the most part. At work, with my friends.

I finally gave in and scheduled a therapy appointment, as apprehensive as I was to do so. I needed the nightmares to stop, the irrational thoughts to cease.

"Why don't you tell me a little about what brings you in today," Dr. Jen said.

"Um...okay. I don't really know where to start." I crossed my legs and leaned back in the oversized chair, only to recross them a moment later. I almost expected Dr. Jen to say more, to give me an inkling as to where she wanted me to start, but she didn't. I continued, "I guess, the biggest issue, is my husband—well, my ex-husband. Or...I guess my *deceased* husband." I stumbled over the words, suddenly aware I was under the microscope. The room was warm, and I wanted to remove my jacket but didn't.

I wasn't sure I'd stay for the full intake hour.

"Your husband passed away?" she asked, her pen hovering over the legal pad that rested in her lap. She was calm, but curious, the wrinkles in her forehead prevalent, evidence of years working in a stress-inducing industry written on her face.

"Yes."

"I'm terribly sorry to hear that. How long?"

"Two years this month."

"Was it sudden? You're pretty young..."

"Um, yeah, I guess you could say that. He died of a heroin overdose." She made a clicking sound with her tongue and tilted her head to the side, her pen making another note on the page but her face stoic.

I always thought therapists were supposed to make you feel at home, comfortable.

I felt neither.

"Oh. I'm so sorry, how terrible." I shifted in my seat again, my hands clammy and folded in my lap. "How long were you married?"

"A few years."

"Were you there when he died?"

"No."

"Do you have any children?"

"Two. My daughter, Ava, is five, and my son, Hayden, is three." I retrieved my phone from my purse and held it out to her, showing her the picture of Ava and Hayden that I kept as my background.

"Aw, they're adorable, thank you for sharing that. What do you hope to get out of therapy, Brynn?"

"I...I don't know."

"Let me rephrase that: have you ever been to therapy before?"

"No."

"Well, I'd like to make this as stress-free for you as possible. This is a welcoming space where I withhold judgment and instead offer you coping mechanisms to help you manage the stress in your life. It would be helpful for me to understand the events around your husband's death, perhaps learn a bit more about your childhood and background. From there, I can work with you to establish those coping mechanisms that I mentioned and perhaps—if necessary—refer you to a psychiatrist on our team that can prescribe some medication. How does that sound?"

I waited a beat before answering, not wanting to be rude. Was I being interviewed? Politely, I stood from the couch and smoothed the seam of my pants, my feet heavy beneath me. Dr. Jen shifted in her chair, as if she wasn't sure whether to stand or remain seated. "I'm sorry, Dr. Jen, I don't think this is for me. I appreciate your time."

She stood, setting her legal pad and pen on the chair she'd risen from. "Are you sure we can't continue the session? I hate to see you leave like this."

"I'm sure." I made my way to the door, placing my hand on the knob. I turned to face her once more. "I apologize for wasting your time."

I left that afternoon and never returned to Dr. Jen's office. Saying the words out loud was just too much, I didn't see how it would help. There was no need to rehash the past; no way for me to describe the true pain I felt in those moments that had forever changed the course of my life. I didn't want to talk about Nathan—not to a stranger, not to anyone. I just needed to suck it up and move on.

He'd already taken enough from me.

CHAPTER THIRTY-FOUR

JANUARY 2010

"So, I DID A THING," I said, smiling nervously as I set my wine glass on the coffee table. Andi and Jerilyn stared at me expectantly, unconsciously leaning forward from their positions on the couch. "I registered for college!" I shouted.

"What? Brynn, that's amazing!" Andi jumped up from her seat and engulfed me in a hug—well, more like a chokehold, but I could only assume her intentions were pure. Her kinky coil red hair tickled my nose as it brushed across my face.

"Wow, that's so great," Jerilyn agreed. "What will you do with Ava and Hayden while you have class?"

Andi released her death grip on my neck and sat back down on the end of the love seat, a hand-me-down I'd received from my parents. I'd finally moved out of their house and back into my very own two-bedroom apartment with Ava and Hayden, truly on my own for the first time in my life. It was a small apartment, but it offered us the space we needed, and while Ava and Hayden shared a bedroom, they were still young enough not to be bothered by such a thing. Truth be told, they'd shared a bedroom from the beginning and seemed to enjoy it; I often found them scrunched up in the corner of their room playing together or snuggled up watching the tiny thirteen-inch television I'd set up for them on the nightstand.

"Well, it's online for the most part," I explained. "I'll only be on campus one night a week, so my parents offered to take the kids overnight those days, which will be a huge help." While I'd been nervous to bite the bullet and register for college, I was also excited. I'd put it off after high school and had always thought I'd get the opportunity to give something, anything, the old college try.

"...and you know we'll help out where we can, too," Jerilyn said, Andi nodding in agreement. She emptied her wine glass and stood. "Definitely," she confirmed.

"This calls for a celebration, ladies! Refills all around!" Andi announced, grabbing the half-empty bottle of Riesling from the coffee table and filling our glasses. "A toast," she said sincerely. We held our stemless glasses in the air. "To our favorite fearless single mama! We're so damn proud of you!" We clinked our glasses together and each took a slow sip, the wine bubbling on our tongues.

"Now all that's left is finding you a man," Jerilyn joked.

"What? No!"

"I mean it! It's time for you to get out there and start dating again. You've been single for almost three years!"

"For good reason!" I argued. "And by choice, I might add." I crossed my arms over my chest, mildly annoyed that we were having this conversation for the umpteenth time. My track record with men was enough to drive a person crazy—and that person was me.

"No, I think she has a point, Brynn," Andi chimed in. "What about one of those dating sites?"

"Gross. No way. Do you have any idea how many creeps are out there?"

"Oh! My friend Ryah's brother, Darren! He's super hot. I can set you guys up!" Jerilyn suggested, reaching for her phone and scrolling through to find Ryah's number. I swatted the phone out of her hand and watched as it landed softly on the cushion next to her.

"A blind date? No, thanks."

"Oh come on, it'll be fun! You've been single for too long," Jerilyn pleaded, her face folding into a pout.

"I haven't been single long enough!"

"We need to get you laid, girl," Andi teased.

"I'll stick with my B.O.B., thank you very much." I sat back in the lounge chair across from my friends and couldn't help but smile. Not only had they helped move me into my new apartment, but they also came over every couple of weeks to enjoy some adult beverages and engage in girl talk, something I'd missed desperately during my years with Nathan.

I was lucky they hadn't abandoned me.

"BORING. I'm signing you up for Match.com," Andi declared and reached for my brand new laptop that sat on the coffee table. It was a gift from my parents after I registered for classes. She flipped it open, but was immediately cock-blocked by the password protection I'd already set up. She pouted and stared up at me with puppy eyes.

"Like hell you are!" I jumped up and swiped the laptop from Andi's death grip and then sat back down in my seat. Jerilyn reached over and placed her hand on my knee, a sincere expression on her face.

"Brynn...you can't hide in your house forever."

"I'm not hiding."

"You kind of are, honey," Andi chimed in. "You never come out with us, and we're always coming over here to hang out with you."

"I don't go out because I hate sleazy bars, not to

mention I have the kids to think about; I hate paying for sitters. Plus, I highly doubt I'd find any decent men lingering around at any of the bars around here." I paused for a beat and then glanced out the sliding glass door at a group of kids running across the parking lot. "I'm really not interested in dating right now, you guys..."

Or ever again.

"What is it, Brynn?" Andi asked genuinely.

"I'm still having nightmares," I admitted.

"The melatonin isn't helping?"

"No." I turned back to my friends and their concerned faces. I admired their ability to go with the flow; to support me when I needed it, but also just to love me in the rare moments when I was feeling normal. I'd been back and forth on that spectrum all afternoon, but they never seemed to fault me for it.

"How often are they happening?" Jerilyn asked.

"Often enough. At least once a week, sometimes more."

"Just playing devil's advocate here," Andi started, "but nobody said the guy has to sleep over...maybe have some fun here and there and then kick his ass to the curb at the end of the night?" She grinned mischievously and offered me a wink.

"Very funny. I'm just saying I don't even know if I'm ready for that much."

"Look, we love you and we care about you. We just want you to be happy."

"I know...I love you guys too. I just don't think I'm ready to start dating. Not yet, anyway." The timer on the oven dinged, signaling that our Totino's Pizza Rolls were ready.

Yes, we were that kind of classy.

I set my wine glass on the table and made my way into the tiny galley kitchen.

"Fair enough," Andi started. "I suppose now is a good time to mention I'm hosting a Pure Romance party next month?" She giggled and one of her signature snorts slipped out. I smiled and pointed in her direction.

"Now *that* I will participate in!"

CHAPTER THIRTY-FIVE
MARCH 2010

THE NERVES SETTLED in my belly as I climbed out of my car and walked through the Rasmussen College parking lot, the snow crunching under my feet. I'd elected to attend the Brooklyn Park campus since it was close to work and a fairly straight shot down US-169, which meant the likelihood that I'd get lost en route would dwindle significantly. I'd planned to take the majority of my courses online but elected to do one class per quarter on campus to avoid my anti-social tendencies, even though class didn't end until 10:00 p.m. and the drive home would be close to forty minutes.

I entered the building and took a right down the hall toward the business center to room 104, where I grabbed a seat at a table near the back of the room.

So much for being social.

I pulled a notebook and pen out of my messenger bag and placed them on the table in front of me, watching as several other students filed in and claimed their seats.

"Good evening, everyone," the instructor announced a few minutes later. She'd stepped to the front of the room and turned around to write her name on the whiteboard. "I'm Marguerite, and I'll be your instructor for this *Principles of Economics* course," she said, her African accent thick off her tongue. She finished writing on the board and placed the cap back on the marker, but still held it in her hand when she turned to face the class. Her short brown hair was cropped into a pixie cut, a flattering look for her high cheekbones, chunky, red-framed glasses and tweed jacket.

"So, we're going to start with a little icebreaker to kick things off tonight," Marguerite continued. A collective sigh reverberated throughout the room. We may have all been adults, but at the mention of forced mingling with strangers, each of us immediately clammed up as if we were back in middle school. We sat on the edge of our seats awaiting further instructions to the game none of us wanted to play.

"Now, I know nobody wants to move from their comfy seats, but hear me out," she started, chuckling to herself. "We can all stand to make a new friend tonight. So, I'd like everyone to get up and find someone new to sit with, someone you don't know. Once you do that, I'll set a timer for two minutes, and you'll talk to your new table mate and get to know each other a bit. After the two minutes are up, we'll go around the room, and you will introduce the rest of us to your new partner."

I groaned along with the twenty-plus others that sat with me. But we did as we were told and stood from our seats. Unlike the others, however, I didn't need to seek out a partner. Within seconds I was greeted by a bubbly woman about my age. We both wore our blonde hair the same way—in a top knot—and I recognized her purple shirt and black cardigan because I had the same ones hanging in my closet. She had come over from a table in the front of the room and set her stuff down next to me, pulling out a chair.

"Hi, I'm Ainsley!" she said, extending a hand. "Looks like we're partners!" She gave a genuine smile, her green eyes sparkling as we both laughed, timidly shaking hands.

"I'm Brynn," I replied, letting go of her hand.

We sat back down in our seats as Marguerite announced, "All right, the timer is starting in ten seconds…" She held up a stopwatch as if it were a bomb detonator and all of us feared for our lives.

Ainsley turned to me. "Do you want to talk or listen first?" she asked.

"Umm, I'll listen, if that's okay?"

"Absolutely!"

"…and go! Two minutes on the clock!" Marguerite shouted. The room erupted in voices, everyone rattling off introductions to their table partners.

"All right, so, I'm twenty-two, and live in Coon Rapids with my brother," Ainsley started. "I'm in the Medical Assisting program and this is my first class on campus. I have a cat named Freddy, who drives me insane, but I love him anyway. Umm…what else?" She paused and looked up to the ceiling. "Oh! My current favorite show is *How I Met Your Mother*." Ainsley stopped, relaxing in her chair and taking a deep breath.

I recognized it as my cue to start talking.

"Wow, okay! Well, I'm twenty-five, and I live in Buffalo. I have two kids, one boy and one girl. My daughter, Ava, is six and my son, Hayden, is four. I'm a single mom and this is my first college course ever for my Business Management degree. And my favorite show is *Friends*!" I finished just as Marguerite pressed an exceptionally loud buzzer to signal the end of the icebreaker.

We spent the next hour listening to the individual

groups recite details about their partners. After, Marguerite announced we'd be working with our new "friend" on a group project to present on a period of economic prosperity. Ainsley and I chose the Roaring Twenties and made plans to get together outside of class to complete the assignment.

"Why don't you come over Saturday? If it's not too far of a drive, I mean," I offered. "I can get a sitter if the kids would be too much of a distraction for you. They can get a little rambunctious sometimes," I admitted. Ainsley flashed a wide smile.

"Are you kidding? I love kids! I'm really excited to meet them."

"Oh, that's great!" I said, relieved. "How's noon?"

"Noon is perfect."

WE WERE DISMISSED for dinner break shortly after and had decided to grab food together. We hopped into Ainsley's car and drove to Subway, each of us ordering a roasted chicken breast sandwich on wheat with a Diet Coke. We drove back to school and ate in her car in the parking lot so we could make sure we weren't late getting back to our first night of class.

I took a bite of my sandwich as Ainsley asked, "So, do your kids stay with their dad when you're in class?"

I took my time chewing and shook my head. "No, actually they're staying overnight with my parents on the nights I have class." Ainsley nodded in understanding. "Do your parents babysit Freddy while you're in class?" I joked.

"Both my parents passed away, actually," she said, very matter of fact.

"Oh, wow...I'm...so sorry to hear that," I said, my

heart instantly aching for my new friend. "How long have they been gone?"

"My mom died of breast cancer when I was fourteen, and my dad died a couple years ago from organ failure."

I didn't know what to say so I just placed my hand over hers and offered a friendly squeeze. I knew from experience that sometimes saying nothing was better than generic condolences. I hadn't planned on telling her about Nathan, but I suddenly felt connected with her in a way I couldn't explain, almost like we'd been friends forever.

"My husband died," I said, my voice quiet. "It'll be three years next month. Heroin overdose." I saw the wheels in Ainsley's head turn as she calculated how old my kids were at that time.

"I'm so sorry," she said. We looked up from our sandwiches, each of us offering the other a nonchalant shrug, one that somehow said, "death sucks" and "I feel for you" at the same time.

————

It's funny how some things seem insignificant while they're happening. Like how a stupid icebreaker game in an Econ class could be the start of a lifelong friendship; the kind of friendship that everybody always talks about after going to college—the kind I'd missed out on before.

But that's exactly what it did for Ainsley and me. I walked away from class that night already knowing this girl would be around for a lot longer than the fourteen weeks it'd take us to get through Econ. If I learned nothing in college, at least I'd walk away with that.

Okay, stupid icebreaker game, you win.

CHAPTER THIRTY-SIX
JULY 2015

"Hey, lady friend!" Andi chirped as she slid into a chair across from me at Caribou Coffee. It was Friday afternoon and time for our monthly Sip N Bitch session, where we met after work and enjoyed specialty coffee while we bitched about the events of our week. I was especially ready for this week's session, thanks to the blind date that had ruined what could have otherwise been a relaxing Thursday evening.

I had reluctantly allowed a girlfriend from work to set me up with her husband's friend, Rick, who her husband worked with at The Auto Shop, and it's safe to say that it didn't go well. Sometimes when you're single for so long you have to wonder if your friends simply run out of worthy suitors or if they just want to say they tried.

Even Elle was unimpressed when I'd called her later that night.

Rick had been nice, sure. He was also quite handsy, and while I don't mind the occasional leading hand on my lower back, I was *not* a fan of his constant need to touch my arm, hold my hand or rub my thigh under the table. I'd known him no less than thirty minutes when the groping started.

We had met at Applebee's, a cautionary measure I'd taken in an effort to keep my escape options open in case this guy wasn't the "charming hard-working man" he'd been advertised to be.

The first of my grievances was that Rick had arrived a good twenty minutes late, leaving me standing by the hostess stand, wondering if I'd been stood up. Anyway, he was late and didn't bother to call to say he would be. He also showed up wearing his work uniform, which incidentally was a pair of oversized cargo khaki pants and a powder blue long-sleeved button-up that had The Auto Shop logo over the breast pocket and had been partially un-tucked following his shift. Judging by the smell of him, I was certain he was attempting to mask the stench of his BO with an extra squirt (or ten) of Axe Body Spray. While I do try not to judge a book by its cover, I couldn't help but do so in Rick's case.

I'd spent most of dinner eyeing a spot of what I assumed was motor oil on the right sleeve of his shirt, a task that was surprisingly difficult since Rick was right-handed and happened to be big on hand gestures when he spoke. At one point he had launched into an eighteen-minute story about a customer, a frail old lady as he'd described her, who didn't understand that she needed to pay for mechanical services before she could leave with her vehicle.

I counted eight times that the stain on Rick's sleeve disappeared from view. Eight times that I nearly sighed out loud in frustration because watching that stain on Rick's sleeve entertained me more than listening to him talk for eighteen minutes straight about a poor old lady—that very clearly had dementia and probably shouldn't have had a valid driver's license to begin with. Halfway through the story, he unbuttoned the top two buttons of his shirt and out popped the curliest, most pube-like chest hair I'd ever seen in real life.

Ron Jeremy ain't got nothin' on you, Rick!

The other half of the date I spent consciously keeping my limbs under the table to prevent the awkwardness that ensued every time Rick reached for my hand with his greasy French fry fingers; I don't think I saw him reach for a napkin once. When he finally noticed I wasn't eating my meal, I apologized and said I had a headache, placed a twenty on the table and thanked him for the date. I hated to be *that* girl, but when your date is *that* guy…I mean, what choice did I have?

I got a speeding ticket on the way home.

Apparently, I couldn't get out of there fast enough.

"WHAT ARE YOU DOING THIS WEEKEND?" Andi asked. She pulled the plastic lid off her Mint Condition and sucked the whipped cream off the top.

"Homework," I replied, taking a sip of my Vanilla Crafted Press and setting my cup back down on the table.

"Wrong. Try again," she teased, a devious smile playing on her lips.

"Sleeping in?"

"You suck at this," she chided. Andi reached into her purse and pulled out an emery board. She inspected her long-rounded fingernails and then casually started filing them as if she wasn't in the midst of harboring a secret. "The correct answer is," she leaned forward in her chair, a cunning expression on her face, "you're going to the cabin with me!" I froze in my seat and stared at her, unsure if I'd heard her right.

"Um, what cabin?" I asked.

"Mom and Auntie Mae are letting us use the family cabin for the weekend."

"Just us?"

"Yes, just us."

A wave of anxiety rushed over me while I tried to imagine where the kids would spend their weekend. At ten and eight, they certainly weren't old enough to stay home alone for that length of time and as a single mom, it wasn't practical for me to engage in spontaneous trips. "I'm not sure I can get a sitter on such short notice..." I admitted, disappointed.

"Already taken care of," Andi said, a Dr. Evil expression on her face. She lifted her pinky finger to her lips and smiled coyly.

"What? How?"

"I arranged it with your parents a couple weeks ago—Ava and Hayden are going to Grandma and Papa's!" She slapped her hand down on the table and a few customers startled from the noise.

"You sneaky little shit!" I squealed.

"You love me." She offered a quick flip of her red curls and stuck out her tongue.

"I *do* love you!" I pushed up from my chair and threw my arms around her.

"I can't even begin to tell you how hard it was to keep that a secret!" We laughed and I sat back down in my chair.

"I'm so excited! Okay, now, tell me the plan; how's all this going down?"

———

Andi and I drove straight from Caribou Coffee over to my place, a split-level home right in the heart of Buffalo that I'd been renting for the last few months. It provided the space to give Ava and Hayden their own bedrooms for the first time ever, and we were already reaping the rewards.

Andi's bags had been packed and loaded into the trunk of her car, which we'd be driving to the cabin that was located on beautiful Knife Lake in Mora, Minnesota. She'd even arranged for my dad to pick the kids up from daycare, and while I was bummed not to get a chance to say goodbye to them, I'd planned to FaceTime them before they were tucked in for the night at Grammy and Papa's house.

I parked my SUV in the garage and watched in the rearview mirror as Andi pulled in behind me in her car. We ran into the house to pack my bags, giddy at the thought of a weekend filled with girl talk and what would likely end up being more than a few too many cocktails and shared secrets.

I didn't care; it was long overdue.

Once I'd packed the essentials, I grabbed a sticky note and scribbled a quick note to the kids and then placed it on top of their bags that were packed and waiting in the entryway where my dad would pick them up later. I fished my phone out of my pocket and typed out a group text to my parents, thanking them for the much-needed weekend away.

"Ready, girl?" Andi asked, lifting my duffel bag and slinging it over her shoulder. I double-checked the locks on the door and stuffed my keys into my purse.

"So ready!" I beamed.

———

After we finished unloading our bags from the car, Andi and I unpacked our groceries and then stood around the center island in the kitchen, snacking on popcorn and drinking Stella Cidres.

"Are you still seeing that guy? Phil, is it?" I asked.

"Oh, hell no!" She waved a dismissive hand in the air.

"Wow, really? What happened there?"

"Too clingy? I think," she said, unsure how to pinpoint their obvious lack of connection.

"That's it?"

"Pretty much. He was kind of controlling and expected me to spend every waking moment with him. Not my jam, ya know?"

"Ah, there it is. Poor guy."

"Do *not* feel bad for him. He can eat a bag of dicks because he sucks." She grabbed a new bottle of Stella from the refrigerator and popped the top.

"Ha! That's a new one," I laughed and took a pull of the crisp apple ale.

"I like that my crazy doesn't bother you," she said, laughing cynically, sticking out her tongue. "Come on, let's head out to the dock." Andi grabbed my arm and pulled me out of the kitchen. I swiped my jacket from the arm of the couch and we made our way through the cabin and out the front door.

We skipped down the sidewalk arm in arm, our beverages sloshing over the sides of their containers. We settled onto the edge of the dock, our manicured toes dangled in the chilly water, the moonlight reflecting across the lake.

"Truth or dare?" Andi asked.

"Truth."

"Wuss," she teased. Then, more seriously she asked, "Do you miss him?"

"Wow, going right for the jugular, huh?" I laid back, hanging my feet over the edge.

"You know me…" Andi shrugged and followed suit. She tossed her sweatshirt down, fluffing it under her head to use as a pillow.

"Sometimes," I admitted.

"But?" she coaxed.

"…but not as much as I used to."

"Good."

"Truth or dare?" I asked.

"Dare."

"You would…"

"Again, you *know* me!" she laughed.

"I dare you to bite your fingernails right now." I glanced over as Andi flinched, an offended look on her face. She pinched her lips together, releasing a slow stream of air like a deflating balloon, a clear indication that the thought of damaging her perfectly manicured nails was *not* a laughing matter.

"Mmm, nope. No. Never."

"You and your nails!" I joked, holding my own fingernails in front of my face and inspecting them in the dark.

"They're jewels, not tools, babe," she said.

"Touché."

"Truth or Dare?" Andi asked.

"Still truth." Andi sighed, well aware that I was chicken shit and wouldn't be caught dead mouthing the word "dare" in her presence. Andi wasn't the type of person you wanted handing out dares and I definitely feared whatever absurdities she might come up with.

"Are you ever going to tell me everything that happened between you and Nathan?"

"On a Nathan kick tonight, huh?" I mused.

"Yes."

We sat in silence for a moment, a calmness settling over us. A loon sang from across the lake, and I inhaled a deep breath of the fresh air before answering.

"He used to rape me," I said, my voice barely above a whisper.

"He…*what?*" She sat up, facing me. "Oh, Brynn…"

"Sometimes I still get mad about it. Like, I wonder why, ya know?" I watched the stars glisten in the clear sky, mentally tracing the shape of the Big Dipper.

"I just…I can't imagine how horrible it must have been for you. I'm so sorry."

"No one really knew about it. Most people still don't. It's just too hard to talk about, and most of the time I don't want to think about it. It still hurts," I admitted.

"That's the thing about pain—you don't always need a visible wound for it to hurt. Sometimes there's no evidence that anything is wrong, it's just there, hidden beneath the surface until it rears its ugly head again."

"Yeah, and when it does, it punches you in the face and then pours salt into the wound and sews it shut so you can feel just how much it hurts."

We collectively sighed, more in tune with one another than ever before.

"I'm proud of you, Brynn…"

"I know…" I said, my words hanging in the air.

"No, I mean it. I'm tired of telling you how proud I am of you and you just brushing it off like there's no way someone could *actually* be proud of you. I wish you knew how amazing you are." She slid her freckled hand over the top of mine and gave it a squeeze.

"Thanks for not giving up on me," I whispered.

"Never."

We sat in silence as we listened to the peaceful sounds of the water against the shore, each of us alone in our thoughts. I was surprised that I was able to open up to Andi. Not that I ever struggled when it came to talking to her; I just liked to steer the conversation away from Nathan. Those secrets had been hidden, tucked away. Nathan was no longer someone with control over my life, but rather a fictional character in my mind.

He'd come to life again, but this time on my terms.

I realized in that moment that it didn't hurt so much, talking about him. I didn't cry, didn't feel the weight of the world on my chest as I admitted to my friend what he'd done to me.

Eight years. That's how long it had taken for me to start healing. The wounds, once stitched to prevent bleeding, now mere scars left as a reminder of what I'd survived.

CHAPTER THIRTY-SEVEN

JUNE 2017

"So, I HAVE A DATE TOMORROW," I told Ainsley as we settled into lounge chairs in my backyard on Friday afternoon. We'd both taken the day off work—me from Regions Marketing where I was now dabbling in project management, and Ainsley from her position as a Registered Nurse at Mayo Clinic in Rochester—and were overdue for a stress-free day in the sun. The carnival was in town for the weekend, so we'd planned to take the kids to enjoy some rides, carnival games and fried food before settling in for fireworks at dusk. We still had a couple hours to go before the festivities began, so both the kids were off riding bikes with their neighborhood friends while Ainsley and I settled in for some much-needed girl-time.

"Oh, my gosh! I need details!" Ainsley cheered, her eyes lighting up. I nodded with a smile. "Finally!" She clapped her hands together like an excited schoolgirl. "Tell me more!"

I took a sip of my iced coffee as Ainsley leaned over in her chair, her hand tucked under her chin and resting on the arm of the chair in anticipation for a good story.

"I'm nervous," I admitted with a half-smile, squinting from the sun in my face. I couldn't believe how anxious I was over this date. I'd been on plenty, but there was something different about this man.

"I get that. But spill."

I wasn't quite ready to spill, not wanting to get ahead of myself and overthink things. It was a strange feeling, one I was having a hard time getting used to. I told my girlfriends just about everything these days, especially when it came to the disaster that was my dating life over the last ten years. We'd laughed over embarrassing moments, drank over dreadful first dates and tear-rendering last dates. There were too many disappointments, and I was left with the overwhelming feeling that no matter how hard I searched, I would never find someone to love.

I'd been on and off dating sites for years and was never really thrilled with the selection of suitors that I'd eventually met in person. I'd grown so tired of the process—of first dates and junk mail notifications, the slew of sex-hungry men that often filled my inbox. Out of sheer frustration, I decided to close my account once and for all—to succumb to the idea that I'd be just fine staying single for the rest of my life.

I logged into my account one afternoon with the intention of closing it, of moving on, but there was a message in my inbox. And how wrong would it feel to just close my account, leaving that message unread, never knowing what could have been?

I clicked on the notification.

Hi Brynn!

My name is Liam. I'm sure you hear this constantly from other guys on here, but you are absolutely gorgeous! And not just for your looks, because unlike half the tools on this site, I actually read your profile and think we are a lot alike. The only difference is that I don't have kids. But I understand how important they are to a mother and how they will always be number one in your eyes.

My parents divorced when I was younger, and I remember my dad telling me to take care of my mom and sister, that I would be the man of the house. So, I get it!

I just wanted to reach out on the off chance that you'd be up for chatting and getting to know each other a bit. If things go well, maybe we can meet up for coffee sometime? Anyway, I really hope to hear from you!

Liam

"I…"

"Oh, no," Ainsley interrupted before I began. She sat up, her hand over her mouth as she stared at me, a smile playing behind her palm.

"What?"

"You already have feelings for him, huh?"

"What? No. That's…not possible. We haven't even met in person yet."

"Brynn…"

I sighed, caught before I even realized I was hiding anything. Ainsley was right—I felt something for Liam, even though all we'd done for the last month was talk on the phone and text—albeit constantly. Was it possible I was falling for him already? My heart felt heavy, but not in the dreadful way I was used to feeling when it came to dating. It was…different. Almost as if I knew something big was about to happen in my life.

Was I ready for it? I wasn't quite sure. Not after Nathan and so many failed relationships—so many let-downs. Outside of my friends and immediate family, I trusted no one. A hazard of the past, I suppose.

"Yesterday when I was at Hayden's baseball game, he

and I were texting, and I kept thinking how much I wished he were there with me. I know it was just *texting*, but Ains, I swear it was as if he was sad that he couldn't be there, too. Like it felt almost wrong that we weren't watching the game together."

She smiled and brought her hand to her heart. "Does he have kids?" she asked.

"No, actually."

"Okay, so does he *want* kids? I mean, obviously, you have Ava and Hayden to think about. Is he okay with you having kids?"

"He says he is, yes. He said he loves kids and just never had any himself because he wasn't with the right person. And—before you ask—yes, he knows that I don't plan to have any more kids. That was one of the first things I admitted when he told me he doesn't have any."

"Okay, that's good then. You've been honest with him and that's huge, Brynn. What else?"

"He knows I was married before, that Nathan died, and how. He has some stuff in his past, too, but we're in our thirties now, so that's to be expected. I just love that he seems to get it, you know? I'm not embarrassed or ashamed of where I've come from, like I was with other guys. I feel…comfortable—like I can be myself."

Ainsley reached over and patted my hand, squeezing it as she pulled away and grabbed the sunblock from the table. "Where's he taking you?" she asked, squirting some of the lotion into her palm and then rubbing it on her arms.

"We're staying local. He wanted to pick me up here, at the house, but with it being the first date I asked him to meet me in town. We're keeping it casual and just meeting at the lake and then going to lunch or something."

"Hun, that sounds…perfect."

I chewed on my bottom lip, trying to hold back the huge grin that was about to be plastered on my face. Ainsley lay back in her lounge chair and I followed suit, sliding my sunglasses over my eyes.

"Just let it happen, Brynn. You deserve this more than anyone I know," Ainsley said.

———

THE NEXT AFTERNOON, after playing yard games with the kids and then doing some chores, I showered and got ready for my date with Liam. I curled my hair and kept my makeup light and simple, knowing I didn't need to try too hard for him; he wasn't into vanity. We would be outside for most of the date, although Liam hadn't yet told me what we'd be doing, and there was no point in foolishly assuming my makeup wouldn't wash away at the first signs of perspiration anyway. Temperatures had been in the nineties most of the week.

I pulled a maxi dress over my head and slid my feet into a pair of strappy sandals that accentuated the fresh pedicure I'd gotten with Ainsley the day before. Butterflies floated around my stomach and I looked at my reflection in the full-length mirror. While the nerves had certainly set in, the excitement seemed to outweigh them, and I was reminded of a quote I'd seen on Pinterest the day before:

Tomorrow could be the first day
of the rest of your life.

No pressure.

I kissed the kids goodbye—having told them I was

going out to meet my Girls' Night crew for lunch—and then climbed into my SUV and drove down to Buffalo Lake, where Liam would be meeting me. I sat, waiting on a bench that overlooked the lake across from the public library, my heart racing with anticipation.

I heard his car before I realized it was him, the engine grumbling low as he pulled into the parking spot next to mine. I turned and locked eyes with him.

His mouth curved into an undeniable smile.

I couldn't help but smile back.

He cut the engine and stepped out of his car and I took in the sight of him: light wash Wrangler jeans, a black V-neck T-shirt that hugged him in all the right places, his hair shorter than I'd seen in the pictures. He trotted over to me, gigantic smile still in place, and pulled me into a hug. Despite the humidity in the air, I didn't want to let go.

"It's you!" Liam beamed, looking me over and holding my hands out in front of him.

"It's me!"

"I can't believe this is finally happening." He hugged me again and kissed my forehead. He smelled incredible—woodsy and aromatic in the most masculine way, and I couldn't help but bury my face in his chest. We stood that way for a beat longer than socially acceptable, but nothing about it felt awkward. It was just comforting, pure and simple. It was as though we'd waited our entire lives for that moment, and neither of us wanted to rush it.

Liam and I took a seat on the bench. The wind had picked up, and the whitecaps on the water lapped against the shore. My hair blew erratically in the wind, and Liam reached up and brushed it off my face.

"You're more beautiful than I imagined," he started, his ocean blue eyes sparkling against the reflection of the water. "Your pictures don't do you justice." I blushed, unsure how to accept such a compliment.

"You're quite handsome yourself." He smiled again, and I was drawn to his lips and wondered when he might try to kiss me. Liam shrugged and a smug look played on his face.

"I know." He winked, and I playfully shoved his arm. We sat back on the bench and he slid his arm over my shoulders. We watched the ducks swim in the water.

"This is nice," he said.

"It doesn't seem real." I met his eyes, and Liam laced his fingers through mine, tracing the scars on my knuckle. He brought my hand to his mouth and pressed his lips to the flawed skin.

"What are Ava and Hayden up to today?"

"Ava was reading *Twilight* when I left, and I hate to admit it, but I left Hayden alone with the Xbox, so he's playing *Minecraft*."

"Oh boy! No turning back now!"

The fact that his first question was about my kids wasn't lost on me. I tried to remember the last time I'd been asked about my kids so early into a first date and realized the answer was never.

"So," Liam said mischievously, "are you ready to get your ass kicked in mini-golf?"

"Shut up! I haven't been mini-golfing since I was a kid!"

"Brynn, wait. Before you get too excited, there's something you should know." He had a pained look on his face, but the twinkle in his eye gave him away.

"Yeah?"

"I'm very, *very* competitive. I won't let you win just because you're a woman."

"Oh, it's on!" I contended. My competitiveness had been known to get me in trouble, but there was no way I would go down without a fight. How hard could a game of mini-golf be?

It turns out, very.

He kicked my ass.

I stood next to no chance in the game of mini-golf when paired against Liam. Less than halfway through the round, I even stopped keeping track of my score and just wrote down whatever number was the closest to what he scored on the hole.

It's not cheating if you still lose, is it?

We made our way through the course and waited for the couple ahead of us to finish the sixth hole. Lingering under a tree so the sun couldn't beat down on us so aggressively, Liam's arm made its way around my back, pulling me in close and allowing me to inhale the intoxicating scent of him. I stood on my tippy toes as he brought his lips to mine and kissed me, each of us sharing what would inevitably be our last first kiss.

When he drove me back to my truck later that evening, he didn't say goodbye from the driver's seat—he had manners and wasn't afraid to use them. He walked me to my car and stood by while I unlocked it and set my purse inside before turning to face him.

His arms were around me in an instant, and I felt his heart racing in his chest. He lifted my chin and kissed me, his hands caressing my lower back.

"I'd really like to see you again," he admitted when he pulled away. "There's no point in waiting to tell you that. Would you like to see me again?"

"I'd really like that."

"You're so beautiful," he said as he tucked a curl

behind my ear before kissing me again, as if he didn't want to let me go.

I drove home in a daze, beaming from ear to ear and wondering how I'd gotten so lucky, already aware that the quote I'd seen the day before must have been a sign from above.

CHAPTER THIRTY-EIGHT

JULY 2017

L<small>IAM</small> and I always joked that we met accidentally on purpose. What were the odds, really, that on the day I'd decided to discard my online dating profile for good, Liam's message would be there waiting for me?

I figured one last-ditch effort couldn't hurt, so I had replied to Liam—my phone number included—before closing my account and deleting the app from my phone. I knew, regardless of the outcome, it would be the last message I'd ever send using an online dating app. Liam's first text came later that day, and we haven't looked back since. Hence, we met accidentally on purpose, very much in search of love but neither of us actually expecting to find it.

We spent the next month exchanging daily text messages and talking on the phone, often through the late hours of the night. Even after those long nights, I still woke up to "good morning" texts from Liam the next day.

I pinned my hopes on the notion that the chemistry would remain once we met in person, although I was apprehensive it wouldn't. I'd been let down plenty of times before and naturally kept my expectations low.

It's incredible to think that it's possible to fall in love with someone before ever meeting them, but Liam and I swear that's how it happened for us. We've gone back through those text messages on several occasions—because we're that couple that saved every single message we've ever sent—and every time I read through them, I can still feel the sentiment of our words.

When we finally did meet in person, it was undeniable that we would be together for the rest of our lives. We'd been struck by Cupid's arrow. But how do you pull back the reins, even when you're so sure? How do you pace yourself when you're certain that after a prolonged, discouraging search, you've finally found your person? We tried. But our union was undeniable—it was instant, and it came at us so hard and fast that I feared my friends and family would think I'd lost my mind.

I could've told him I loved him after that first date.

He's admitted the same. We were ridiculously in love, and time would play no part in its quantification. Sometimes love is like that; it's reckless abandonment at its finest.

———

"Soooo, how's the new man?" Harper teased. She tucked her long blonde hair behind her ear, took a sip from her wine glass and leaned over the center island, her head resting on her hands.

I blushed, as I did every time Liam came up in conversation. I had intended to show up to Girls' Night with a bit more reserve than I was demonstrating, but I'd blown my cover and they could see right through me, the evidence riddled on my face the second Harper mentioned Liam.

The Girls' Night Crew met once a month, and it was Harper's turn to host. We rotated hostesses with a food and wine sign up that resembled the traditional Minnesota potluck, each of us bringing something to contribute to the theme-based meal. The tradition had gone on for years, although none of us could truly pinpoint when it had started.

Some of the girls' friendships went way back—all the way to high school—while others joined later, having met through college, work or other acquaintances, like Ainsley, who wasn't able to join us often since she was living a couple hours away in Rochester. But we'd all grown close, having seen each other through weddings, births of our children, birthday parties and every other event you could imagine in between our monthly gatherings. I relied on these girls throughout the years and cherished every one of our get-togethers.

"Oh my…" Harper said when I failed to respond to her question.

"Oh my, what?" Jerilyn asked, taking a seat on the bar stool to my left.

"Brynn has it bad."

"She does? Oh em gee, let me in on this!" Jerilyn's friend from college, Mindy, exclaimed. She had just come through the front door and had joined the lopsided group as we hovered around the kitchen island. She reached for a carrot from the veggie platter and dunked it in ranch dressing before chomping into it.

"You guys, stop." I covered my face with my hands, surprised to find that I was crying. "I…he's—"

"She's in looooove!" Harper declared, her arms around my shoulders.

"This is so not like me at all!" I swore, embarrassed by my emotional state. I didn't cry over guys anymore.

"It's okay to be happy, hun. You deserve it!" Jerilyn reached over and laid her hand on top of mine, each of us giving a gentle squeeze that said so much more than the words that came from our mouths.

"Somebody pinch me," I said through my sniffles.

"So, when's the wedding?" Elle asked, a sly smile on her lips. A couple of the other ladies were gathered in the living room and their ears perked up at Elle's question, their conversation quieting.

"Oh, God, don't jinx me and start talking about a wedding already!" I laughed and held my hands up in the air before turning back to Jerilyn. "Remind everyone when the baby is due?" I hinted, in hopes that the conversation would naturally sway in her direction.

"You know when the baby is due," Jerilyn chided, a devilish look on her face. She winked before running her hand over her baby bump. She and Jackson had celebrated their eight-year wedding anniversary over the winter, and baby number two was on the way. Their son, Remy, was four and beyond thrilled to be a big brother, which he'd dutifully told Ava all about the week before while she babysat him.

"Well, even if you don't want to gush about your new boy toy right now, just know that we're all ecstatic for you," Meg declared and several others nodded in agreement.

"All right, ladies, food's ready!" Harper announced, taking the hint. She placed a tray of chicken kabobs on the counter next to the salad, fruit and veggies, and the rest of the ladies flocked over and dug in. I was grateful for these nights, for the opportunity to share these moments with my girlfriends.

I'd seen them get married and start their families with the support of their partners. I had been jealous, and at times felt I couldn't relate to them. Most of them were just starting to have kids, now in our thirties, yet mine were old enough to babysit for them. We were often at different chapters of our lives, and because of that, I'd felt alone and left out, even though they did their best to include me. I was the first of us to have children, to go through a terrible marriage. The first to mention the word divorce; the first to become a widow.

I didn't openly share my story with many of them—Jerilyn and Meg were the only ones in the group who knew the worst of what I'd been through with Nathan. And even though Harper was Jesse's sister, she wasn't privy to the nightmares that haunted my past, and I was grateful she didn't mention her brother often. Although last I heard, he was clean and engaged to a woman he'd been dating for several years.

But none of that ever really mattered; we all had each other's backs through thick and thin, this crew and me. And it was finally my turn for a happily ever after.

———

I STROLLED IN FROM GIRLS' Night shortly after 9:15 p.m. Liam and the kids were in the living room, in the midst of a high stakes Mario Kart tournament, and by the sound of things, Liam hadn't shown any mercy.

When I'd mentioned my plans for Girls' Night to Liam earlier in the week, he'd jumped at the chance to spend time with the kids and volunteered himself to hang out with them. I loved that he felt comfortable with them and that the three of them wanted to spend time together, even though they hadn't known each other for long.

I slid my feet out of my flip-flops and hung my purse on the banister and headed up the stairs to the living room.

"Oh, come on!" Ava shouted, her body leaning left and

right in tandem with the Wii controller. "You're driving dirty!"

"I am not! I'm driving to win, there's a difference." Liam challenged, his eyes focused on the flat-screen in front of him.

"Hi, Mom!" Hayden shouted over the noise of the video game.

"Hey, bud. Did you guys eat dinner?" I asked, and motioned to the leftover kabobs I'd brought home, the Tupperware still warm.

"We ordered pizza," Liam admitted, a sheepish look on his face. "I'm sorry!"

"Why are you sorry?"

"I should have cooked or something..."

"Don't feel bad! Even great cooks like myself order pizza sometimes," I joked, heading into the kitchen to place the leftovers in the fridge. "All right, kiddos, it's close to bedtime and you have school tomorrow. Can you finish up your race and then go brush your teeth?"

"But Mom!" Ava and Hayden said in unison. It didn't take much more than a "Mom Look" to get them to their feet. They even still hugged me before running downstairs.

I took the win.

———

ONCE THE KIDS were down for the night, I joined Liam on the couch; we were halfway through the first season of Shameless on Netflix and hoped to get through an episode or two before turning in for the night. He'd planned to stay over in case I'd gotten home late from Girls' Night. Truth be told, I never wanted him to leave.

"Hi," he said, pulling me in close. "I missed you."

"I missed you, too. Did you have fun without me?"

"We did, but we feel terrible about it," he teased, breaking into a sly smile.

"Thank you for watching them tonight."

"Oh, it's no problem at all. They're really great kids."

"Thank you. I just feel bad. I hope you didn't feel like a babysitter…"

"Babe, the closer we get, the closer your kids and I will get. I will love those kids and I will do anything for them. They're just as important to me as you, I promise." He pulled me closer, and I buried my head into his shoulder to hide the tears that I knew would fall. I'd been on an emotional roller coaster for weeks as I tried to make sense of what was happening between us. It seemed surreal, almost too good to be true.

"It means so much to me that you just said that."

"You're an amazing mother and have done such a great job with Ava and Hayden, sweetie. You should be proud."

"I am," I mumbled into his shirt, and he rubbed my back while I cried, wondering how I'd gotten so lucky after all that time on my own. We'd come so far since that first date, even though we'd only been dating for just over a month. It felt like we'd been together forever.

I snuggled in under the crook of Liam's arm and he pressed the "play" button on the Roku remote. But my mind was elsewhere, lost in daydreams and the realization that all the walls were finally tumbling down.

CHAPTER THIRTY-NINE

AUGUST 2019

I WATCHED as Hayden swung the aluminum bat and a loud crack echoed across the field, the baseball ricocheting down the third baseline. He tossed the bat aside and sprinted to first base, passing the bag just before the third baseman could get the ball over.

"Safe!" the umpire yelled, throwing his arms in a lateral motion to relay the signal. Hayden removed his shin guard and batting gloves and handed them to Coach Mills, who gave him a pat on the back. He adjusted his helmet and led off toward second.

"Nice hit, bud!" I shouted, clapping in unison with fellow spectators. My phone vibrated in my pocket, and I fished it out and brought it to my ear. "Hey, babe!"

"Hi, Sweetie! How's the game?"

"It's good! Hayden just hit a single," I said, pride for my son reflecting in my voice. He'd pitched the first inning, striking out the first two hitters and earning a ground out on the third.

"Nice! I should be there in about fifteen minutes. Did you save me a seat?"

"Of course!"

"Are your parents still joining us?"

"Yep, Mom called and said they should be here within a half hour," I confirmed, excited to have the family together in support of my son.

"All right, babe, I'll see you soon," Liam said, and I heard the engine of his Subaru WRX roar to life after he turned the key in the ignition. "I love you!"

"I love you, too."

I smiled to myself as I recalled my parents' reactions when they first met Liam, my dad's silly list of "Ten Rules for Dating my Daughter" that he handed over to him amid our backyard barbeque—playful, but there was so much truth in the items on that list, too. Where Liam laughed and appreciated the gesture, Nathan would have yelled.

But most touching was Liam's recollection of my mom's reaction the day he showed her and Dad the engagement ring he'd picked out for me, when he asked them for permission to marry their daughter, to adopt their grandchildren. The uncontrollable tears they shed together as they embraced him, grateful for the man he was, for the husband and father he would be.

I STUFFED my phone into the pocket of my chair just in time to watch Hayden safely steal second. He slid feet first into the base and looked up as the catcher overthrew the second baseman. The ball sailed over his head and rolled into center field, and Hayden took off running again. He rounded third and the coach waved him around to home where he slid into the base, covering it with dirt right before the ball hit the catcher's mitt.

"Safe!" the umpire shouted again, while the home field crowd erupted.

270

"Way to go, Rockets!" Ava and I shouted, giggling at the looks we gave each other in realization that we'd simultaneously shouted the same words.

Ava leaned her head on my shoulder, her long hair tickling my skin and fluttering in the breeze. I inhaled the scent of her shampoo from the top of her head, like I used to do when she was younger. Now fourteen, she was developing into such a beautiful young woman; I was grateful for the snippets of affection she still awarded me and wondered for the gazillionth time where the years had gone.

I'd spent those years as a single mom, relying on the support of my family and dear friends who had somehow, throughout the years, brought me back to life and given me a voice. There were lonely days, sure, but most of them were filled with happiness— with friendship and family. Game nights, celebrations of birthdays and holidays, each filled the calendar year after year. And through it all, despite my disastrous dating life, I felt so loved and supported by the inner circle of people that enveloped me and my children.

But I'd been cautious where my heart was involved. After Nathan, there was no other choice but to keep my guard up—for the sake of these kids that I adored with every part of my being. And because, for once in my life, I actually believed I was worthy of love.

I was one to love hard—to love deeply—and that wall that I'd hidden my heart behind so many years ago had been built up so high that I had started to wonder if it would ever come down. I'd developed a hard exterior, one that took so much strength and trust to penetrate. All because once, all those years ago, I'd given my heart to the lowest bidder and carelessly allowed him to break it; to tear it into a million tiny pieces that had taken an army to put back together.

And once it had finally healed, I found Liam.

It's ironic, actually, how much truth there is to the notion that once you stop looking for love, it finds you. Now, just one short month away from marrying the man I'd waited years for, I was finally at peace with my past.

"Liam's here," Ava said, pulling me from my thoughts, her index finger aimed toward the parking lot. I popped up from my camping chair and jogged over to my Liam's car. He climbed out of the driver's seat, a smile on his lips. "Hi, babe!" I said, and he pulled me into a hug.

"Hi, sweetie. How's the game going?"

"Really great! Hayden just scored a run. We're up five to two." I beamed. Weekends at the ball field were well-favored in our family. The smell of the fresh-cut grass, the dirt on the field and the sounds of baseball always brought me back to my childhood. Of the nights when my parents and I sat in the stands and watched the Jacksonville Suns play during the two-year stint when we'd lived in Florida. They were some of my most cherished days, and I was thrilled to see my son had inherited the same appreciation for the game.

"That's great, they're doing so well this year," Liam replied. He stuffed his keys into the pocket of his jeans and closed the car door before locking it with a chirp of the key fob. We laced our fingers together and made our way over to our seats, where Ava had set out an extra chair for him.

"Liam, you should have seen Hayden's hit!" she said, proud of her not-so-little-anymore brother. I glanced over at the two of them and couldn't help but smile; Ava stood from her chair, she and Liam sharing a hug. Rogue tears trickled down my cheeks as my soon-to-be husband listened with laser focus while his soon-to-be stepdaughter gushed about her latest crush.

It's funny how when you've been through hell and back, the simplest things can wreak havoc on your emotions, tugging on your heartstrings when you least expect it. When it took a village to break down that wall, how could they not? There I stood, on a Saturday afternoon, watching my son play our favorite game at Jim Thome Park and yet, I was crying.

My heart was full of love as I watched my accidental family laugh and smile together on that sunny day at the ballpark. I swiped at my cheeks and took my seat next to Liam, sharing a glance with the man who'd finally mended my broken heart.

CHAPTER FORTY

SEPTEMBER 2020

If you'd asked me seventeen years ago why I was so against drugs, aside from the obvious reasons, I wouldn't have had a good answer; I just was. The D.A.R.E. program must have sunk in a little deeper for me than most, I guess. For some reason, even without ever experimenting with drugs myself, I'd always been against them. You could ask me the same question now, though, and I'd give you the only answer that actually matters: drugs destroy families.

Drugs destroyed *my* family.

Nathan wasn't all that bad when he was sober—I think that's part of the reason I held on as long as I did. I kept convincing myself that he could be fixed, that he was only at his worst when he was using. I held onto those happy moments in hopes that we could find our way back to them, that we could create new happy moments. It's ironic though—when I look back I often have a hard time recalling those happy moments at all and instead focus on the bad ones—they're the ones that stuck with me the most.

What I could never comprehend was why I was never

enough for Nathan—why Ava and Hayden were never enough. I think that's a common mistake that the loved ones of addicts make; we're often oblivious to the fact that the addiction actually has nothing to do with us, that we're not the ones battling the demons.

See, if there's anything I regret during those years, it's that I didn't understand that Nathan's recovery was actually about him and not about me. I made demands under the assumption that Nathan was capable of meeting them. But he wasn't. Not really. Because he hadn't had the chance to fight the demons inside him first. If I could go back and do anything over again, it would be that.

I'd give Nathan the time he needed to heal.

The time to find the strength inside himself instead of always trying to be strong *for* him.

There have been times throughout my life that I questioned everything: did I ever really love Nathan? Did I support him enough? Should I have left sooner? Why had I married him when I wasn't even sure it was what I wanted? I can say with confidence that Nathan and I would never have survived in the long run.

We were destined to fail.

We never would have found our way back to one another, not when so much damage had been done. I exhausted myself during those years with him. I lived in fear. I inhaled the toxins each and every day that followed the After; ever since the day he wrapped a telephone cord around my neck and tried to strangle me.

And yet, despite everything, I like to think that if Nathan were alive today that he'd be in a better place. That he'd have found happiness; that he would have overcome his demons.

I'd wish that for him.

In the years after his death, I still had so much to be

grateful for. My children. My family. My many dear friends who helped me find myself again—who helped me see who I was underneath all the angst and heartache. Who helped bring the vibrato back to my laughter.

Even now, so many years later, the pain is still there. Time doesn't really heal anything, it just makes the pain more bearable, idling in the background while the scars fade. It wasn't until after I ruined myself that I was able to start the process of fixing what had been broken. There's always time to forgive yourself and start over. To mend those tattered relationships you once cherished and unintentionally burned.

To right the wrongs.

Addicts do it all the time; it's one of the core principles in the recovery process—no matter what the addiction. Everything we do in life comes with a choice. We may not always make the right one the first time around, but in the end we're only human.

I still catch myself wondering how someone like Liam chose me in the end; how deep within the depths of our souls, from the moment we met, we just simply knew that it was meant to be us together.

You see, when you find your person after you've already been someone else's damaged goods, you have to accept their past just as you hope they accept yours. It should be a no questions asked kind of acceptance, a give and take.

You tell each other about the things that broke you— maybe not all of them, but the important things—and then together you put those broken pieces back together one by one. You have that "aha!" moment where you suddenly understand the meaning of the phrase, "everything happens for a reason." You may both be flawed, but together you're actually kind of beautifully flawed;

two souls that otherwise never would have fit together, be it not for your triumphs. That your damage is kind of the reason it works in the first place. Neither of you will ever be perfectly innocent again, but you'll probably be perfect together. You'll start to forget that you were broken to begin with, because all those broken pieces no longer fit with the new puzzle you've assembled. They're just extras; they're the pieces that you leave behind in the box just in case you ever want to look at them again—to go back and paint that picture one last time. But you don't actually need them to complete the puzzle, not anymore.

That's what Liam did for me. He stored all my extra pieces in a box that we stuffed in the back of our closet. Sometimes I remember that they're there, but I don't need to take them out anymore because my puzzle is finally whole.

I tell my daughter every day how much I love her. How much I hope she shoots for the moon and doesn't give up until she catches it. She is, and always has been, the North Star in my sky; guiding me home even when I wasn't sure we had a home to go to.

And my son, my handsome, goofy and loving son— who still gives me a hug every single day even though he's a hormonal fourteen-year-old boy. He has a heart of gold and will do great things in this world, even if it's just to make his mother proud. I have no doubt that he will be a good man, that he will treat women with respect and decency. His mama taught him that, you can be sure of it.

I've been so blessed throughout my life—in family, friendship and love. I will never regret my past, no matter how much it may hurt from time to time. I walked away with two incredible kids who I've gotten to raise with so much love. I've walked away with strength, a confident woman and a loyal friend. I walked away with an open heart and a willingness to grow.

And then I found Liam.

I've never needed extravagant gifts or boatloads of money. I just needed someone to love me. Someone who isn't afraid to tell me how he feels, to hold my hand and pinch my ass in public just because he likes the way it looks in my yoga pants, even though I'm only wearing those yoga pants because my favorite skinny jeans are too tight. Someone who makes me feel beautiful even without makeup and with a head full of frizzy, untamed waves. I needed someone who could show me the true meaning of love—that love sometimes makes you feel like a silly schoolgirl and you're pretty sure you're trapped in a fairy tale, but somehow you really are the princess and you finally kissed the right frog. Life does that to us sometimes —it gives us something we never knew we needed.

It gives us a Liam.

It gives us an Ava.

And it gives us a Hayden.

And if you're one of the lucky ones like me, it gives us sunshine.

EPILOGUE

Ava

I CAME across an article a few years ago that claimed that a high percentage of kids resulting from teenage pregnancies and raised by a single parent end up dropping out of high school and battle life through addiction, some form of crime or living off the system. I hated the statistics that supported that statement and I'm beyond grateful that my mom did everything in her power to make sure I didn't end up as data in favor of the argument.

She worked her butt off to create a better life for us, and I never once felt like I was missing out or that I didn't have all the opportunities that other kids had. It's weird to think that I'm the same age now as my mom was when she had me—I can't imagine what it would be like to have a kid right now.

I don't remember much about my dad. I remember being sad, though. Mom used to have to explain it to me all the time, "Daddy is with the angels, sweetie." It's confusing to go through something like that as a kid, and sometimes I'm really glad I don't remember much, especially now that I understand the circumstances around his death.

Growing up, my mom didn't really talk about him unless I asked, and honestly, I didn't ask all that much. I was used to him not being there, so I guess I didn't really notice the difference—at least not until I started school and every one of my friends had a dad. I remember one time asking my mom to get me a new one. I think that was about the time I started realizing our family was different.

I didn't notice it until I got older, but my mom kind of gave me time to idolize my dad a bit. Like, even though she had good reason to, she never really spoke ill of him. She just spoke *of* him. I don't know many people that could do that as gracefully as she did, especially considering what I know now.

Sometimes I wonder if things would have been different if he had been around. Would he have wanted me? Would he have wanted Hayden? Who knows...maybe if he'd lived, he still would have left us behind. I wish I had those answers. But maybe it'd hurt less just to know he was still breathing, you know? I don't really know what's worse —a dad that leaves by accident? Or one that leaves on purpose? One that lives less than an hour away from you nearly your entire life and literally knows your address but never makes an effort to see you anyway?

Yeah, I definitely think that would be worse than him dying.

It wasn't until my teenage years that Mom started opening up a bit about my dad. Not that she was offering up information; I could kind of tell it was a touchy subject even before I knew anything significant. I had always just assumed it was because a little part of her still missed him. But when I started asking her about him—I think I was around thirteen—she wasn't really sure how much to share. She took a deep breath, sighed and then asked if I wanted the whole truth or just the truth as it pertained to me. I didn't really know which one I wanted; I just knew I wanted *some* truth. I was holding on to these snippets of memories of him, and I needed something more. I had so many questions...

Am I like him? *Not at all.* Would we have had anything in common? *I'm not sure...*what kind of music did he like? *Rap.* Would he have hugged me every day like Mom does? Tell me he loves me? *Maybe?* Would he have tucked me in at night and made my stuffed animals talk and dance and sing me stupid songs until I almost pee from giggling? *No.*

Mom did those things.

All I'd really known outside of what my mom had told me was what I found through a *Google* search. I'm not entirely sure why I did that, but other than a bunch of arrest records and a MySpace profile—whatever that is—I didn't find much. But I felt guilty every time I typed his name into the search bar. I don't really know why; he was my dad—it made sense to feel curious about him. I guess I just didn't want to hurt Liam's feelings by wondering about my dad, even though he'd been gone for so long by that time.

Anyway, I know you're not supposed to speak ill of the dead, but given what I know now about my dad—which isn't the full story, more like the PG-13 version—some days I have a hard time comprehending how his DNA makes up fifty percent of who I am.

Mom and I cried together as she told me about those years with my dad. I was somewhat surprised by her honesty and raw recollection, but I think it was the only way she could talk about him without experiencing it all over again. *Conceal, don't feel, as Elsa would say*—Frozen *refer-*

ence here! God, I loved that movie when I was little. She spoke like it was just a story and not actually something that happened to her. I think she just wanted me to know that I deserve better than someone like my dad, too.

I spent a lot of time after that hoping like hell that I didn't turn out like him.

It's like I almost have a fear of being anything like him and because of that my immediate response to conflict is always to distance myself from everybody. I mean, not entirely; I always have my music and I'm grateful that Billie Eilish gave me the refuge I needed some days—to just plug in my earbuds, lay back on my bed and get lost in her voice, in her stories. If there's anyone other than my mom that I aspire to be like, it's her. She just gets it—she's unapologetically herself, and that's what I want to be, too.

I don't want to be a product of something; I just want to be me.

Knowing my mom and how strong she is, how strong she's always been, I never would have guessed she was a domestic abuse survivor. But I guess that's the thing about survivors—they do what they have to do to make it to tomorrow, and sometimes that includes beating the odds, no matter how hard it may seem.

When I started to research schools to go to for college, Mom and Liam insisted I explore my options and consider out of state schools, just because they didn't want me to miss out on anything. But there was no way in hell I was going to move thousands of miles away from my mom. I applied and was accepted to the University of Minnesota later that year, deciding to major in Social Services and Psychology.

Now, Mom and I meet for lunch every other Friday at the Applebee's a few miles from the U of M where I've now just started my sophomore year. I've always felt guilty that she drives out here all the time, but she says she doesn't mind and that she'd drive five-hundred miles a day to see me if she had to. Then, of course, she immediately breaks into song, belting out "I'm Gonna Be" by The Proclaimers and dancing like a weirdo. *And I would walk five-hundred miles, and I would walk five-hundred more...*I literally laugh out loud every time she does this, it doesn't matter that I've seen her do it more times than I can remember.

Sometimes Liam and Hayden join us for lunch, but Liam's busy this weekend and Hayden's celebrating his seventeenth birthday with his friends. So it's just Mom and me today, which is totally okay because I actually have a surprise for her.

For my Creative Writing class my freshman year, I had to write a paper about someone who has inspired me. Out of the forty-six students in the course, my professor said I was the only one who wrote about their mom. The only one! I wish moms got more credit. I guess that says a lot about mine, huh?

As I wrote the paper, I thought about the little music box she always used to turn on when she tucked me in at night. I remember her winding up that music box as she tucked me into bed and pulled the covers tight around me so the bed bugs wouldn't bite. There was a tiny ballerina on top of a carousel that spun around and projected tiny clusters of stars on the ceiling as it played the instrumental to "You Are My Sunshine."

I've never told her, but I brought that music box with me to college and keep it in the drawer of my nightstand. Every once in a while when I miss her, I wind it up and watch the stars dance across the ceiling, humming along as the melody plays, just as my mom did for me all those years ago.

You are my sunshine, my only sunshine
You make me happy when skies are gray
You'll never know dear, how much I love you
Please don't take, my sunshine away

My mom's birthday is coming up, and even though I'll see her at the surprise party Liam, Hayden and I planned for her next weekend, I asked her to come for lunch today so I could give her birthday gift to her a little early.

After I had finished my inspirational paper for Creative Writing, I wound up the music box and then went to the International Star Registry website. Within a few clicks, I picked out a star and named it after my mom. I also purchased a bracelet with three charms: a star, sun and moon, and then I had the star engraved with the coordinates of the constellation I had named after her. My mom always says that I'm her North Star, but she doesn't seem to realize that she's mine, too.

She's literally my favorite person in the entire world.

If you or someone you know is a victim of domestic violence and could use assistance in leaving a dangerous situation, please visit www.thehotline.org or call 1.800.799.SAFE.

ACKNOWLEDGMENTS

To my husband: I love you more than there are words. Thank you for taking the pieces of my shattered heart and showing me that they could be mended back together. You are the peanut butter to my jelly, and I love growing old with you. I love you (more than coffee)!

To my children: My beautiful babies...my sunshine on cloudy days. I would do anything for you. I'm so damn proud of who you've become and know you will do great things in this life. Despite the odds stacked against you, you're both so kind, loving, talented and caring. At my lowest points, you've made me laugh, smile and cry and gave me every bit of strength imaginable to get through those dark times. It's hard putting this book out there, knowing you might read it one day. I'm the proudest mama in all the world and love you to the moon and back! P.S. De, thanks for the assist writing the epilogue!

To my parents: I'm sorry...for so much. For all the things I couldn't find the words to tell you back then and for all the things I said but shouldn't have. Thank you for helping me navigate through the uncharted waters of single parenthood. I'm beyond grateful for your love and support of everything I set out to do. I love you, and while I hope like hell you don't read this book, please know that I needed to do this for me. I know it's a tough pill to swallow…just focus on the happy ending part. This is my closure, my acceptance.

To my brothers (yes, I have *two* of them! #middlechild): I'm sorry for excluding you from Brynn's story and hoarding you for my own life story instead. I love ya—even though you're both turds.

To my beautiful nieces (all five of you!): I truly hope you don't read this book unless/until you're actually old enough to read this book. But when and if you do, please learn from it. Don't be stubborn like your Auntie and think you need to make all the mistakes on your own; I promise you, you are beautiful and you deserve the world. I will forever treasure our Summer Olympics, endless sleepovers, movie nights, arts and crafts, nail painting, baking/cooking, Justin Bieber dance parties and every other random thing we got to do together while you were littles. Auntie loves you all very much! My door will always be open.

To every one of the amazing family members I inherited when I became a Jump: You've welcomed not only me, but also my (nearly grown) children into your family with open arms. We came to the door with a lot of baggage, and you simply picked up our bags and helped us unpack. We are so grateful to be a part of your family.

To Jennalynn: Every girl deserves to have a best friend like you! I will forever cherish our lifelong friendship more than you could possibly know. Through all the ups and downs, you never gave up on me, Ketchup. I can't wait for our next Hanson concert. Love, Mustard.

To Mandy: My seester from another mister. I truly

cannot imagine my life without you. I love your crazy. TIAB. Muah!

To Ashley: Wifeyyyyyyyy!!! You are, hands down, one of the kindest souls I've ever met. I hate Econ almost as much as I love you. I'm grateful for you every single day.

To Heather: I can't say the words, they'll make me cry. You know I luh you. You know I love our Yahtzee games, our stupid catch phrases and our ridiculous ability to break into song and change the lyrics. I'll never eat Top the Tator and Ruffles without thinking of you—cheers, Heg. Also, we can't go to the liquor store!

To Becky: You're the inspiration behind beautifully flawed, my sugar shorts…man, I love the heck out of you. You saved me back then. I hope you know this. Thank you for be-friending me when I had nothing to give. Could I BE any more grateful?!

To my Soup Mate: We'll always have fry-days!

To my dear friends and family whose "characters" went unnamed in this book, you are no less important, I just couldn't possibly write you all into one tiny book (I'm not *that* talented yet): my cousin, Lindsay, Krista (RIGHT!), my rent-a-brother Jeremy (thank you for answering all my law enforcement questions!) and Sadie (truly one of the BEST fans and friends I could possibly have supporting me, even though I know you prefer Harry Potter!), Adrine, Nikki, Brandi, and every single one of the ladies in my Girls' Night Crew and my many amazing coworkers who have become more like family throughout the years—I love you all more than you know! Maybe I'll have room for you in a future novel. *Maybe.*

To my overzealous and highly encouraging alpha and beta readers: You guys ROCK! Thank you for giving me the kick in the ass that I needed to get this book finished after thirteen friggin' years. I appreciate the hours you spent reading, sharing feedback and excitedly awaiting the next chapter! I heart you all. Special thank you to Mandy Henkelmann, Ashley Heck, Lisa Lonesky and Sami Matthews for their willingness to read this story several times, offering feedback and proofreading for the low price of a free paperback with my autograph slapped onto it. Ladies, you're amazing and I cannot thank you enough for all you've done to help turn this story into a book!

To my editor, Kiezha Ferrell, with Librum Artis Editorial Services: Thank you for encouraging me throughout this process! I was terrified to put my manuscript into the hands of a professional, but you made me feel at ease right from the start. I'm so incredibly grateful for the opportunity to work with you. You, my dear, are one of the best.

Most importantly, to the victims and survivors of domestic abuse: I hear you. I see you. I am with you. #SurvivorsNotVictims

ABOUT THE AUTHOR

Shannon Jump is an avid reader of multiple genres, with a passion for writing and storytelling. She refuses to start the day without the perfect cup of coffee, is a die-hard Minnesota Twins fan and Food Network junkie. She lives in small-town Minnesota with her husband and two teenage kids. *My Only Sunshine* is her first novel.

———

If you enjoyed this book, please consider leaving me a quick review—even just a sentence or two will do! Who knows? Your review could be the reason a future reader says "yes" to *My Only Sunshine!* To leave a review, please visit any one of my pages on Amazon, Goodreads and BookBub.

I love connecting with readers and hope you'll come say "hello!" on social media! I also send out a monthly newsletter that offers behind the story insights, exclusive giveaways and updates on my current projects.

http://www.shannonjumpwritesbooks.com
info@shannonjumpwritesbooks.com

Newsletter Subscribe:
https://www.subscribepage.com/y6t3n6

Social Media:
www.facebook.com/ShanJumpMNAuthor
www.instagram.com/sjump4203

Goodreads:
https://www.goodreads.com/author/show/
20979307.Shannon_Jump

BookBub:
https://www.bookbub.com/profile/shannon-jump

Made in the USA
Monee, IL
10 March 2021

61399414R00177